Highland Renegade

CHILDREN OF THE MIST SERIES

CHILDREN OF THE MIST SERIES

CYNTHIA BREEDING

This book is a work of fiction. Names, characters, places, and incidents are the product of the author's imagination or are used fictitiously. Any resemblance to actual events, locales, or persons, living or dead, is coincidental.

Entangled Publishing, LLC
10940 S Parker Rd
Suite 327
Parker, CO 80134
rights@entangledpublishing.com

Amara is an imprint of Entangled Publishing, LLC.

Edited by Erin Molta
Cover design by Bree Archer
Cover photography by Period Images
clu, undefined undefined, and nikpal/Getty Images

Manufactured in the United States of America

First Edition September 2020

Chapter One

Scotland, July 1774

"I do not understand why you are taking us into barbarian country," Juliana Caldwell complained as their carriage hit a rut in the road and rocked precariously.

"We could very well get killed," her sister Lorelei agreed, grabbing a side strap to keep from slipping off the seat.

Emily, Countess Woodhaven, shook her head at her younger siblings. "Scots do not go around murdering innocent women."

"No?" Lorelei sniffed. "I heard they are lawless cattle thieves."

"And I heard they steal women and force them to marry," Juliana added.

Emily put her fingers to her temple and rubbed, hoping to forestay a headache that was already forming. They had been on the road from London for six days and her sisters' admonishments had grown more stark with each passing day. At first, they had been upset about leaving London and not retreating to a country estate—not that they had a country estate any longer—but as they'd traveled north, their agitation had grown more dire. Yesterday, they had passed over the border at Gretna Green and the landscape had become rockier as they traveled toward Stirling. Looking out the windows at the increasingly barren terrain had sparked another deluge of anticipated horrors. She certainly wasn't going to admit that she also felt a bit of trepidation.

"Would you rather have been taken into the convent?" she asked.

That quieted both of them, and she felt a bit guilty over using the threat. But it was true. They had no other place to go. Albert Prescott, the Earl of Woodhaven—her recently deceased husband—had had a penchant for gambling and opium that had left her with a mountain of debt after his death. Creditors had circled like sharks scenting blood—not to mention a mistress the old lecher had apparently had for years—all wanting money. She'd sold the house in Mayfair to pay off the debts, but not the mistress. The country estate was entailed, and a cousin who had claimed the title didn't feel charitable about housing a widow and two young, attractive women. Or maybe it had been his wife, the new countess, who didn't. Either way, they no longer had a home.

"We are sorry," Lorelei said, her voice subdued. "You are doing what you think best for us."

Juliana nodded. "We would *truly* die if we had to live in a convent."

"Or take the veil." Lorelei shuddered.

Emily had to smile at the idea of either of them retreating into silence and prayer. At seventeen, Lorelei was vivacious and a natural flirt. Juliana, a year older, was willful and opinionated. "I doubt the nuns would even consider such a thing."

Lorelei's expression grew wistful. "We just wanted a

Season like our friends."

Juliana gave her a sharp look. "I told you not to bring that up."

"It's all right," Emily said. "If things go the way I hope they will, you can both return to London for next year's Season."

While Lorelei's face brightened, Juliana shook her head. "I do not care if I have a Season or not. What is the point? To marry someone who will try to control me? I will not be forced into that."

Like I had been.

"You should not bring up Em's marriage, either," Lorelei said accusingly.

"It is all right," Emily said again. "It does not matter now."

Initially, she'd had no choice. When their parents had been killed in a carriage accident five years ago, her father, Baron Caldwell, had very little in his bank account. Ever the hopeful entrepreneur, he'd sold his land to invest in new inventions, always telling them that the latest one was sure to be a success and they would soon have money to burn. When the Earl of Woodhaven—forty years her senior—had come calling afterward, with his proposal of marriage as well as the offer to take in her sisters, she hadn't seen how she could refuse. She'd been only ten and nine with no idea of the man's rotten soul.

But that was in the past. Through some miracle—or perhaps because King George had a passion for science himself and had met her father several times—he'd seen fit to petition Parliament for a special dispensation awarding her the land title to forfeited holdings in Scotland that had belonged to the outlawed Clan MacGregor. She had decided, like Juliana, that no man was ever going to control her again. She was determined to handle the land operation herself.

She had been advised that some MacGregors still occupied the land, courtesy for *not* having fought at the Battle of Prestonpans nearly thirty years ago. She suspected King George also allowed them to stay partially because his mother's confidant was Lord Bute, a Scotsman whose estates were near Glen Strae.

However, she had also been told after receiving the land deed that she was within her rights to have the clan vacate the land. From the records she'd seen, the holdings didn't seem to be doing well. The profit wasn't much, but Emily was determined that would change. Since she would need someone's help in learning everything about successfully managing the land, she'd decided she would simply explain that she intended to be accommodating and allow the clan to stay. The situation would be beneficial to all of them.

Emily smiled at her sisters and leaned back against the squab. "Everything is going to be fine. You will see."

• • •

Ian MacGregor watched incredulously from the battlements of Strae Castle as a carriage followed by three…no, four… wait…*five* wagons made their way up the perilously steep, winding road that led to his home. The carriage must belong to the Countess of Woodhaven, but by the devil's own horns! How long did the old dowager plan to stay?

He knew his lands—*MacGregor* lands—had been annexed by the Crown and sequentially leased to an earl years ago, simply because his father had refused to change his surname. He had refused to do the same when his father died. MacGregors were the purest branch of Gaels in Scotland, descended directly from Albiones! Their motto wasn't *My Race is Royal* for nothing. That their name, and the clan itself, was still considered banished by the English government made no sense. The grievances that had impelled Queen Mary to issue the edict were long past. Hopefully, Lord Mount Stuart would be able to persuade the present monarch to restore their rightful name and place in history. And soon. Ian wanted to start the process of gaining back the legal right to his lands. *MacGregor* lands.

Meanwhile, there was this… He squinted at the caravan plodding its way closer. He'd received notice a fortnight ago from the local magistrate that the widow of the Earl of Woodhaven had decided to visit. The earl had been in his mid-sixties and Ian had no idea why his wife, who had to be close in age, would make the trip all the way from London. He'd been careful in the reports he had to make to the earl's estate to undervalue both the crops and livestock so the Englishman wouldn't come snooping up here.

Now it seemed the old dowager had decided to come sniff around. He grimaced when he looked at the line of wagons. She wouldn't need to unpack any of it. He'd already come up with a plan, aided by his brothers and uncles, to make sure her visit was neither comfortable nor accommodating. The grimace turned to a smile. She'd soon be wishing for a return to the luxuries of London.

Turning, he made his way down the steps and across the bailey to the massive front door where his sister Fiona, his ward Glenda, and three of his brothers awaited him. He had no idea where Devon might be, but no one ever knew where his fourth brother was most of the time.

"Ye must have heard the noise of them approaching," he said.

"Aye," his brother Carr answered.

"Sounds like a cavalry unit comin'," his other brother, Alasdair added.

"Why would they be bringin' so many wagons?" Fiona asked, her eyes growing round as the whole line came into sight.

Rory, his third brother, snorted. "'Tis just like a woman, thinkin' she canna exist less she changes her gown every five minutes."

Ian had an uneasy feeling those wagons didn't contain just clothes, but he kept his thoughts to himself as he watched the carriage come through the open arch of the gateway. The portcullis always stayed up these days and the drawbridge down, since Scotland was not at war, but for a brief moment he almost wished he had barred the entrance. Then he shook his head. He was nine and twenty. It was ridiculous to let some little old lady intimidate him.

The carriage finally rolled to a stop in front of them. Ian motioned for a groom to open the door and assist the woman down. He had no intention of paying homage, but Highland ways did call for hospitality. At least, initially.

His eyes widened as a girl stepped down who couldn't be any older than Fiona, except where his sister's hair was as black as his own, this one's was pale as moonlight. Her eyes had a silvery cast that made her look almost otherworldly. He caught Alasdair, who always had an eye for the ladies, staring and gave him a poke. "Probably a daughter."

Then another one stepped out whose hair was the coppery color of sunset. She looked around, her ginger-colored eyes practically snapping as she frowned.

"Looks like she wants to pick a fight." Rory grunted. "Women should nae argue with a man."

Fiona shot him a look. "Ye doona do so well keeping me quiet—"

"Probably another daughter," Ian interrupted before a real fight did break loose. At least that might explain the need for a lot of gowns. Even though Fiona preferred breeches, he knew most young women didn't.

"How many children do ye think the dowager has?"

Carr, ever the analytical one, asked as a third woman stepped down.

"I…doona…ken." Ian's breath caught. This last one looked like an angel descended from heaven. Her hair was like spun gold, her complexion like fresh cream, and her eyes a deep blue that reminded him of Loch Awe on a cloudless day. He found himself moving forward in spite of planning to wait at the steps.

"I am Ian MacGregor, the…" He'd almost said laird, but, since the word was banned—by the English, at least—and he didn't need to stoke any English fires. "…one in charge here. The missive I received dinna say the dowager would be bringing three lovely daughters." He smiled at her, then peered inside the carriage, which was empty. "Where is your mother?"

"Resting in peace beside my father," the angel answered.

Even her voice sounded heavenly, clear and melodious as harp strings being plucked. Then the words registered. He drew his brows together.

"Your mother is…nae with ye?"

One golden brow arched. "It would seem not."

He suddenly felt like a green lad or, at least, a dolt. Of course her mother wouldn't be here if she was dead. But what the devil… He straightened to his full height and squared his shoulders. "Where is the dowager Countess of Woodhaven?"

Her lips curved in the slightest of smiles and he noticed how full and lush they were. Very kissable. Mayhap…

"I am she."

It took a moment for those words to sink through his rapidly lustful thoughts. Then he blinked. "*Ye* are the dowager?"

She nodded. "I am Emily Woodhaven. These are my sisters, Miss Lorelei Caldwell…" She gestured to the blonde and then to the redhead. "…and Miss Juliana Caldwell."

"But I thought…that is, I mean…I dinna…" He stopped himself before he sounded even more like an eejit. "We were nae expectin' three lasses."

"Do not worry about accommodations." Emily pointed toward the wagons. "We brought our own beds."

He frowned. Did the woman think a MacGregor could not offer a bed… Er, *accommodations*? His mind didn't need to be thinking of beds right now or the pleasures to be found in one. He turned his gaze to the wagons instead.

"What else did ye bring?"

"Just the things that are valuable to me and my sisters. I am sure it will all fit into a room or two at the most."

His frown returned. "But why? Ye'll just be staying long enough to see the property, aye?"

"Well…no." She looked at her sisters and then back to him. "We plan to live here."

"*What*?" He heard the word spoken in unison behind him where his brothers lingered.

She glanced at them, then opened her reticule to withdraw a document and took a deep breath.

"I am sure you will find everything in order," she said as she handed him the papers. "This is the title deed. I am the new owner here."

• • •

For the space of a full minute, Emily could have heard a needle drop on the soft ground. No one spoke. But then, they probably didn't have to. The stunned looks on the faces of the men behind Ian slowly changed and she could almost see a dark cloud building over their heads.

The cloud could have been her overactive imagination, since the three men and the one girl all had raven black hair. The younger girl had lighter brown hair. The men's eyes—

narrowed at the moment—ranged from blue to green to hazel. As she tried not to overtly stare at them, they seemed to increase in size, which was already formidable, both in height and width of shoulders.

Emily tore her gaze away and looked up at Ian defiantly. "Up" being the operative word, since he was even taller and broader than his brothers. She was not exactly short herself, at five and a half feet, but she barely came to his shoulder. She squared her own and refused to look away.

It was only then that she noticed the unusual golden color of his eyes. Like a wolf's. And he was eyeing her as a wolf might its prey. She could almost feel the tension in his body, as though all those muscles were coiled and ready to spring. A sudden scraping sound nearly caused her to jump. Then she realized he had crumbled the papers in one large fist.

Perhaps announcing that she was the new owner could have waited, given that his face looked like it were chiseled out of stone.

She took another deep breath and hoped her voice wouldn't shake. "Were you not informed about the deed?" For a moment, she didn't think he was going to answer.

"Nae. I wasna."

It sounded like a growl and for a brief second, she wondered if there was any truth to the myth of werewolves. She gave herself an inward shake. If nothing else, she had to *appear* brave for her sisters who for once were silent and watching her. Nor would it do to show fear in front of the MacGregors. She'd learned that much from her husband. She lifted her chin.

"I am sorry you were not informed." She gestured to the crushed papers. "That *copy* of the deed should make it quite clear once you read it." He made a sound that was definitely a growl this time, and she forced a smile. "But do not worry. I have no intention of asking you to leave." This time she distinctly heard a series of growls from the group behind Ian and swallowed hard. Somehow she managed to keep the smile pasted on her face. "In fact, I would like to ask your help in teaching me to manage this holding. That should be to all of our benefits, do you not think?"

For a moment he stared at her with an expression between wary and cautious, as though he might be dealing with someone not quite sane. Then he turned to his brothers and all hell broke loose as they started shouting in Gaelic and gesturing wildly.

Emily tried not to cringe. This wasn't turning out exactly as she expected.

Chapter Two

"What do ye propose we do?" Rory asked yet again.

"Damned if I ken." Ian poured a dram of whisky, drained it, and leaned back in the leather chair behind the massive desk in the library. The brothers had retreated there as soon as Maggie, their housekeeper, had taken charge of the Sassenachs. The idea had been to plan strategy, but so far none of them had come up with anything. They just kept shaking their heads as though they'd all been clouted with the hilt of a claymore.

"I will ask our solicitor to make sure the papers are legal," Carr said.

"'Tis the king's seal on them," Ian replied bleakly, then pushed the crumbled sheets across the desk. "Look for yerself."

Carr smoothed the papers and glanced at them before folding them neatly to tuck into his shirt. "Still. We want to make sure."

"That doesna solve the problem," Rory grumbled. "Those women want to *live* here."

"Well, it wouldna be so bad to look on the one called Lorelei," Alasdair said with a chuckle. "She's verra bonnie."

Rory snorted. "Ye think all women are bonnie."

"Well, they are." Alasdair didn't seem the least bit affronted. "But ye have to admit, that one looks like the faeries sent her, with her pale hair and silvery eyes."

"More apt, the demons sent the other one," Rory said.

In spite of the dire situation, Ian grinned. While Maggie had been leading the women into the castle, one of their wolfhounds had enthusiastically tried to make Juliana's acquaintance. Unfortunately, he had barreled into her from behind, causing her to stumble and fly forward like a leaf in the wind. Rory had, by instinct, leaped forward, too, catching her before she'd sprawled on the ground. She'd been furious by the time he'd set her back on her feet, whether from embarrassment or the guffaws from his brothers or both, she'd offered a string of English curses that would have been hard to rival.

"Well, ye did hold her a wee bit longer than necessary," he said.

Rory scowled. "Only to teach the lass a lesson that they doona have free rein. The MacGregors are in charge here."

"We hope," Carr said.

"Aye," Ian responded before Rory could argue the point. "Assuming the deed is legal, the countess could make our lives miserable."

"Which is what I thought we were supposed to do to her," Rory replied. "Wasn't that the original plan?"

"Aye, but that was when we thought she would just be visiting and the leasehold was still in effect. I doona ken that is the best thing to do now."

Rory eyed him suspiciously. "Are ye having a change of mind because the *old* dowager isna quite so old?"

"And bonnie," Alasdair added.

"Nae!" Ian realized his overly quick denial belied the fact. It didn't help when Alasdair and Carr both grinned at him. His face warmed like a green lad when he thought of where she was right now... Probably soaking in a bath, her naked body all pink from the warmth of the water... Then he remembered his instructions and which room she'd been given and where it was. His conscience niggled at him. With an effort, he dismissed it and returned to his fantasy of her bathing. He hadn't had a chance to glimpse much of her, other than her face with its lush, kissable lips, since she'd been wearing a travel pelisse that had covered most of her. Was she...? He shifted in the chair, aware that his breeches had grown tighter. "'Tis a fine line we walk, right now."

Carr inclined his head. "We might need to reconsider, since she could send us all packing."

"Doona be an arse!" Rory frowned at both Carr and Ian. "And doona tell me ye are thinking of welcoming them!"

"Nae, but..." Ian held up his hand before Rory could retort. Carr was right. They couldn't just make life miserable now for three young women. "Mayhap alter the plan a bit. We can still make sure the lasses are shown how hard life can be here, but we can also impress on them what good stewards we are, so they'll ken there is nothing to worry about when they go back to London."

"How soon will that be?" Rory asked.

From the way his body was reacting to Lady Woodhaven, the sooner the better. What he didn't need was to get involved with her. Apart from the fact that she must be very manipulative—how else had she been able to secure the deed in her own name? And she'd chosen to marry a man near old enough to be her grandfather, no doubt for his money and title—but his clansmen would consider him a traitor if he colluded with a Sassenach countess. These were *MacGregor* lands, regardless of what an English king decreed. His duty to his clan—who did exist, regardless of legal proclamations—was to hold the lands for his kin.

"Just long enough to assure the countess that everything is being managed well and she can count on her profits being sent to London on a regular basis."

"I think that's a good idea," Carr said, "but Devon will nae like it."

He probably wouldn't. Their younger brother hated anything to do with the English. He'd even offered to make sure the old dowager didn't enjoy a single day while she visited. Who knew what he would do once he learned of the new situation. Ian sighed.

"We will just have to deal with that when he returns."

"And what about our uncles?" Rory asked. "They're due to arrive in a day or two. They'll nae be pleased, either."

Probably not, but at least they wouldn't be as obvious about their feelings as Devon. Donovan and Broderick had taken the surname Murray and were thus able to move more freely in both English and Scottish society but that didn't mean they were more likely to want an English countess here.

Ian heaved another sigh and reached for the bottle of whisky on the desk. He would have to handle one crisis at a time.

• • •

Emily, along with her sisters, followed the middle-aged housekeeper—Ian had called her Maggie—into the castle and up a winding, narrow flight of stairs. Besides issuing a terse "Follow me" the woman hadn't said a word, nor did she pause in the entryway to give Emily a chance to look around. She'd gotten only a glimpse of a large room beyond double doors to the left and a single door to the right that was closed, before they'd ascended the stairs. When they'd crossed an actual drawbridge and approached what looked like a truly medieval castle, Emily had felt a twinge of excitement. It had a thick crenellated curtain wall surrounding it with merlons and embrasures, and she could picture archers posed along the battlements, bows drawn, ready to do battle with any enemy that approached. The castle itself was an imposing square granite structure, several stories high, with round towers at each end. It was like walking into the world of several centuries ago.

And maybe she had. Inside, the walls were stone, and a wooden staircase they were climbing spiraled upward with uneven steps and no railing to hold on to. She'd read in a history book that they'd been deliberately built that way so invaders would have a hard time brandishing a sword while keeping their balance.

"This looks primitive," Lorelei whispered.

"I hope there are not bats in the rafters," Juliana replied.

"*Shhh*!" Emily hissed at them. The last thing they needed was to insult the housekeeper and, by extension, the MacGregors who were their hosts, but the woman didn't appear to have heard. Still. The meeting outside had not been exactly cordial and they didn't need to ruffle anyone's feathers.

Her sisters said no more, but perhaps that was due to the effort of climbing. Maggie didn't pause at the first landing but continued up another flight of stairs to the second floor. Then she led them through what seemed a maze of dark interior hallways, lit only with candles stuck in wall sconces. Finally, she stopped in front of a door at the end of the hall. Pushing it open, she looked at Emily.

"This is the room the laird made ready for ye." She glanced at Lorelei and Juliana. "I'll have the room across the hall aired for them."

"Thank you." Emily shot her sisters a warning look. The

lack of addressing her properly with "my lady"—especially when the housekeeper gave Ian the respectful term "laird," even if it was banned by the English—wasn't a point she wanted to argue at the moment.

"Could we have some water brought to tidy up a bit?" Lorelei asked.

"There's water in the pitcher there." Maggie pointed to the dresser. "And a basin beside it."

Again, Emily gave her sisters warning looks. "That will be fine."

The housekeeper gave a curt nod, then stepped back and shut the door, leaving the three of them alone. Emily looked around the room. Besides the dresser, there was a small table and two chairs by a very narrow window—probably an arrow slit, she realized—a single bed, a wardrobe against one wall. There was also a screen behind which, she hoped, was a chamber pot. A large hearth took up most of the remaining wall. Logs had been laid, but not lit. At least, she wouldn't be cold later.

"That woman is horrible," Lorelei said, interrupting her thoughts.

"She certainly would not find herself employed in any London household," Juliana added.

"I doubt that she would want to be," Emily retorted. "And we were warned that Scots could be taciturn, so we will just have to adjust to her personality."

"And what about the men?" Juliana asked. "They were rude as well."

Lorelei giggled. "But you have to admit, they were all very good-looking!"

Juliana rolled her eyes. "Is that all you ever think about? They were *rude*."

Her sister stuck out her tongue. "You are just angry because you tripped and one of them caught you."

"Caught me? He *held* me…and wouldn't let go."

Lorelei grinned. "I would not mind being *held* by an attractive man."

Juliana frowned. "I felt like his bloody captive."

Emily frowned, too. "You might want to check your language. I am sure you have already created quite an impression with the litany you loosed in the bailey."

"*Hmph*." Her sister folded her arms defiantly.

"Please, Juliana. For me. For *us*," Emily said. "From what we witnessed outside, the MacGregors did not seem to have been warned that King George had actually *transferred* the deed instead of holding it. That had to have been a shock. We do not need to be alienating our reluctant hosts."

"I can try." Juliana lowered her arms, looking somewhat mollified. "Just do not expect me to act like some sweet, demure, *biddable* lady."

"I…" Emily began but was interrupted by a knock on the door.

"Maybe the housekeeper sent up some hot water after all!" Lorelei went to open the door, only to stare at the girl who'd been in the courtyard earlier.

"May I come in?" she asked.

"Certainly." Emily moved forward, but not before she pinched Juliana's arm. "Please."

"We have nae been introduced, since my brothers are all *eejits*… Idiots." She smiled at all of them. "I'm Fiona."

They reintroduced themselves and Juliana, taking care to stay out of Emily's arm's reach, added, "I agree with your assessment of your brothers."

Fiona laughed. "Och, well. Ye took the wind out of their sails, had them in irons, ye did."

"Irons?" Lorelei asked. "None of them were shackled."

"Not that *that* would have been a bad idea," Juliana said.

Fiona laughed again. "Sometimes I would like to see it as

well—they can be a wee bit bossy, all of them—but I meant, when ye take the wind out of sails suddenly, the boat stops dead in the water and canna make headway. 'Tis what 'in irons' means." She looked at the puzzled faces. "We do a lot of sailing on Loch Awe."

"I am afraid we have not had experience with sailing."

"I'll be glad to teach ye, if ye plan to stay."

Emily smiled. "We definitely plan to stay."

"Good." Fiona paused, as though contemplating, and then took a deep breath. "I think ye should ken something, though."

"Ken?"

"Ken…know. Know something."

"What is it?"

Fiona hesitated once more. "My brothers hatched a plot before ye came."

"A plot?" Juliana asked. "What kind of plot?"

"It was to get ye to go back home."

We are home, Emily wanted to say, but thought better of it. Evidently, the MacGregors didn't want to welcome an Englishwoman, even for a visit. "Can you tell us about this plot?"

"They were nae going to hurt ye or anything. They figured an old lady was coming—on account of the earl being in his sixties—and thought if they made life verra uncomfortable, ye would nae stay long."

"I see," Emily said.

Fiona looked around. "'Tis why they gave ye this room."

Emily frowned. "This room?"

"Aye. 'Tis on the old side of the castle."

"There is nothing wrong with it."

"Nae, but 'tis *old*." When they all looked at her blankly, she went on. "The back side of the castle is newer and has conveniences. There is a cistern with hot coals banked beneath it to provide pumped hot water for the bathing room, oil lamps and chandeliers, wood paneled walls, rugs, and comfortable furniture. My grandfather even built a wide staircase. And," she added, "all the rooms have proper windows."

Emily was beginning to understand. No doubt the MacGregors had thought that an elderly countess, one used to luxury and being waited on, wouldn't last long under these conditions. They hadn't planned on someone younger and more adaptable to show up. Nor did they know that she was destitute and had no place else to go. Everything they owned was in the wagons that had followed them. She set her jaw.

"But why would your brothers do this?" Lorelei asked.

Fiona grimaced. "Because they are eejits."

"You will not get an argument from me," Juliana said and glanced at Emily. "We may not be a clan, but I think your brothers have just declared war."

For once, Emily agreed. It seemed she was going to have to do battle. But knowing what she did now, it would be on *her* terms.

Chapter Three

By the time the big gong sounded in the bailey, signaling the evening meal, Emily and her sisters—with a bit of help from Fiona—had hatched their own plan.

Fiona escorted them through the twisted hallways until they reached the spiral staircase leading down. "'Tis better my brothers doona see me with ye just yet, but all ye need to do is go through the double doors in by the entrance. Ye'll be in the Great Hall where the clan eats."

Thanking her, Emily led her sisters down the stairs—careful to stay on the broader side of each curved step—and then through the doors she'd spotted earlier. Once inside, she stopped so abruptly that Lorelei and Juliana bumped into her. Ignoring their chiding, she gazed around the huge room.

She could very well have stepped back a century in time. The hammer-beamed, wooden ceiling was two stories high. Three large iron chandeliers hung from heavy chains. Tapestries depicting hunting scenes and warriors in battle lined the walls between the arrow slit windows. Four hearths were set in the stone, two on either side of the long, rectangular room, fires blazing with warmth to ward off the dank chill. The long tables and benches that took up most of the floor space were filling with MacGregors of all sizes and ages, many of whom were armed.

At the far end of the hall, a raised dais held the high table. The MacGregor crest—a buckled belt around a lion's head with a royal crown—graced the wall directly behind the large, intricately carved armed chair which obviously belonged to the leader of the clan. To either side of that hung various types of weapons.

"I thought the MacGregor name was banned." Juliana gestured to the round wooden crest and then looked around. "And didn't our solicitor say only a few MacGregors were allowed to live here?"

"He said the MacGregors who did not fight at Prestonpans were given a retreat. I'm sure that included their families as well."

"You are quite right."

Emily turned at the sound of Ian's voice behind her. He and his brothers still wore the same clothing they had earlier in the day, which was a relief, since their own baggage had not been unpacked from the wagons yet and they remained in their traveling clothes. After what Fiona had told her, she suspected not delivering the trunks promptly was another ploy to make them uncomfortable, but obviously dressing for dinner was not a main concern.

"I am glad they were not separated."

"Too many of our clan are still forced to hide in the hills. Some have sought refuge in Ireland." He pointed to the girl Emily had seen on her arrival. "That one—Glenda—is my ward, since her parents were killed trying to flee."

Emily looked at the girl seated at one of the long tables close to the dais. She appeared to be perhaps four and ten at the most and she was watching them sullenly. "It must be hard for her."

"I've tried to help her adjust to the change," Ian replied.

"And other changes, too. Hopefully, soon," Rory said. "Lord Mount Stuart will see to it."

Emily drew her brows together. "The son of the former prime minister, Lord Bute?"

"Aye. He's already talking up members of Parliament to restore our name...*and* our lands," Rory answered. "So ye shouldna plan to stay—"

"I am quite sure I have not been the first to tell you that you are quite rude," Juliana interrupted.

He grinned. "Do ye nae want to add a 'bloody' to that?"

She glared at him. "Barbarian."

His grin widened. "Is that the worst ye can do?"

"Please! Do not encourage her." Emily leveled a look at her sister. "We do not intend to be rude, either."

"Aye, well. We have manners, too," Alasdair smiled at Lorelei and offered his arm. "May I escort ye?"

For a moment she looked flummoxed and then she smiled prettily while Juliana rolled her eyes. "I suppose you might."

"And allow me to escort ye," Ian said to Emily, extending his arm as well. "We have a table especially reserved for ye."

Emily put her hand on his sleeve, not surprised that his arm felt like steel beneath it. Oddly, the sensation sent a tingle up her arm. She didn't have long to ponder on it because she heard Juliana behind her.

"I do not need assistance," she practically hissed.

Rory chuckled. "I just dinna want to see ye sprawl on your face again."

"I did not sprawl!"

"Aye. Because I caught ye."

This sounded like it was going to escalate, but before she could turn around, she heard Carr's voice, soothing as a zephyr wind.

"If ye will allow me, Miss Caldwell, I'm sure Rory can find his own way."

There was an audible sniff. Then, "Thank you." Emily gave a silent sigh of relief.

"It seems my brother and your sister are peas in a pod," Ian said as they walked toward the dais.

"Juliana can be a bit bristly." She had her own reasons for that, but Emily wasn't about to disclose such personal information. "But she has a kind side, too."

"Well, a symbol of Scotland is the thistle," Ian replied, "but it does have a pretty flower." Before she could respond, he stopped and gestured. "Here ye are."

She wasn't particularly surprised that the small table he'd led her to was in a corner off to the side of the dais. After what Fiona had shared, she hadn't expected to be seated as guest of honor on the dais. But Ian was watching her covertly, probably wondering if she were going to protest. She affected one of Lorelei's smiles, the one she used with beaus in ballrooms. "This is just perfect. We can observe without being noticed."

"That's...good, then." His expression didn't change, but one brow lifted almost imperceptibly. "And is your room to your satisfaction?"

Given that there were better-appointed bedrooms—not to mention an actual bathing room—in the newer part of the castle, he was well aware that it was not. But she wasn't about to give him the satisfaction of complaining about the room or, for that matter, the lack of hot water, either.

"The room has a wonderful medieval feel to it and the unusual staircase as well." She gave him another of her sister's smiles. "I love medieval history so I am sure I will be quite happy living in this castle."

He looked a little disconcerted, then he gave a brief bow. "Enjoy your dinner then."

She allowed herself a genuine smile as he walked away. The games had begun.

• • •

"I doona think I was really expecting better news, but there's naught we can do," Carr said the next afternoon as the brothers met in the library once more.

Ian looked at the somewhat smoothed deed Carr had put on the desk. "The solicitor says 'tis legal, then?"

"Aye." Carr helped himself to the open bottle of whisky. "Even if Lord Mount Stuart is successful in getting our clan cleared this year, only the lands annexed as leaseholds would be returned."

"Mayhap we should get a second opinion?" Rory asked.

Ian shook his head. "Carr's going to Oban was risky enough, since we are MacGregors. I willna risk anyone going to Fort William."

Alasdair nodded. "Too many soldiers with ne'r much to do might enjoy arresting a MacGregor."

"To say nothing of the Camerons around the place," Rory said.

"We never ken which way the wind blows with them," Alasdair replied.

Cameron lands bordered theirs to the north. In the past, when all clans had been forbidden to give aid to any MacGregor who hadn't changed his surname, the Camerons had taken particular delight in cattle-reiving, knowing the MacGregors could file no complaint. That had, of course, resulted in MacGregors responding in kind and adding a sheep or two for good measure. Ian almost grinned as he recalled the stories his grandfather had told. The cattle, like the clan, had disappeared into the mists, causing folks to speak of fae help or, for the more superstitious, that the clan itself consisted of changelings…which might actually have been useful at the darkest point in their history. Recently, especially after Culloden, there had been an uneasy truce, oft broken, between the Camerons and MacGregors.

"I agree with Alasdair. 'Tis nae worth the risk of clashing with either soldiers or Camerons." Ian opened a desk drawer and tossed the deed into it. "For now, at least, our people think the countess is here on a lengthy visit. Only we four—and Fiona—know about the deed."

"And where is Fiona?" Alasdair asked. "I've nae seen her today."

"She invited the Sassenachs to the solar this morning," Ian answered. "She said she was going to show them around the castle and gardens."

"Do ye think that wise?" Carr asked. "When they see the modern half they will wonder why—"

"'Tis the point, brother," Rory said. "They have to realize they are nae welcome without our saying it. 'Tis brilliant."

"Until she decides to wield her authority and choose her own room," Carr answered.

Ian's conscience niggled at him again, although he pushed it aside. "Last eve she said she liked living in a medieval castle."

"That was before she kenned what the rest of the place looked like," Alasdair said. "And if she decides to exert her ownership rights, then the whole clan will ken about the deed."

"We can still deny it," Rory said. "We can say Carr took the deed to the solicitor—which is true—and we are going to make sure 'tis authentic."

"Didna I just do that?" Carr asked.

Rory waved a hand. "'Twas the solicitor's opinion, nae *ours*."

"Regardless," Carr answered, "I think Ian needs to talk

with the countess about what she intends."

"And it would nae hurt to apologize to the ladies and offer them better rooms," Alasdair added.

Rory frowned at him. "Are ye going soft on the fae-looking one?"

Alasdair frowned back. "Do ye ken nothing about women? If ye expect one to do what ye want, ye have to offer her something she wants first."

"When did ye become an expert on women, little brother?"

"I was nae the one who got rejected leading the ladies into dinner last night." Alasdair quirked his mouth up. "Ye were, if I recall correctly."

"I dinna get rejected!" Rory defended himself. "I dinna *ask* to escort that redheaded harpy."

"But ye wanted to."

"I dinna—"

"*Enough.*" Ian glared at them both. "Ye are nae bairns. And apart from what either of ye think about the Caldwell ladies, we have the dowager countess to contend with. 'Tis what's important."

"I agree," Carr said. "The sooner ye talk to her, the sooner we ken where we stand and…" He glanced at his other brothers. "…the sooner we can plan a real strategy."

Ian sighed inwardly. Carr was right. He was going to have to talk with Emily Woodhaven and, to alleviate the prickling of his conscience, he would offer better rooms. Mayhap, he would even let her have her choice, now that Fiona had shown her the castle. That might make her more amenable to his plan—*suggestion*—about keeping the deed's existence private for now.

Alasdair was right. Give a woman something she wants. In return, she will be more pliable. That strategy had worked well enough on previous conquests. Not that he saw Emily—

the Lady Woodhaven, he mentally corrected—as a *conquest.* In a sense, she was the "enemy" or an "obstacle" at best. Certainly not someone to lust after. He needed to put that idea out of his head and concentrate on what really mattered. Holding the land, not holding *her.*

But his traitorous body was already looking forward to seeing her again.

Chapter Four

As it turned out, Ian didn't have to go looking for her. She came looking for him. His brothers had left the library only moments earlier when he, having finished the single dram he allowed himself and was putting the bottle away, heard a light tap on the closed door.

"Enter!" he'd called. He'd asked Maggie earlier to give him a full report on how the day had gone with the Sassenachs, so he supposed it was she. Instead, when he looked up, it was Emily who stood in the doorway.

He blinked, hardly recognizing her. Yesterday, when she'd arrived, she'd been wearing a pelisse and last evening at dinner—no doubt because her trunks hadn't been taken up to her room—she'd worn her traveling dress, which had buttoned up the front with a high neck, long sleeves, and loose fit, to accommodate the lengthy time spent in a carriage. Her hair had also been pulled back in a tight chignon.

The woman who just entered truly could have been an angel descended from heaven, although Rory probably would have said she was sent from hell to bedevil them. Her golden hair was gathered loosely at the base of her neck, tendrils escaping and framing her face which, after a night's rest, glowed with health. For the first time, he understood why the English popinjays waxed poetically about a "peaches and cream" complexion. Her eyes were even bluer, near violet, but perhaps that was because of the lavender dress she wore. He remembered that lavender was the color of half mourning that widows wore and wondered if she truly mourned her husband. The man had been decades older than she. From the cut of the dress—just low enough, in spite of its fichu, to offer a suggestion of breast swells—and its much more formfitting design that accentuated a small waist and just the right amount of hip flare, it appeared she was observing proprieties with only the color.

"Please come in. Have a seat." He gestured to one of the chairs by the hearth. "Can I help ye with something?"

"Actually, yes." Emily eyed the whisky bottle still in his hand as she sat. "I could use a drink, if you do not mind."

He blinked again. "I'll see if I can find some sherry."

"I would rather have the whisky, if you please."

He glanced down at the bottle, then back at her. "This is called *uisge-beatha*, the 'breath of life.' 'Tis quite strong."

"For a woman, you mean?" She arched one brow. "Or do you caution men not to drink it as well?"

"Nae. Aye. Nae..." *Why am I stumbling over words?* "I mean, it takes a wee bit of getting used to."

"Then as soon as you pour it, I can start becoming acquainted."

"I..." Ian clamped his mouth shut, reached for a whisky glass, and poured a dram into it. He was tempted to pour more, just to prove his point when she sputtered and spit it out, but that would be a waste of good whisky. He handed her the glass, his fingers brushing hers.

"Thank you." She took a healthy sip—near half the

dram—closed her eyes while rolling the liquid in her mouth, then swallowed and looked up at him without so much as a twinge. "Excellent."

He blinked once more, vaguely aware he might be taking on owlish tendencies, and watched as she drained the rest.

"Would ye like some more?"

"No, thank you." She handed the glass back. "That suited me nicely."

"Do ye drink often?"

She gave him a sharp look. "Are you asking if I have a problem with spirits?"

"Nae..." Damnation. That wasn't what he meant at all. "I...just have never seen a woman...*enjoy*...a dram so quickly."

"I find, at times, that whisky puts things to rights." She pointed to the bottle. "Is that distilled here?"

"Aye." When his father had refused to give up his surname, he'd had to turn the distillery over to Donovan and Broderick. That might be to his advantage now. "My uncles run the distillery."

"Do they own it?"

He drew his brows together. She was obviously trying to find out if it went with the deed. "Nae completely."

"Are there shareholders?"

His frown deepened. Women weren't supposed to know anything about business. "'Tis more of a clan operation."

"Who reaps the benefits? Apart from consuming the product, I mean." She rose and walked closer to him. For a moment, he wondered if she were going to try and seduce him...but she only reached past him to pick up the bottle. "I am not familiar with this label. Where do you distribute it?"

He was distracted by the faint floral scent wafting from her hair. She must have washed it in rose water. He had the oddest urge to bend his head and bury his nose in the curls atop her head. Luckily, she set the bottle down and turned away, allowing his good sense to return.

"Mostly just to Glasgow."

"Well, then. The first thing we will need to do is increase production. I would wager a number of gentlemen's clubs in London would buy all you have immediately."

He stared at her. "Do ye have any idea of how long it takes to produce Scotch?" Then he went on before she could answer. *"Years."*

She waved a dismissive hand. "All the more reason to increase production now."

By the devil's own horns! Was Emily Woodhaven thinking to take over the distilling process? His uncles would be fit to be tied. He needed to change the subject.

"Perhaps we can. However…" He swallowed hard. "I believe I owe ye an apology."

Her brow lifted again. "For what?"

The woman was going to make him spell it out. "Yesterday's meeting was a wee bit awkward. We were nae expecting three young women to arrive. Thought was nae given as to which rooms would suit ye best." When her brow rose slightly higher, he rushed on, not allowing time for her to criticize. "Now that ye've seen the rest of the castle, ye can be the best judge of which rooms would suit ye and yer sisters."

"I told you last night that I *liked* my room."

"Aye, but ye had yet to see the rest of the castle. In the light of day, ye must prefer one of the other rooms."

"Not really. The one I have will make do quite nicely."

He wasn't sure he'd heard correctly. What woman wouldn't want the luxury the more modern rooms afforded? "I'm sure yer sisters will want ye all to move."

"If my sisters wish to move, they may do so, but Fiona was kind enough to have a tub delivered to my room, so I will be content."

"But..." If he couldn't get her to accept his offer, how was he going to get her to agree to staying quiet about the deed ownership? This wasn't going the way he planned. "Tell me if ye change your mind, then. Meanwhile, I will have a maid assigned to meet yer needs."

"That is not necessary. The gowns I brought do not need assistance to don."

Was the blasted woman not going to accept any of his help? "As a countess, ye must have all sorts of servants to do yer bidding." An odd expression crossed her face, one he couldn't read, and it was gone before he could ponder on it. "I am sure a village girl or two would be glad to come here to assist ye."

She shook her head. "I did not seek you out to discuss servants. What I want to know is when can I tour my—the—holdings? I would like to see what opportunities there may be for me to improve things."

Ian swallowed his pride at that remark, remembering how he'd deliberately sent in reports that didn't tell the whole story of just how profitable the lands were. And now, if he were going to convince her that he would be the perfect steward, he'd have to show her. And perhaps that could be an advantage, since offering a better room hadn't worked.

"I can arrange that in a day or two," he said, "but mayhap it might be wise nae to divulge that ye have the deed just yet. The clansmen will need a wee bit of time to get used to the idea that an English countess is wanting to ken their business." He gave her a beguiling smile, one that usually worked. "MacGregors are a bit wary of strangers, given our circumstances."

Emily tilted her head to one side to consider him. For a long moment she didn't speak, then she nodded. "I suppose there is a benefit in letting your clansmen get to know me first. To realize I am not a ninnyhammer who needs smelling salts when something goes awry. I agree to withhold the information. For now."

He breathed a sigh of relief. "Thank ye. I am sure ye will nae regret it."

She smiled as she turned toward the door to leave, but she looked like the cat who'd just discovered the door to the creamery open.

Ian wondered if the imaginary comment he'd thought of Rory making might not be true, after all. That she'd been sent from hell to bedevil him.

• • •

The whisky had definitely been excellent…and a bit potent. Emily left the library with a rather fuzzy feeling and wished the hallway wasn't tilting. *Uisge-beatha* Ian had called it. Water of life. A much better description than the blue devil that Londoner's commonly called gin. But then, this *uisge… oosh-ka.*something—she forgot the word—was so much smoother than gin. Why, she had hardly noticed the whisky slide down her throat like liquid silk. No indeed. And it left her all warm and tingly inside. Or maybe she'd felt all warm and tingly when she'd gone to pick up the bottle to check the label. For just a moment, she'd gotten the impression that Ian had moved closer to her, his body heat wrapping around her like a warm blanket. And oddly, she had felt safe.

What a ridiculous notion. Her head was finally clearing as she walked back to her room. She—and her sisters—were hardly welcome guests here. The apology and offer to move to the modern part of the castle had been a ploy, not a change of heart. She was quite adept at recognizing ploys. Albert had used them often when he'd needed something from her—usually a piece of her mother's jewelry to pawn to pay for his habits—and she'd learned early that his compliments were not sincere. Slowly, she'd built a wall around her heart as she also learned the hurtful consequences when she didn't acquiesce to his wheedling and cajoling. The fewer feelings she allowed herself, the less pain she felt.

In this case, Ian had wanted her to agree to keep her ownership of the castle quiet. He had not threatened her in any way nor did she think he would. He had simply made his point, albeit with a practiced smile that she was fairly sure worked on a vast majority of women. Not that she would be taken in by such. However, it wouldn't hurt her to keep the deed under wraps for now, until she learned the things she needed to know. It wasn't as though King George was going to rescind the title to the lands. She could agree with Ian to bide her time. So, for now, she'd let him think his beguiling smile had worked to persuade her.

Her sisters nearly pounced on her when she entered her bedchamber.

"How did your conversation with Mr. MacGregor fare?" Lorelei asked.

"No need to pussyfoot around." Juliana gave Emily a direct look. "Did he finally decide the deed was legal? That you own this place? And that you intend to run it as you see fit?"

"Is that all the questions you have?" Emily smiled at Juliana, used to her directness.

"For now."

"Yes, for now," Lorelei repeated. "And the answers? Was he rude? Were all the brothers there? How did they react?"

"That's three more questions. The brothers were gone when I arrived, so—"

"You were alone with Mr. MacGregor?" Lorelei's eyes grew round. "Did you leave the door open?"

"For pity's sake," Juliana said. "Emily's a *widow*. She does not need a chaperone."

Her sister was right, although the emphasis on *widow* made her feel like she was ancient. She was only four and twenty, although to her young, unmarried sisters that probably seemed like she was doddering on old age. "I closed the door because I did not want our conversation to be heard." The moment when she'd stood close to him flashed through her mind, but there was no reason to mention it. Or the instant tingle she'd felt when he'd handed her the glass and his fingers had brushed hers. She certainly wasn't going to admit that easy smile of his had any effect, either. That was very dangerous ground she wouldn't tread upon. "And, no, Mr. MacGregor was not rude."

Juliana lifted one brow skeptically.

"In fact," Emily went on before her sister could remark, "he apologized and offered us accommodations in the newer part of the castle."

"Thank God," Lorelei exclaimed. "These rooms are horrid."

"Agreed," Juliana said, her voice wary, "but why would he do that?"

Emily grinned. "It was a bribe."

Lorelei looked puzzled. "A bribe?"

"He asked me not to mention that the deed had been transferred and let his people think we are just on a visit."

"I knew it was too good to be true!" Juliana snorted. "I hope you set him to rights."

"Actually, I did not."

"What? Does that mean we have to stay in these rooms?" Lorelei all but wailed. "I did so love that room all done in blue that Fiona showed us—"

"And you may have it if you wish," Emily replied. "Or any other of your choosing. Both of you."

"Why would Mr. MacGregor be so considerate all of a sudden?" Juliana narrowed her eyes in consternation. "What did you do?"

She hoped her sister wasn't implying that she would act inappropriately or, worse, seduce the man. Lorelei looked at her with wide-eyed innocence, but Juliana had, unfortunately, had firsthand experience with propositions and she knew, more than Lorelei, how Emily had had to act to appease Albert.

"I did not do anything other than agree that it would be wise to give his people some time to get used to us before giving them all the details."

"But why delay?"

"Is it not better they know why we are here?"

Her sisters often lacked patience. "First, I want to tour the property and ask questions of the crofters and merchants. It will be easier if they do not know I am the new owner. Second, there is a distillery on this estate that makes excellent whisky. The kind that White's, as well as some of the other gentlemen's clubs, would love to stock. I gather that two uncles run it. I would like to meet them before I disclose who I am or my plans."

"And when is all of this going to happen?" Juliana asked.

"Mr. MacGregor is going to arrange a tour tomorrow or the next day," Emily replied, "and I will ask about the uncles."

"We do not have to go on the tour, do we?" Lorelei asked. "The weather is cold up here, even if it is summer."

"Neither of you has to go. In fact, it will be easier for me to get the locals to talk if they are not bombarded with all three of us."

"I am not sure it is smart to ride out without at least one of us," Juliana said. "What if the man—or his brothers—decide to do you bodily harm? Maybe even kill you? It could look like an accident and no one would ask questions."

"Why would anyone want to do such a thing? Especially if they do not know I have the deed?"

"Mr. MacGregor knows. So do his brothers." Juliana grimaced. "And that Rory… Well, I would not put anything past him."

"Just because the two of you struck it off on the wrong foot, does not mean he is malicious," Emily replied. "I will be fine, even if he does ride along."

But for some odd reason, she hoped he wouldn't.

• • •

Ian made himself scarce the next morning. As he rode out shortly after sunrise, letting Paden, his big stallion, have his head and enjoy a full-out gallop, he told himself he wasn't running away. He wasn't even avoiding the prospect of taking his Sassenach *guest* around MacGregor lands. He wasn't doing either of those two things. He truly wasn't. He simply needed time to think. And strategize.

His instincts told him that the dowager Countess of Woodhaven—the *young dowager* Countess of Woodhaven—hadn't deferred to his request because he was laird, at least to his clan. Nor did he think she'd acquiesced because she thought him wise. He suspected she was formulating some plan that would benefit her. She was a wily one, acting every inch the proper English lady and then downing a full dram of whisky without so much as a sputter. She bore watching.

The problem was, watching her made his male libido spring to life, much as he tried to ignore the fact. He couldn't help being aware of her alluring feminine curves—breasts that would fit nicely into his palms, a small waist his hands could encircle, a plump bottom that he could cradle against him—to say nothing of the golden halo of hair that suited her angelic-looking face. Angelic? Ian snorted in derision. Angels didn't drink whisky like she had. If he were a superstitious sort, he'd think the fae had a hand in sending her to Strae

Castle.

He reined in the stallion once they were well out of sight from anyone on the battlements—just in case his *guest* had a notion to climb up on them. He had a more immediate problem to solve, one in which he'd have to reconcile the low profit margins of his reports with the robust crops that promised a good harvest, as well as the obvious abundance of sheep grazing everywhere that wasn't planted. If only the countess had waited to come north for a couple of months, the fields would be tilled and the animals sheltered in pens for the winter. But then, anyone with a few ounces of common sense would travel north while the weather was good, and Emily Woodhaven had already proven that she didn't lack intelligence.

Of course, there was the off chance that she had not seen or read any of his reports. They'd been sent to the earl's man of business. Even as the thought entered his head, he tossed it aside. She wouldn't be here if she hadn't been aware of the reports. His only hope was that he could convince her that several years of too much rain had drowned out crops, but this was a bumper year. And that he was perfectly capable of being the steward for these lands. Then he would pray for an early, harsh winter to set in that would send her and her sisters fleeing to the relative comfort of London.

Ian spent the rest of the morning stopping at different crofters, explaining the earl's widow was *visiting* and, when he brought her around, to do their best in rejoicing over the blessing of crops this year. And, since most of his clansmen had taken surnames of Murray or Grant, they could also bear witness to how well he managed the holdings, even when times had been hard. He didn't have to spell it out for any of them, since once the Sassenach was back on her side of the border, they could resume acting like MacGregors.

By the time Ian returned to the castle he was feeling quite

satisfied with himself. The countess would get glowing reports of everything going well and have no need to oversee anything herself long-term. If he were lucky—and persuasive—she might never tell anyone about the deed. And, if his luck held, Lord Mount Stuart and his father, the Earl of Bute, would be successful in returning the MacGregor name and rights to their lands this year. All would be well then.

He felt much more hopeful as he rode through the raised portcullis. The bailey was full of clansmen—also Murrays and Grants—who were headed for the Great Hall for the noonday meal. As he turned his horse toward the stable, an angry shout came from the open front doors as a young man bolted down the steps toward him.

"Tell me 'tis nae true that the damn English king has given away the deed to our castle!"

Ian's hopes were dashed like a skiff on hard rocks blown by a harsh wind. Dozens of his clansmen had just heard what he wanted to keep secret. He glowered at the man whose eyes glittered back at him, black as coal.

Devon had returned home.

Chapter Five

Ian glared at each of his brothers, all of whom had sat as far away from his desk as possible with the exception of Devon, who stood directly in front of it, arms folded across his chest, legs splayed.

"I am still waitin' on an explanation," he said.

Ian gestured toward the others. "Which of these eejits told ye?"

"I was the one who explained the situation," Carr said.

Carr was by far the most diplomatic of all of them. If anyone could have *explained* the situation tactfully, or at least created a buffer from the harsh truth, it would have been Carr. That Devon was livid meant he'd failed.

"And did ye two"—Ian looked at Rory and Alasdair—"offer your opinions as well?"

Both of them shrugged a little too nonchalantly.

"Doona be blamin' our brothers," Devon said. "I've eyes in my head. Trunks and personal effects from five wagons being carried into the castle and then seeing three—*three*—Sassenachs supervising the unloading made me a wee bit curious."

So that's how Emily and her sisters had spent the day. He supposed he'd find out soon enough what rooms they had decided to claim with their belongings. But one calamity at a time.

"Curious? Ye were bellowing like a mad bull out in the bailey."

"Curiosity turned to anger when I learned the truth." Devon adjusted his stance. "We need to fight this, nae let those women move in."

Ian sighed. Devon was itching for a fight, and it would take all four of them to hold him down if he lost control now. He'd become violent after their father had married an Englishwoman, but he'd been a lad of twelve then and easy to subdue. He hadn't had a violent outburst in years, but this could certainly kindle the embers of the fire that stayed inside him.

"Carr had our solicitor check the deed. 'Tis legitimate."

"The damn king has nae right!" Devon leaned forward, placing both hands on the desk. "Old King George promised our grandfather he would only leasehold these lands—*MacGregor* lands—in return for our nae backing Bonnie Prince Charlie."

"'Twas George II who made that promise, nae his grandson."

"*A mhic an Diabhail*!" Devon straightened and began to pace. "That son of the devil should return to hell for nae honoring his grandfather's oath."

"Ye expect the English to understand honor?" Rory asked.

"Nae." Devon paused to look at him, then turned back to Ian. "Those women are going to be nothing but trouble."

"Ye have the right of that," Rory said. "The redheaded one has a tongue like a viper."

Alasdair chuckled in spite of the tension in the room.

"Ye say that because she didna succumb to yer charms."

Rory snorted. "I didna even *try* to charm the hellion."

"Be that as it may," Ian intervened before another argument ensued. "Now that our clansmen have heard the news, we must find a way to calm them."

"Calm them?" Devon asked, eyes blazing again. "If the Sassenachs were men, we'd send one of their heads back to London on a pike."

"Which would guarantee that the MacGregor name will never be cleared," Ian answered.

Devon glowered. "The old earl never stuck his nose in our business. Why did his widow decide to venture up here?"

"'Tis a good question." Ian was still trying to make sense of it himself. Aside from the rarity of a woman being able to own land in her own right, why would someone bred for the parlor rooms of Society want to come to Scotland? Londoners thought they were barbarians.

"We are hoping they willna want to stay," Carr said.

Devon narrowed his eyes. "They were moving their belongings in!"

"There will be nae lack of help to get them packed back up again."

"And how do ye propose to get them to agree?"

"The plan is to show the countess what a good steward I can be," Ian said. "Once she's assured of money continuing to come in, there will be nae reason for her nae to return to London and leave us in peace."

This time Rory spoke. "And we also plan to let them find out just how harsh life can be here."

"By letting them move into the new part of the castle?" Devon gave him a skeptical look and crossed his arms again.

"That was Ian's idea."

Ian shrugged. "I figured they would be more cooperative if they had better accommodations."

"Oh, aye," Devon said. "And have our clanswomen act as their servants, too."

Ian ignored the sarcastic tone. "I will make clear that the people who work in our castle are treated as equals. And we can make sure they ken Scots are independent and fend for themselves."

"*For sure*, we doona intend to make things easy for them," Rory said.

"Ye can count me in for that," Devon replied.

"I ken ye doona want them here." Ian looked at each of them. "But until—or *if*—the Earl of Bute can get our names cleared, we canna fight for our lands."

Carr nodded. "Meanwhile, we must take care nae to anger the countess too much lest she sets us out on the road and we must needs disappear into the mists again."

Ian raised a hand before Devon could protest. "Ye need to have a care for what ye do. 'Tis a fine line we walk."

He had the odd feeling he was already teetering on it.

• • •

"Who is the new man on the dais?" Lorelei asked that evening as they'd gathered in the Great Hall for the meal.

Juliana rolled her eyes. "Is it not plain as day that is another brother? They all look alike."

Lorelei tilted her head and considered. "There is something that is different about this one."

Emily looked at the dais and then to her sister. "Besides the fact that he has been scowling at us since we came in?"

"All of them have been scowling, ever since we had the wagons unpacked." Juliana glanced sideways at the raised table. "But I agree that his staring is somewhat unsettling."

"He looks really angry," Lorelei replied.

"He was not here when we arrived," Emily said. "Finding

out about us was probably a shock."

Lorelei shook her head. "Everyone else was shocked, too, when they heard the news, but mostly they are just ignoring us."

That was true, although where they were seated at the small square table to the side of the dais it was easy enough for no one to pay attention to them. Emily wasn't sure if Ian had meant it as an insult to tuck them away practically out of sight, but she considered it a kindness, whether intentional or not. It would have been very uncomfortable to try to mingle with the clan seated on the benches of the long tables—at least until they had a chance to get to know them—and she certainly didn't wish to be a spectacle on the dais. The more unassuming she could be right now, the better.

"It will take time for them to accept us," Emily answered.

After the conversation with Ian yesterday, she was under the impression that they would not announce her actual ownership until the clan, at least most of them, had gotten used to the idea of her sisters and herself living at the castle. That had all changed with the brother's outburst this afternoon. She'd heard several servants talking in low tones as she descended the spiral staircase from the old part of the castle earlier, and they'd quickly gone silent when they'd seen her. She thought they were probably speculating on why three women had brought five wagons worth of items that, somewhat grudgingly, Carr and Alasdair had been pressed into service to unload and take to the rooms that Lorelei and Juliana had chosen to use. Little did anyone know that those wagons contained *all* their worldly possessions.

"We may have to wait a long time for that to happen," Juliana said. "I could not get more than a 'yes' or 'no' out of any of the servants, and that was before everyone found out about the deed."

Emily had had similar experiences herself. When she'd

introduced herself to Hamish, the castellan, he'd looked at her with an attitude that would have done justice to any Mayfair butler. She'd been able to get only short, terse answers from Maggie about the household schedule and, when she'd gone to the kitchens, the cook made it clear whose domain that area was. She'd heard shouting in the bailey earlier but she hadn't thought much of it, since there was always noise outside.

"I thought you were not going to tell the clanspeople about the deed yet," Lorelei said.

"Yes. That is what Mr. MacGregor and I agreed to."

"Then what happened?" Juliana asked.

"I do not know." She'd taken some cheese and bread off the morning sideboard so the three of them could work through the midday meal. It wasn't until she was returning to her bedchamber to change her dusty dress for supper that she'd overheard two maids talking about the announcement that had been made. If it could be called that. It seemed that the lately arrived brother was fit to be tied. She sighed.

"It seems I will have to corner Mr. MacGregor again and get some answers."

• • •

"You are not planning to disappear again this morning, are you?"

Ian paused in saddling Paden and stared at the wall over the horse's withers for a moment before he slowly turned to face his nemesis.

Emily stood in the open doorway of the stable, the rising sun silhouetting her in a reddish glow as if she had stepped through a circle of fire. Or, as Devon or Rory would probably put it, *stepped from the gates of hell.* But demons didn't have golden hair or eyes the color of a mountain loch. Should they? He briefly wondered if either Jezebel or Delilah, the great seducers of biblical times, had been blond. He gave himself a mental shake. He doubted very much that the countess had her mind on seduction, given her no-nonsense expression. It was his own head—albeit probably not the one on his shoulders—that fancied that notion. Mayhap he needed to pay a call to a tavern wench in Dalmally to rid himself of this untoward lust he felt. He forced himself to gather his thoughts.

"I have crofters to see. Best to get an early start."

One delicate brow arched. "I believe that I asked for a tour of the lands. Since I am already dressed for riding, I will accompany you."

That was the last thing he needed. His plan had been to ride to all the crofters he'd contacted yesterday and revise the version of the story he'd given them. News from the castle spread more quickly than the River Awe overflowing its banks after a hard rain. And *this* news was tantamount to Loch Awe itself rising.

"I really have business to attend to today," he said. "Ye can plan on tomorrow, though."

She stepped inside. "As I said, I am dressed for riding."

Now that she was out of the sunlight, he could see that she was in a riding habit of dark-blue velvet with a long, divided skirt, a short, fitted jacket with braid, and a white shirt with high-necked ruffles. Her hair was secured in a tight bun at her nape and in her hand, she held a bonnet with enough ribbon to wrap around a sheep. She looked every inch an English countess…and completely, totally, inappropriately dressed to go visiting crofters.

If he wanted his clansmen to instantly dislike her, he should take her up on her offer. MacGregors, even more so than most Scots, had no tolerance for English aristocracy. Seeing her in her finery would make the women who toiled alongside their husbands equally shun her. His mission would be half accomplished if he took her with him dressed as she was. He sighed.

"Ye canna go dressed like that."

A slight frown creased her forehead as she looked down. "Why not? It is what I wore in London."

"Aye. Which makes it wrong for here."

She contemplated him for a moment. "Do your people hate the English that much?"

He shrugged, for some reason not wanting to be too blunt. "Ye canna blame them."

"Well, I will have to change their minds then."

He nearly laughed at the idea but managed to quell the thought. "Ye will nae be changing any minds dressed fancy like that."

"Fine." She folded her arms. "Then what do you suggest I wear?"

"Breeches." The word was scarcely out of his mouth when a vision filled his mind of how she would look in them. "With a long tunic and coat."

Both brows went up this time. "Your women wear men's breeches?"

"Ye are in the Highlands, lass. 'Tis practical clothing."

"And where would I find something like that?"

"Fiona can find something that will fit." The image in his brain sharpened at thinking how well breeches would fit. He refocused. "I doona think she is awake yet, though." His sister was an early riser, but, since she and Emily were in different parts of the castle, she probably didn't know.

"She is not only awake, but up and about. I saw her as I was coming out here."

So much for that hope. He smiled wanly. "It will take her a bit to find something and have it altered for ye."

"Nonsense." Emily gave him an angelic smile. "She and I are about the same size. It should not take me more than ten minutes to get changed." She turned toward the door. "Meanwhile, would you have a horse saddled? I am an experienced rider, so I prefer a mount with a bit of spirit."

If she rode like she drank whisky… He put that thought out of his mind. "I will think on that."

"All right. Ten minutes then."

Ian watched as she hurried across the bailey and then he led Paden to the back door of the stable. In another moment, he was mounted and galloping away.

He would face Lady Woodhaven's wrath tomorrow. For today, he needed to still the waters that would be churning among his people.

• • •

Unfortunately, when Emily returned to the house, it took her several minutes to locate Fiona who, she soon found out from a maid, liked to go up on the battlements to watch the sun rise.

The staircases leading up to them were located in the side towers of the old part of the castle. As she passed the Great Hall, she saw Ian's brothers inside. Not having time to stop and speak, even though it was quite rude, she hurried past as they neared the door. She felt eyes penetrating her back, but she didn't turn around.

Once inside the tower, the stairs spiraled upward, much like the staircase to her bedchamber, but these were more uneven. Luckily, they were built against the right wall although there was no railing. This, too, was a form of defense when the medieval castle had actually been used as such. An enemy trying to make his way up the stairs would not have his sword arm free to attack while defenders coming down from the battlements would be able to wield their swords easily. She wondered what other protections were in place. When she had time, she was going to fully explore. For now, though, she needed to find Fiona.

By the time she reached the door that led into the battlements, she was feeling a bit dizzy from circling four flights. Catching her breath, she stepped outside, nearly blinded by the sunlight after the darkness of the tower.

Sunlight. The sun had clearly risen. How much time had she wasted? She'd said ten minutes. How long would Ian wait?

At least Fiona was not far away. She had walked about halfway across the front of the castle, hands lightly on a merlon, her face lifted, her eyes closed as she breathed in the fresh morning air. Emily hesitated to disturb her, but she needed those breeches.

"Good morning."

Fiona's eyes popped open and she turned her head, then she smiled. "Emily. Do ye enjoy sunrises, too?" She gestured. "Come and look."

Emily did enjoy getting up early, although seeing a sunrise in London was near to impossible, but it afforded her a quiet time of day. Even though there were no social calls until near noon and Albert had never stirred until well past that time, the duties of running a household—actually, the whole estate, since her husband had rarely been fit to do so—had made her appreciate those few quiet moments shortly after dawn.

Carefully, she made her way along the ledge. Although it was wide enough for a man to pass by, the stone was slippery with dew. She stopped a few feet from Fiona to take in the sight and gasped.

The hills near the castle were blanketed in lush green, the mountains beyond steeped in the darker brown shades of dormant heather. Far to her right, she could make out a winding silver strip of river as the sun glistened on it. To her left, below the craggy top on which the castle sat, was a small village. And the expanse of fields in front of her were dotted with sheep and crofters' huts.

"It is beautiful! I can see why you come up here."

"Aye. And a bit of silence before I have to deal with my brothers."

"Speaking of your brothers...or, at least, Ian... I have come to ask you to lend me a pair of breeches," Emily said. "Ian told me my London riding habit would not be accepted well by your clan."

"Aye, it wouldna, but I do like it." Fiona gave her a wistful look. "I would like to go to London. Can ye tell me about it?"

"Yes, of course. Later." Time was of the essence right now. "I would really like to change into the breeches, since Ian is waiting for me."

Fiona frowned slightly. "He is nae waiting."

A sense of wariness rose. "Why do you say that?"

"I saw him ride out just as the sun rose."

"You saw..." Emily didn't finish the sentence. The sun had just risen as she'd returned to the castle. That meant Ian hadn't waited ten minutes. He hadn't even planned to. As soon as she'd turned her back, he must have left through the the other side of the barn.

She quickly squelched the hurt—no, the *anger*—that tried to surface. She'd learned long ago neither of those emotions did her any good. Only cool, calm logic had worked when dealing with Albert.

Cool, calm logic would work with Ian MacGregor, too. He had just declared war, even if he didn't know it.

Chapter Six

Ian could no longer put off the inevitable. He waited in the breakfast room of the newer part of the castle the next morning for Emily to put in an appearance. He had thought to check the stables first when he rose to see if she were already waiting, but then had abandoned the idea. If she were lying in wait, it would only look like he was trying to escape her company once again.

It really had not been escape, he told himself…again. Two mornings ago he'd ridden out with the grandiose notion of warning the crofters and clansmen that the *visiting* countess would be coming round. Then yesterday, thanks to Devon's outburst in the bailey, he'd had to go to those crofters and clansmen and explain that the "visit" might be prolonged, due to some entanglement with the deed. Being a MacGregor, he was not about to surrender to the whim of an English king or his writ.

MacGregors hadn't taken Mary, Queen of Scots kindly for bequeathing some of their lands to Campbells, and they'd taken a dim view of her son James as well. If they could defy the Scottish monarchy for centuries, they certainly didn't have trouble ignoring the present English king. Or, at least, until it suited them otherwise. If—no, *when*—the Earl of Bute's son could persuade Parliament to restore their name. Once that happened, Ian would petition George to restore the deed as well. Most of the people he'd spoken to yesterday had agreed to the pretense of not refuting the deed. For now.

The battle would come later.

Hearing footsteps—feminine ones—in the hall, he braced himself for another kind of battle.

He rose as Emily appeared in the doorway, and a breath caught in his throat. He should never have mentioned her wearing breeches. The pair that Fiona had lent her fit like a second skin and were far too tight, showing the curve of her hips and long, slender legs. As she walked past him to the sideboard, he got a glimpse of a very nicely rounded bottom. The glance turned into an ogle. Every step she took made that bottom wiggle. He flexed his hands, wanting to fill his palms with her and splay his fingers into that soft flesh while pulling her against him. He balled his fists behind him. It was a good thing she had her back to him because he probably looked like a gawking fool. He'd managed to get his idiotic lust under control when she turned, and he inwardly groaned.

He hadn't noticed that the short-waisted riding jacket had been open when she walked in, but now he saw that it was. The shirt she wore—he recognized it as one of Fiona's—fit her just as snugly as the breeches. The faint outline of her breasts was visible against the material. He said a silent prayer of thanks that the shirt was buttoned to the collar at least.

Evidently his sister was smaller than Emily. He narrowed his eyes thoughtfully. Actually, his sister was a bit *taller* than Emily. Where had these clothes come from? He seemed to recall the jacket from several years ago, but why would Fiona give the Sassenach clothing that was so tight when her own would have fit?

Emily smiled at him and set the plate down across from him. "There is no need for you to stand while I get my breakfast."

Nimble though he was, she sat down before he could get to her chair. He eyed her warily as she dug into coddled eggs and cut a slice of ham. She was acting as though nothing were wrong.

"Did you get your business settled yesterday?" she asked.

"Aye." Cautiously, he sat back down and resumed eating. It was an innocent enough question, but he wondered what she really wanted to know.

She gave him another smile. "That is good then."

"Aye," he said again, beginning to feel like a parrot, but not wanting to offer too much information. When he'd returned yesterday, barely in time for the evening meal, Fiona had informed him that Emily had asked for a tray, so he'd assumed she was angry.

Her pleasantness was making him uneasy, somewhat like when the woods were too still and something lurked out there. He just didn't know what was lurking in her mind. Perhaps he should just pretend that all was well between them.

"My schedule is free today. What would ye like to see?"

"Where do you suggest we start?"

She was making this too easy. Which made him *un*-easy. Something was amiss, but he didn't know what it was.

"Ye mentioned ye wanted to ken about the whisky business. We could ride to the distillery, if ye like."

"That would be wonderful. Is it far?"

"Nae, only about a mile."

"Did you say your uncles run the distillery?"

Ian nodded. "They actually live here at the castle, but they've been out inspecting the barley and the peat bog the past few days."

"Peat bog?"

"'Tis a marshy field with decayed vegetation. Large chunks of it are turned over to dry and then it's used to heat crofters' homes. 'Tis used in the kiln to dry the barley as well. The smoke gives our whisky a distinctive flavor."

"That sounds...interesting." She laid down her fork. "Perhaps we could visit the bog first?"

He frowned slightly. "We will ride past it, but it can be a dangerous place."

"How so?"

"As I said, 'tis a marshy field. If ye venture into the part that's more mud and water than peat, it can suck ye down."

"Does that happen often?"

"Nae, the peat diggers ken where to cut."

"Well, I shall take great care to stay on my horse then."

"Speaking of horses, I ken I have the right mount for ye." There was a gentle, old nag that was slow as ice melting in January, which would mean they wouldn't see much today besides the distillery. And, if Emily were the expert rider she said she was, it would be completely frustrating to ride such a horse. And, if she weren't a good rider, he wouldn't be putting her neck at risk.

"I hope you did not spend much time thinking on it." Emily rose, forcing him to pop up as well. "While you were gone yesterday, I chose my mount myself." She put down her napkin and smiled. "Shall we go?"

He had a feeling he wasn't going to like this.

• • •

Emily watched Ian covertly as the head groom, Jamie, led out the horse she'd chosen yesterday. As she suspected, Ian was not pleased. In fact, he glowered.

"This is nae a suitable mount for a lady." He turned his

glare on the groom. "What were ye thinking? That one is barely gentled to the saddle."

The poor man looked like he'd been caught between a wolf and a bear. She took pity on him, since he *had* tried to talk her out of the spirited black filly, appropriately named *Muirne* for "fiery one." He'd wrung his cap in his hands and it wasn't until she assured him—in front of several stable hands who had gathered around—that she would take full responsibility if she fell off. In her peripheral vision she'd seen the men start to grin and knew silent wagers were being made. One had even goaded him into "letting the Sassenach try." He'd reluctantly given in, muttering something in Gaelic that she hadn't understood.

"Do not blame Jamie." She noticed that none of the wagerers from yesterday were hovering today, probably because most of them had lost and none wanted to be pointed to as having encouraged her ride. "I insisted."

Ian turned his attention back to her. "Ye *insisted*? And what do ye ken about horses?"

She fixed a cool look on him. "I would say the animal is of Friesian blood, which stud line was ancestor to both the British shire and the Fell pony. In medieval times, they carried knights into battle, which makes her both surefooted and sturdy for the hills of Scotland." She smiled at Ian. "A wise choice on your part to purchase her. I assume she will be bred to that bay stallion of yours?"

Jamie gaped at her.

Ian blinked, opened his mouth, closed it, then grudgingly nodded. "In a year or two when she is ready."

"Yes, breeding a young mare risks the chance of a weak foal."

Jamie began to grin, something he quickly hid behind his hand and a cough.

Ian stared at her. "Is husbandry a topic of discussion in

London parlors these days?"

"*Husbandry* is often and widely discussed in social circles, since it is the objective of nearly every young woman to catch one, preferably with a title and wealth to accompany it." Her smile widened. She couldn't help it. "But that may not be the kind you mean?"

His ears turned slightly pink, a rather endearing quality.

"Ye ken 'tis nae what I meant." He looked around the stable to where the men were industrially applying themselves to various tasks and appearing to pay no heed to the conversation. "I thought ladies dinna discuss *breeding* of any kind."

It was her turn to blush as she caught the innuendo. She had never been able to conceive a child with Albert, although she wasn't sure if that was a blessing or a curse, considering. A fleeting thought crossed her mind. What would a child of Ian's look like? She pushed the thought away. Good heavens, discussing the filly's mating with the stallion must have turned her mind. She and Ian were barely civil to each other. He certainly wasn't entertaining ideas of *mating* with her. Not that she was, either. Thinking such thoughts. She wasn't. Taking a deep breath, she lifted her chin.

"You are quite right. The subject of one being *enceinte* is not broached in London parlors."

Ian raised a brow. "But ye pay nae heed of what is proper?"

She wasn't quite sure how to take that. "I am not overly fond of parlor conversation. Or London Society, for that matter."

"Is that why ye came north?"

"Partly." She certainly wasn't going to tell him she and her sisters had no place else to go. "I am quite interested in learning about distilling whisky."

A corner of his mouth quirked up. "I would say ye have a

fair passing acquaintance with the whisky process already."

He was obviously referring to the way she'd finished off that dram, which certainly hadn't been ladylike, but she'd had enough experience sneaking into Albert's library to take a quick swig of cognac to ward off the pain of the latest bruise she'd received. She had not had time to linger and sip. But Ian didn't need to know that, either.

"I am interested in learning about sheep farming, too."

His brow lifted again. "To supplement your knowledge of horse breeding?"

"Not all women limit themselves to playing the pianoforte and embroidery."

"A fact I'll tuck away." He studied her. "How do ye ken about horses?"

"The estate next to the earl's—my husband's—country house bred horses. Hunters, mostly, but the owner was interested in developing good saddle horses as well. He'd invested in several Andalusians and Friesians." The man and his wife had taken pity on her and invited her and her sisters over often to get away from Albert. Another fact Ian didn't need to know. "Since I enjoy riding, I took an interest."

He gave her a skeptical look. "I still doona think Muirne is the right horse for ye."

Having heard her name, the filly snorted and pawed the ground. Emily ran a hand along her sleek neck and led the animal to a bale of hay. Before anyone thought to stop her, she used it as a mounting block to slip into the saddle. "Let's find out, shall we?"

Tapping the filly's flanks gently, she rode out of the stable, leaving Ian gaping at her.

• • •

Ian muttered a curse and leaped onto Paden. The stallion

didn't need any urging to catch up to the filly. His hooves clattered over the drawbridge directly behind Muirne, causing her to shy suddenly to the left. For a moment, Emily swayed in the saddle before catching her balance. If she'd been using a sidesaddle, she doubtless would have been tossed over.

"I told ye that filly is nae ready for the road," Ian said. "Turn around. We will get ye another mount."

"We will do nothing of the kind," Emily replied, her hand stroking the filly's neck to calm her. "You should not have galloped directly behind her. You practically overrode us."

Ian opened his mouth to retort, then closed it. Emily had already ridden on ahead. Besides, she was right. Even a mature horse didn't like being crowded, and loud noise could make one skittish. And, he had to admit, Emily did seem to know how to handle a horse. With a sigh he nudged Paden forward, this time staying to the side where the filly could see him approach.

She glanced at him as he came alongside. "Tell me about your distillery. I do not recall seeing it listed as a source of revenue."

She had definitely read the reports he'd sent. And understood them. Which meant she was probably going to demand to see the ledgers he kept here as well. He suddenly felt like he was treading on very boggy ground that had nothing to do with the peat bog nearby.

"They were nae mentioned because 'tis mostly a local business we do."

"Did you not say you sold the whisky in Glasgow?"

"Well…aye. But nae that much. 'Tis more for local consumption." He waved a hand vaguely. "Every clan has its own stills."

"But your whisky was excellent," she said. "How many bottles do you produce a year?"

The woman was as tenacious as a terrier at a rabbit hole.

"I would have to check with Broderick and Donovan."

"Your uncles?"

"Aye. They keep the books, since they run the distillery."

"But you cannot give me an estimate?"

A very stubborn, obstinate terrier she was. "'Tis better if I check with them first."

She gave him a look as though he were daft. "I can ask them myself."

No. That would not do at all. The income from the whisky—which was substantial, if unreported—was distributed among the clansmen, since they harvested the barley and dug the peat. To take that money away from them would limit their ability to purchase supplies and would prove a hardship come the winter.

Equally as important, he needed to talk with his uncles to alert them about the deed. Neither would be happy to learn of the new circumstances, and that would be putting it mildly.

"Changes canna be made overnight as ye will discover once ye see the kiln and stills. 'Tis a long process that canna be rushed, so the question can keep a day or two, nae?" Ian asked.

"I suppose," she said as they approached the large rectangular building not far off the road. "But I do intend to inspect the distillery and its books *soon*."

He wasn't sure what *soon* meant to a terrier determined to root its rabbit, but he let it go for now. He had a bigger problem. Actually, two of them, since his uncles had emerged from the distillery and were walking toward them.

As they dismounted and he made the introductions, he watched both of them carefully, hoping they wouldn't get off to a bad start before he had a chance to explain everything. Donovan was in his late fifties, remembered the defeat at Culloden well, and resented having to use the surname Murray.

Broderick was his father's youngest brother, only about fifteen years older than himself. He had traveled to London once and seemed to get along fine with the English—or at least as well as any Scot could—but his goal was to run the distillery when Donovan retired. He'd even talked to Ian about buying it outright...hence another reason to keep the profits close to home.

"I am pleased to meet both of you," Emily said. "I have sampled your fine whisky and am looking forward to learning about the whole process of making it. If we can increase production, I am sure I can arrange to have it sold to some of London's best gentlemen's clubs. But..." She glanced at Ian, then smiled at the men. "I promised I would not launch a barrage of questions at you today."

Although they both nodded cordially and smiled back, Ian didn't miss the look his uncles exchanged. It was a look that meant they weren't agreeing to anything.

Chapter Seven

"You summoned us here?" Juliana asked as she and Lorelei joined Emily in her bedchamber late that afternoon.

"I do not know why you insist on staying in here." Lorelei sank down on the bed. "It's drafty and those twisty stairs aren't safe. Why do you not pick a room near us?"

Emily shook her head. "I like having this part of the castle to myself. Its creaks and groans at night let me imagine the ghosts of old lairds are walking about."

Lorelei shuddered. "Do not even jest about things like that."

Juliana rolled her eyes. "Stop being superstitious."

"I heard all old castles are supposed to be haunted," Lorelei retorted. "Another reason I am glad we are in the newer part."

Emily smiled at her. "You do not think a spirit could wander there?" The remark brought a look of consternation to her sister's face. "Never mind. I am sure Fiona would have said something if Strae Castle has a resident ghost."

Lorelei's eyes rounded. "She has. Said something, that

is."

"About a ghost?" Juliana laughed. "Let me guess. Somebody was murdered—actually, a lot of somebodies, considering this place was used for battle—and some old warrior cannot rest."

"No. Fiona told me it was a woman who was murdered." Lorelei gave her sister a reproachful look. "Her stepmother."

"*What*?" That Ian had a stepmother was news to Emily, but then it wouldn't have been in any financial reports sent and she was hardly on personal terms with Ian or his family.

Lorelei nodded and sat up straighter now that she had their attention. Emily suspected she was about to launch theatrically into a lengthy telling of the story and that wasn't why she'd asked them to come up here. "Just tell us what Fiona said. No embellishment please."

Lorelei frowned. "Fiona said her own mother caught a fever shortly after she was born and that her father was miserable—at least that is what he told his children—and that—"

"Please," Juliana said. "Fiona's version?"

"I am getting to it. Fiona was four when her father remarried. She remembers that the lady was blond and English—"

"English?" Emily asked in surprise.

"Yes. Her name was Isobel. She was the daughter of a dragoon officer. It is all rather romantic," Lorelei said with a sigh. "They eloped to Gretna Green because her father did not want her marrying a Scot, especially a MacGregor, since they were—"

"How was she murdered?" Juliana interrupted.

Lorelei stuck out her bottom lip. "You are ruining my story."

"One that we really do not have time for right now," Emily said gently. "I have matters to discuss with you, so just tell us what happened."

"Oh, all right. She was murdered in her bed." Lorelei paused for effect. "Stabbed. Blood everywhere."

In spite of trying not to look interested, Juliana finally gave in to the silence following that remark. "Who did it?"

Her sister gave her a triumphant look. "Nobody knows."

"Was Ian's—Fiona's—father not here?"

Lorelei shook her head. "He had gone to Dalmally and did not return until the next morning. He is the one who found her."

"There were no suspects?"

"Oh, yes. There were *lots* of suspects." Lorelei started warming to her subject again. "Isobel was much younger than her husband and very pretty. *And* very friendly. Fiona remembers whenever her father was away, gentlemen would call—"

"I think that is enough," Emily cut in. "We do not need to gossip about the dead."

"But—"

"No more."

"So how does it end?" Juliana asked. "Does Isobel wander the halls crying or something?"

"No. It is Fiona's father that is said to wander, searching for whoever murdered his bride." Lorelei glanced from one sister to the other. "He opens and closes doors. Sometimes the door to her bedchamber is left open."

Emily pursed her lips. "Are you going to tell me that I am sleeping in the murdered lady's bedchamber?"

"No," Lorelei answered. "It is the one next door."

Emily released a breath she didn't know she'd been holding. How silly to get absorbed in such a tale! "Well, that is a relief then," she said briskly. "And now I would like to tell you about the uncles I met today, since they will be arriving at the castle later and Mr. MacGregor has invited us all to dine in a smaller room." She looked at both her sisters. "I want each of you to be on your *best* behavior."

"Did they act like eejits, too?" Juliana asked.

"*Eejits*?" Emily replied. "Are you taking to the Scots language?"

Her sister shrugged. "I like the way the word sounds."

"So were they?" Lorelei added. "Eejits?"

"No, and we do not need to refer to Ian—Mr. MacGregor's—brothers in that way." Emily went on. "Donovan Murray is older and rather aloof. The younger one, Broderick, was reserved, although he did answer questions I had about the distilling process."

"Were they friendly, though?" Lorelei asked.

"Well…"

"That means *no*," Juliana said. "Are they like that annoying Rory?"

"Or worse, Devon?"

"Neither. Just…quiet." Emily couldn't quite explain the unsettled feeling she'd had, and she didn't want to alarm her sisters. "Our arrival has been a shock. They will all need time to accept us."

"Which is why you want us to behave properly," Lorelei said.

"Yes." She looked askance at Juliana who grudgingly nodded and gave them both a smile.

She hoped she was right. All they needed was time.

• • •

Ian rose from his chair as Emily and her sisters entered the smaller dining room that evening. He'd purposely invited them to arrive a few minutes earlier than his brothers and uncles so they would already be seated. He knew he could count on Carr and Alasdair to act like gentlemen and rise—

and even Rory, for all his blustering, but Devon was another story. He'd been sullen when told they would all be eating dinner together. The last thing his uncles needed to see was one of his brothers being deliberately disrespectful.

"You have a round table in here," Emily said, looking surprised.

Lorelei giggled. "Just like King Arthur's."

Juliana started to mutter something under her breath but stopped after a sharp look from Emily. Ian suspected it was a remark about no gallant knights being present. Before he could respond to Lorelei, his brothers and uncles entered the room. With small nods of acknowledgment, save for Devon, they took their places.

"Ye are nae far from the truth about the intent of the table," Ian told Lorelei when all were seated. "This is actually our council room used, in better days, for the lairds of neighboring clans to meet twice a year."

"Would you have a banquet and a ball?" she asked.

"A banquet. 'Twas a time for each laird—Campbell, Cameron, Buchanan, Graham, Murray, Grant—to air grievances and settle accounts, instead of declaring war on one another."

"That sounds like a smart thing to do," Emily said.

"Aye. Some of the clans may be rivals, and feuds do endure, but we had a greater common enemy to face."

Juliana raised a brow. "Us?"

Rory snorted, but Ian ignored him. "The English soldiers. There's nae a Scottish lad who doesna ken what King William did at Glencoe in 1692."

"That was a long time ago." Emily frowned. "Did the Campbells not direct the slaughter of the MacDonalds?"

Ian blinked. That Emily knew anything about Scottish history was interesting. Most Sassenachs didn't bother.

"'Tis true Archibald Campbell was nae happy King

James would nae restore his father's lands, so he turned his support to King William and Queen Mary. As colonel to Argyll's Foot Regiment, he sent the order William had signed."

Emily glanced around at the men. "Forgive me if I stir bad memories, but were the Campbells not responsible for the MacGregors' original plight as well?"

Again, Ian was taken by the fact that the dowager Countess of Woodhaven had obviously done some research. Looking at his brothers, he saw looks of astonishment—in varying degrees—on their faces, although Devon scowled. His uncles were studying Emily as though she were some sort of new species.

"I suppose ye could say that. Queen Mary gave John Campbell of Glenorchy the authority to pursue MacGregors with fire and sword—"

"And your clan had done nothing to deserve this?" Juliana asked.

"We didna." Devon glared at her. "Robert the Bruce shouldna have given MacGregor lands to Campbells."

"But if it was done legally—"

"Ye are in the Highlands, lass," Rory said. "The lands we lost had been ours for centuries."

"And England was once under Roman rule," Juliana retorted. "Thank goodness we do not speak Latin!"

Rory leaned back and crossed his arms. "'Twould be better for me if ye did, so I would nae understand it."

Juliana narrowed her eyes. "Are you telling me to be quiet?"

"I think that would be an excellent idea." Emily gave her sister a warning look. "We are guests here."

"Guests?" Juliana gave her sister an irritated look. "Everyone at this table knows that you hold the deed to this property. Why not just be honest about it?"

The remark was met with total silence...the kind of silence that preceded a battle charge. Before a verbal attack could ensue, servants came to the rescue, albeit unknowingly, by bringing in platters of food. Fiona followed them in.

Ian hoped no one would start throwing the victuals, for there certainly wasn't peace at this round table.

• • •

Emily could have throttled her sister. And she might try if they survived the frigid blast of coldness that suddenly surrounded them. Every man sat motionless, as though they were ice carvings.

Fiona looked around as she took her seat. "What is going on?" When no one answered, she gave each of her brothers a thoughtful look, but waited for the servants to leave. "What did I miss?"

"We've just been put in our place by the very privileged *Lady* Caldwell," Rory said.

"Which one—"

"Need ye ask?" Rory reached for his ale. "The one with the viper tongue."

Juliana narrowed her eyes. "Now you are calling me a snake?"

"*Enough*." Ian spoke the same time as Emily did, his baritone harmonizing with her alto to blend into one sound. She gave herself an inward shake. This was not the time to be thinking of making music.

"I know that our arriving as we did has been dismaying," Emily said. "I apologize for my sister—"

"You do not have to apologize for me," Juliana interrupted. For a moment, Emily was afraid she was going to launch another tirade, but instead, she took a deep breath. "I spoke hastily when I should not have."

Rory raised a brow. "Is that an apology, lass?"

"It is enough of one." Ian looked expectantly at his brother. "Do ye think another might be in order?"

Rory held his gaze, then finally turned toward Juliana. "I should nae have compared ye to a snake."

"And is *that* an—"

"Yes, it is, Juliana," Emily finished for her. "And I really think we are not doing justice to the food if we let it get cold."

"I agree," Ian said. "We can discuss what measures will be taken regarding the deed tomorrow."

Carr nodded. "'Tis nae like the ladies are going anywhere."

Emily noticed Donovan and Broderick exchange a look. Hoping to mollify them and offer words of encouragement, she spoke. "I saw so many possibilities this afternoon at the distillery. I am quite sure, with your help, we can turn a very nice profit."

"We shall see," Donovan said.

"'Tis a lot ye doona ken about the process, though," Broderick added.

"Sassenachs." Devon stabbed a piece of meat. "Bloody English—"

"*Gabh air do shocair!*" Ian glared at his brother.

"Aye, do shut your gab," Alasdair said. "Nae need to be insulting the ladies." He smiled at Lorelei. "'Tis nae the lasses' fault we are in this predicament."

Devon glowered at him and stabbed another piece of meat.

Lorelei smiled back at Alasdair. "I do appreciate a gentleman with manners."

His smile widened. "Some of us do have them."

Emily sighed inwardly. As much as she wanted to find a way to establish an agreeable settlement to the issue of the deed, she didn't need Lorelei to practice her charms on one of the MacGregors. This was not London where flirtation was a fine art and every male understood the rules. She would need to talk with *both* of her sisters.

But not tonight. It had been a tiring day. She couldn't really tell if she'd made headway with the uncles. They both remained stoic, giving nothing away. Of course, she hadn't expected to be welcomed with open arms, but still…

At least she'd won a small battle with her choice of horse. On the way back to the castle, Ian had grudgingly admitted she'd handled the filly well. And she—although she didn't voice it—had noticed just how well he sat his own stallion, strong muscular thighs guiding the animal. And his hands had been light on the reins. She wouldn't have expected such a gentle touch… Emily blinked and refocused. Good lord! Why was she thinking about Ian's *hands*? Or how his touch would feel? She must be more exhausted than she thought because, for her own sanity, she needed to curb any personal reactions to him.

Thankfully, the meal was short, since all the courses were brought in at once. She made her excuses to retire. It didn't take her long to perform her ablutions in her bedchamber and don a serviceable, warm night rail. Banking the fire, she turned back the thick wool blanket and sank gratefully into the feather mattress that she'd brought with her. Closing her eyes, she burrowed into the pillow. Tomorrow, she would start assuming duties. But for tonight…umm, sleep…

Some hours later, Emily bolted upright in bed, aware that her heart was pounding and her breathing was shallow. She looked around the room quickly, the embers from the fire casting long shadows, but all was still.

She shook her head to clear it. She'd been dreaming of a man standing by her bed, watching her. She hadn't been able to see his face in the near darkness, and he said nothing. Then, there'd been a small movement of his hand and she'd glimpsed the steel of a blade...

This was ridiculous. There was no one here. To reassure herself, she slid her legs over the side of the bed and padded to the door to look into the hall. Nothing stirred. She closed the door and slid the bolt, feeling rather foolish at taking such a precaution.

Fatigue is affecting me, she thought as she returned to bed. That, and Lorelei's story about how Fiona's stepmother had died. Her weary mind had entangled bits and pieces, causing her to have a nightmare.

There had not been anyone in the room.

Chapter Eight

Emily could hear shouting as she made her way down the winding staircase the next morning. It seemed to be coming from the Great Hall, which was unusual, since the clanspeople broke their fasts early to go about their daily tasks and chores. Most of the time she and her sisters had the huge room to themselves.

As she entered, she saw Juliana and Lorelei seated at their table, although neither of them were eating. They were too enthralled with whatever was taking place.

She turned her attention to the group near the dais. Ian, his brothers, and his uncles had circled around a man who she assumed was cursing in Gaelic, while a younger lad wildly waved his arms in what looked like an attempt to explain something.

"Ye say two dozen sheep are missing?" Ian asked when the man stopped for breath.

"Aye. Damn reivers!" He gestured to the boy. "Neither of us saw or heard anything."

"And we spent the night in the shepherd's croft," the boy

piped up.

"This morning when I was ready to move the flock, it seemed smaller," the man continued. "Then I did the count."

"Could be Camerons," Alasdair said. "They ken how to be stealthy."

"Their holdings are a hard day's ride from here," Carr said. "Why would they bother coming this far south to take sheep?"

"Colquhouns then? Or Buchanans? They're both close."

Ian shook his head. "The Colquhouns would nae have stopped at two dozen. They'd have tried to take the whole flock. And we've nae quarrel with Buchanans."

"Campbells, then," Rory growled. "The whole bloody lot would like to make sure we doona get our name restored."

"Excuse me." Emily stepped up to the men. "What does having your name restored—which is a matter for Parliament—have to do with someone stealing our sheep?"

There was a moment's total silence as her use of *our* sheep sank in. The shepherd and the boy she assumed to be his son turned wide eyes at her.

"Ye are the English countess, aren't ye?" the boy asked.

His father swatted the side of his head. "'Tis obvious, nae?"

The lad rubbed his ear and stepped out of his father's range. "A Sassenach will blame *us* for the theft." He turned to Emily. "Please, your ladyship. Doona turn us out."

"Nobody is going to be turned out," she replied. "But please explain to me how the two matters relate?"

"Yes, please do," Juliana said as she and Lorelei joined the group. "None of this makes sense."

Rory shrugged. "Because ye are nae a Scot."

"Are you—"

"*Hush*," Emily hissed at her. "Not now." She smiled at Ian. "Please continue."

"The feuding is nigh five hundred years old," he said.

Emily felt her own eyes widen. "Five hundred *years*? Is that not a bit long to sustain an argument?"

Devon glowered at her. "Scots have long memories."

"Och, well," Ian said. "We have nae been fighting the entire time."

"True," Alasdair added. "Some MacGregors even took the Campbell surname."

"Traitors," Devon muttered.

Carr gave him a reproving look. "And there have been intermarriages amongst us as well. Nae all of them are enemies."

"I am confused." Emily turned to Ian. "I still do not understand how the two matters relate."

"If everyone will be quiet…" Ian gave each of his brothers a warning glance. "After Bannockburn—in the fourteenth century—Robert the Bruce awarded the Campbells Kilchurn Castle and the lands around it."

"Which had been MacGregors?"

"Most of it," Ian answered, "but land titles and legal documents were just beginning to be used."

"So the land was in dispute?"

"Nae!" Devon glared at her. "'Twas ours!"

Ian ignored him. "The Campbells grew more powerful over time—"

"Because they sided with the bloody English when it benefited them," Devon said.

Carr put a hand on his brother's shoulder. "Let Ian finish."

"Devon is right to some extent. They have amassed great swaths of land to the west and north of us. Presently, we are nae threat to them, but if the Earl of Bute and Lord Mount Stuart are successful in Parliament, we could reclaim some of those—*our*— lands."

Emily drew her brows together. "I still do not see the connection."

"'Tis simple." Donovan spoke up. "They will expect us to retaliate and not only steal back our sheep but some of theirs as well, or possibly some coos."

"And that will make us look like thieves, since the English doona see reiving as a time-honored tradition," Broderick said.

"But if the Campbells—or whoever—started it, why would you be blamed?"

"Because, as Devon said, the Campbells have sided with the Crown enough to have the king's ear in such a matter. King George also made the Duke of Argyll commander in chief for Scotland, so ye can see who will be believed," Alasdair explained. "The Campbells will simply claim we were the ones who stole their livestock."

"But that is not right." Emily looked at Ian again. "What can we do?"

"First, we canna just put the blame on the Campbells, since we have nae proof." Ian turned to Rory. "Ye are our best tracker. If anyone can find the trail, 'tis ye."

Rory gave Juliana a smug look before he nodded. "I'll leave right away."

"And if he finds out you are right?" Emily asked as he left. "What will you do?"

"Since the duke's duties keep him away most of the time, he will nae have had a hand in this, but his cousin Henry oversees things, so we can ask him to come speak to us," Alasdair said. "I canna see him ordering something so petty as this, but he may well ken who wants to create mischief."

Lorelei smiled at him. "How clever of you to suggest that."

He grinned back. "I am the smart one of the bunch."

"That is in dispute," Carr said. "Do ye not remember me

thrashing ye in chess?"

"Be that as it may." Ian gestured to Alasdair. "Ye do have a good idea."

"And it wouldna hurt to find out which way the wind blows with the Campbells," Carr added. "Mayhap if the duke hears the Countess of Woodhaven—an *Englishwoman*—has taken up residence with us, he might be inclined to support Bute and Mount Stuart…or at least, not oppose the petition to regain our name."

Ian gave him a thoughtful look. "I had nae thought of that. Campbells do favor the English. Mayhap having the lady as our guest will benefit us after all."

Emily looked down so her emotions wouldn't show. She was a pawn in the MacGregors' game of parodied chess. She'd also noticed the phrase "taken up residence" instead of "ownership." And "guest." *Guest.* Ian thought of her as such. That she was planning only to visit and not stay.

She understood that the concept of her having the deed to the holdings was difficult for them, but would they ever accept her?

• • •

"Can you imagine someone wanting to steal smelly old sheep?" Lorelei asked when they'd retreated to the solar after the furor in the Great Hall earlier.

Emily didn't answer immediately, instead choosing a chair near the easterly window where the late morning sun poured in. It was her favorite room in the castle. She'd discovered it while exploring on the second day she'd been here. It had been empty, since it was in the old part of the castle and another solar had been built, but she'd had most of her personal belongings, as well as the few pieces of furniture from the wagons, brought in here, and she'd made a nest of sorts. The hearth was empty this morning, since it was late summer, but she envisioned a roaring fire come winter, with sunshine streaming in the window and herself curled in this very chair with a good book. But for now, she had to address stolen sheep.

"Those sheep are income," Emily replied. "At least, their wool is. I am not sure how losing more than a score of them will affect our profits."

"What did those boring financial reports you keep looking at say?"

"They did not show a large income, which is why I think we cannot afford such a loss."

"There are a lot of sheep in other fields around here," Juliana said. "Do those not belong to Strae Castle as well?"

"I think they do."

"Maybe you should take a look at the ledgers and find out exactly what you own."

"I intend to, but first I wanted to see the lands and fields for myself," Emily answered. "Once I do that it will be easier to understand the amounts shown in the accounts."

"The sooner the better, then," Juliana said.

"I want to be able to have a thorough understanding of the situation here first, then I plan to take my time going over each separate entry."

Lorelei sighed. "That sounds terribly dull and tedious to me."

"It may be dull and tedious, but if you want to return to London and enjoy a Season, I have to know how our finances stand."

Her sister cast her eyes down. "I had not thought of it like that."

"It is a sorry state we are in." Juliana stood. "The earl should have provided for us. Or, at least, for you—"

"If only we could have kept the house in Mayfair." Lorelei

sighed again. "I did like that house."

Emily had not been particularly attached to it, probably because it held no good memories. "You know why we had to sell it."

"We know. The bloody earl gambled his fortune away." Juliana began to pace. "And filled his damn head with opium smoke most days."

Emily didn't chide her for cursing, although she probably should have. But there was no defense she could offer. Not that she wanted to. "It is in the past."

Lorelei sniffed. "That nasty cousin could have at least offered you a dower cottage."

"I had no right to demand that since I got the Mayfair house."

"Which you had to sell."

"You might remember that neither Albert's cousin nor his wife wanted us there."

Juliana stopped pacing and turned. "And the MacGregors do not want us here, either!"

Lorelei nodded. "Not even Glenda, who will not speak to us. She just stares like she hates Emily."

"Hate is a strong word." Emily paused, thinking how to continue. "I did not expect to be welcomed, given the circumstances, but most of them have been…cordial."

"Cordial?" Juliana resumed pacing, then stopped again. "Devon continually glares at us and Rory is just plain rude. The man has the audacity to call me names—"

"You do seem to bring out the worst in him," Lorelei said.

"*Me*? Bring out the worst in *him*? How—"

"Why is that?" Emily asked before Juliana could work herself into full-fledged indignation. "The two of you do seem to be at each other's throats."

"You will have to ask him that."

"Maybe he likes you?" Lorelei offered.

Juliana scoffed. "If that is the Scottish way of showing it—"

"I wonder..." Lorelei went on without letting her sister finish. "Remember when we were girls and that horrible Floyd Bentley used to pull my braids and threaten to throw frogs at me? A year later, when he went to Eton, he sent me flowers and candy for my birthday."

Juliana leveled a look at her. "I doubt very much that Rory MacGregor has *flowers and candy* on his mind."

"Still. It would not hurt you to be polite to him." Emily turned to Lorelei. "As for you, it would be wise not to practice your flirtation skills with Alasdair."

Her eyes widened innocently. "All I did was tell him he was clever."

"Your tone and expression caused him to respond."

"It meant nothing."

"Perhaps not to you," Emily replied, "but these are Scottish Highlanders, not accustomed to the art of London parlor flirting."

Lorelei thrust out her lower lip. "How am I going to be successful next Season if I do not practice?"

"For heaven's sake!" Juliana shook her head. "Why do you need to practice flirting? Those silly young lords will wax poetic, even if you do not say a word. Just wave your fan or something."

"My fan. Goodness gracious, you are right! I need to practice that, too. How one holds a fan signifies—"

"You will not be doing any fan waving around here." Emily frowned at her. "I do not want you to encourage Alasdair when you have no intentions of allowing him suit."

Juliana nodded. "I agree. It is not honorable to let him think you like him when you do not."

"I did not say I did *not* like him," Lorelei protested.

"Even so, there is no reason for you to toy with him

and possibly cause hurt feelings." Emily turned her gaze on Juliana. "And that goes for you as well. Stop provoking Rory."

"I do *not*—"

"You *do*." Emily looked from one sister to the other. "It behooves all of us to behave properly and remember why we are here. Are we in agreement?"

They both stared at her for a long moment before reluctantly nodding, but somehow Emily didn't think she'd won the battle.

• • •

A brisk knock on the library door the next morning made Ian look up from the numerous papers he had scattered over the desk.

"May I come in?" Emily asked.

The English had a rather odd sense of protocol, he thought as he stood and gestured for her to have a seat. She owned the castle—at least for now—and yet, she knocked. The door was open, yet she asked to enter. He doubted it was out of deference for him, the *rightful* laird of Clan MacGregor, as it was because she didn't want to escalate the tension and resentment that hung heavy in the air. Which made her a savvy woman.

And also a pretty one, although he pushed those thoughts away. She was dressed in a light-blue gown, modestly cut, but fitting well enough to outline her narrow waist and the flare of her hips. The library had no windows—to preserve the book bindings from damage by sunlight—but the light from the oil lamp on his desk cast her face in a warm glow and made her golden hair seem like a halo. Pity the woman was a Sassenach and, by holding the damn deed, a foe.

"Rory hasnae returned, if that is what ye are wondering."

She smiled slightly and took the chair beside the desk

instead of the one in front of it. "I assumed as much when I did not hear voices raised in the Great Hall."

"I've nae time to take ye on a tour of the land today," he said as he sat down. "I've business matters to see to."

"Precisely." She edged her chair closer to the desk. "I want to know what the business matters are."

For a moment, the scent of rose water wafting from her hair distracted him. Why was she deliberately sitting so close to him? Then he realized it was because she wanted to see what was spread on the desk. *Eejit.*

"What did ye want to ken?"

She blinked at him. "Everything. Expenses, invoices, receipts, inventory... You do have ledgers for all the accounts?"

He felt like Paden had kicked him in the stomach with a well-shod hoof. He had hoped to placate her with copies of the reports he'd sent to the earl's estate, but damn it, the lady sounded like she knew what to ask for.

"It will take days, if nae weeks, to sort all that out for ye."

She smiled again. "I have time."

Time. Perhaps he should rethink his strategy and gather the information—at least, the minimal—she asked for quickly and convince her all was being handled. His brothers, and most likely his uncles, wanted her and her sisters back in London before the first snow fell, and in Glen Strae that could be as early as October.

"I will get ye the reports ye need."

"I have already read the reports you sent last spring," she said. "What I am interested in is the actual accounting books."

He frowned. "Ye have knowledge of accounting?"

"When the earl became...ill...I took it upon myself to learn."

An odd expression that he couldn't decipher had crossed

her face when she mentioned her deceased husband. "I didna ken he had been ill." Another strange expression flitted briefly before she dipped her head slightly.

"It was a lingering illness."

Which could be any number of things, given the man's age. Women were used to managing household expenses, but he wondered how diligently she'd applied herself to other financials. Cautiously, he asked, "Did ye find the reports I sent satisfactory?"

"As far as they went." She leveled a look on him. "You do seem to have more sheep than I expected, given the yield of wool listed."

He nearly groaned aloud. Emily had been applying herself. She might not know exactly how much each coat was worth, but he suspected it wouldn't be long until she discovered the numbers he'd given were low.

"We've been trying to increase the flocks." That much was true, albeit they'd been increasing them ever since the king had given his grandfather permission to reside at Strae Castle.

She frowned. "How much is losing two dozen sheep going to affect profit?"

"It will nae be overly significant," he answered. "Reivers are nae interested in starting a clan war."

The frown deepened. "Does this happen often?"

He drew his own brows together. "Nae recently."

"So you think the Campbells are behind this?"

"I doona ken…" He stopped as he heard voices along with boots tramping down the hall toward them. "We may soon find out. It sounds like Rory has returned."

In another minute, all his brothers stomped into the room. From the look on Rory's face, the news was not good.

"Ye didna find the sheep?"

His brother shook his head. "I picked up the tracks right

enough, but about a mile down the road, the varmints had two carts waiting. I followed the tracks until they blended with others near Crianlarich. It was market day so the town was packed. No sign of our sheep, though."

Devon cursed while Carr and Alasdair exchanged looks. Ian caught their meaning.

"Crianlarich lies next to Campbell lands." He clenched his jaw. "Send for the duke's cousin Henry."

• • •

Emily led her sisters to the library the next afternoon, since the Duke of Argyll's cousin Henry was supposed to meet with Ian to discuss the stolen sheep. She hadn't even had to insist she be allowed to attend, since she *was* English and Ian intended to use her as a pawn to win favor with the Campbells. She just hoped his brothers—particularly Devon and Rory—would maintain decorum. And—she glanced at her sisters just before they entered—that they would as well.

"Remember what I said. *Best* behavior. Both of you."

Juliana looked heavenward as Lorelei started to nod, but then her eyes went round and she made a cooing sound.

"That is the cousin? I thought he would be old."

"Hush!" Emily looked around to see who had attracted her sister's attention. Ian's brothers and uncles milled about, and she spotted Ian standing next to his desk. Then there was movement to his right and she saw what had caused Lorelei's reaction.

Or, rather, *who*. A man, nearly as tall and broad-of-shoulder as Ian, stepped forward. He appeared to be about the same age. His chestnut hair, sun-streaked to burnished gold, set him apart from the black-haired MacGregors like a phoenix among falcons. His eyes were the blue-green of a summer sea and his teeth white and even when he smiled at

Emily and her sisters.

"I daresay civilization has arrived." He made a short bow. "Allow me to introduce myself. Gavin Campbell, at your service."

Lorelei started to extend her hand, but thankfully Juliana took a firm grip on her arm and turned her in the direction of one of the stuffed chairs by the hearth. Emily glanced at Ian and then back to Gavin.

"I thought we were expecting a Henry Campbell?"

"That would be my father. Alas, he left for Inveraray day before last. The duke, of course, is in London." Gavin grinned. "So, when the gauntlet was thrown for a Campbell to come to Strae Castle, I picked up the glove."

"It was nae a gauntlet," Ian muttered, having come up behind him.

Gavin shrugged. "A summons then."

Ian frowned. "A request."

Before the meeting would break into a complete melee, she intervened. "An invitation. I suggested it, since I seem to be missing some sheep." She kept her attention focused on Gavin, although she could see Ian behind him studying her like a hawk might its prey.

"Your sheep?" Gavin asked, a quizzical look on his face.

Ian moved beside him. "Allow me to introduce the dowager Countess of Woodhaven."

"*You* are the *dowager* countess? I had heard you would be paying a visit, but…" Amusement lit Gavin's eyes. "I doubt you were what MacGregor was expecting."

"Considering my husband was forty years older than me, I am sure I was not," Emily answered before Ian could. "And, to clarify, I am not visiting. I intend to live here."

A corner of Gavin's mouth quirked up. "That should make life interesting."

Ian made a sound, suspiciously like a growl. "Shall we all

have a seat?"

"Of course." Instead of joining her sisters by the fireplace, Emily moved toward the desk and took the same chair she'd sat in yesterday. If she was going to be recognized as the owner here, she needed to establish some authority. She'd also spent enough time in London Society—not to mention with her own husband—to understand that usurping a man directly never worked. Ian could have his chair behind the desk. She smoothed her skirts and smiled.

Ian shot her a look as he slid into his seat. She suspected they might be having words later about her actions and she found herself oddly looking forward to standing her ground with him. Over the past two weeks, she'd had time to observe him. He dealt with his quarrelsome brothers without a show of temper. As strong as he was, she had no fear that he would hit her if she spoke her mind. Unlike the earl. She gave him a sideways glance. He narrowed his eyes, but it was more a speculative look than anything. She managed to keep from grinning as she turned away.

"Well..." He refocused his attention to Gavin. "I asked ye to come here because two dozen of our sheep were stolen night before last."

"And?" Gavin asked.

"Did ye ken about it?"

Gavin flicked an invisible piece of lint from his sleeve. "Do I look like a bloo...a *reiver*?"

"I doona suspect ye had a direct hand in it," Ian replied. "The question I asked was if ye kenned about it?"

"I do not. In case you've not noticed, we have plenty of sheep roaming our hills. We do not need to be stealing MacGregor sheep."

"Actually, they are *my* sheep, too." Emily ignored the look Ian was giving her. "King George—Parliament actually—deeded the Strae holdings to me. That includes the livestock."

Gavin studied her as though she were some strange species he'd never seen. And perhaps she was. It was rare for a woman to own property in her own right, but it was a subject she didn't want to discuss. "As I said earlier, I intend to make my home here. However, I have no intentions of putting the MacGregors out, so I see this…thievery…as an insult to me as well."

"I see." His expression changed slightly. "In that case, my lady, I will do some investigating."

"Thank you, Mr. Campbell. I shall look forward to a report in the near future."

"Perhaps sooner than you think," he answered. "I do not get to London as often as I would like, so it has been a long time since I have had the pleasure of visiting with a lady of Society. May I have leave to call on you?"

"That would be lovely."

Ian made that strange sound again, but Emily ignored it. What was he growling about? He'd wanted to use her *Englishness* for his benefit with the Campbells, didn't he? She was only complying.

She smiled and rose, causing both men to leap up. "If you will excuse me, gentlemen, I will leave you to the rest of your discussion." Gesturing to her sisters, she made her way to the door.

A good general knew when to retreat. And this was war, after all.

Chapter Nine

The sooner the dust disappeared from Campbell's horse, the better. Ian watched the animal cross the drawbridge, hooves clopping across the boards, before its rider nudged him to a trot. He turned from the steps to enter the castle, knowing his brothers and uncles would be waiting in the library.

As least they'd had the wherewithal to pour him a generous two drams of whisky that waited on the desk. He swallowed half of it in one gulp before setting the glass down.

"That bad, eh?" Alasdair asked.

"We didna get a confession, but I was nae expecting one."

"'Tis nae what I meant." His brother grinned at him. "Campbell seemed quite taken with the countess."

Ian managed not to scowl. Gavin Campbell's reputation as a rake had followed him from London to Argyll. Did Emily not recognize a scoundrel when she met one?

I would like leave to call on you, he'd said. He probably said that to every woman.

That would be lovely, she'd said. Lucifer's horns! Did she actually think to entertain him?

“’Tis true,” Carr agreed. “I suspect we may be seeing more of young Campbell than we anticipated.”

He hadn’t *anticipated* the whelp coming over at all. Henry was the one who had been asked. Ian shrugged in what he hoped was a nonchalant manner. “At least Campbell agreed to investigate the reiving.”

“Only because he wants to sniff around the Sassenach’s skirts,” Devon said. “Too bad he didna take the lot of them with him.”

Alasdair gave him a reproving look. “The lasses are nae so bad.”

“Speak for yerself.” Rory snorted. “Juliana could make a fishwife blush with her language.”

“Juliana?” Alasdair flashed a grin. “Ye are on first name terms, then?”

“Nae!” Rory’s voice might have been a bit too loud. “I just…I just doona like calling her *Lady* Caldwell or *Miss* Caldwell, however they call themselves.”

Devon nodded. “Damn English and their titles.”

“Titles aside,” Broderick intervened, “we need to use Campbell’s interest in the countess to our advantage.”

“I agree,” Donovan said.

Ian wasn’t sure he did. When they’d talked about it earlier, it had seemed a good idea, in theory. But he hadn’t known Henry was in Inveraray or that Gavin would show up in his stead. The fact that Emily was English was supposed to be common ground for establishing a peace of sorts, not a *personal* interest.

“We canna just throw the countess to the wolves.”

“Do ye mean *wolf*?” This time it was Carr who grinned. “As in young Campbell?”

“Doona tell me ye are going daft on the Sassenach!” Devon glared at Ian. “Ye are completely barmy if ye favor that bloody woman over your clan!”

"I never said that. Ye are daft if ye think I would favor *anyone* over clan." Ian glared back. "And ye need to keep a civil tongue in your head."

"Can we return to the subject at hand?" Broderick cut off the argument. "If Gavin Campbell intends to come calling, we can use that."

"Do ye have a plan?" Carr asked.

"Nae a completely hatched one," Broderick replied, "but Henry will nae doubt want to support the countess's claim on Strae Castle."

Devon glowered. "That doesna help us, does it?"

"It might nae seem so, but if Argyll thinks our holdings are firmly in English hands, he will nae oppose the petition that Mount Stuart will bring to Parliament."

"The duke doesna ken that Bute and Mount Stuart will be asking to restore lands as well as the MacGregor name," Donovan added.

"Nor does the countess," Ian said. "If she has the support of Argyll—and the Crown—we may nae get anything restored."

"'Tis Parliament that will decide," Donovan said. "Doona forget, since Bute was prime minister, he still holds sway with both the Lords and Commons. King George favors him as well."

"It could mean clan war with the Campbells, though, if the countess loses her deed to the land and they support her."

Rory snorted. "Are ye forgetting how many of the clan are still in hiding? We are nae called 'Children of the Mist' for nothing. All MacGregors will rally to us."

"And doona forget the large numbers that fled to Ireland," Alasdair added. "Once the petition had been proposed, we can send word they should make ready to return."

"If Argyll wants war because of that bloody"—Devon stopped as Ian shot him a warning look—"that *Sassenach*, then we will have our men ready."

"It might be good if one of us traveled to Ireland to explain the plans," Carr said. "Sending a missive can be misleading, or it could fall into the wrong hands."

"'Tis true." Ian looked at Alasdair. "Ye speak Irish Gaelic better than the rest of us so ye could blend in best. Only MacGregors would ken why ye are there."

"That would take some time," Alasdair answered. "Our clansmen are scattered throughout the counties."

"*Hmmm.*" Carr knit his brows. "Parliament will convene in late October and Bute plans to present the petition as one of the first items. 'Twould be good if ye could leave as soon as ye can."

Alasdair widened his eyes. "Nae before the harvest festival, though?"

"Ye doona want to miss a chance to flirt with our bonnie Scots lasses?" Rory winked. "I understand the Irish lassies are friendly, too."

"'Tis nae reason I canna charm all of them," Alasdair replied.

"Aye, and mayhap Lorelei as well?" Rory asked innocently.

To Ian's surprise, his brother's face turned pink. Was he interested in Emily's sister? Or did he intend to lead Lorelei on a bit? Either way, it was probably better that he did leave for Ireland. "Sooner would be best."

Alasdair raised a brow. "Harvesting begins in two weeks. We need every hand here to bring in the barley and cut the peat. I willna leave before 'tis done."

Ian suppressed a sigh. His brother had a stubborn streak that usually remained below the surface of affableness, but on those occasions when he took a stand, it was doubtful armed dragoons could change his mind. "After harvest then."

Alasdair grinned, sunny disposition returned. "That will

give me time to say a proper goodbye to our lasses."

Ian wondered if that meant Lorelei, but perhaps it wasn't prudent to ask. No use in borrowing trouble that might not exist.

• • •

Emily and her sisters had retreated to the solar after the meeting with Gavin Campbell to mull what had taken place when Fiona rushed in.

"I heard Gavin Campbell paid a visit earlier," she said as she plopped down in an empty chair. "Tell me what I missed!"

"I was surprised you were not there," Emily said.

"I took one of Maggie's tisanes over to an elderly widow who's ailing," she replied, "and she wanted me to stay and visit. Poor thing is lonely."

"I would like to accompany you next time. It would be good for me to know who is in need of help."

Fiona nodded. "We have a number of elder clanswomen who would appreciate that."

"I did not know the housekeeper made tisanes," Emily went on. "Is she considered a healer?"

Fiona shook her head. "That would be Old Gwendolyn who has a cottage near the peat bog. Maggie's tisanes consist mostly of whisky and honey. 'Tis good for a rheumy cough."

"I will keep that in mind." It was good to know the grouchy housekeeper had a soft spot for the neighbors, since, on a good day, Emily could get no more than a few words from the woman.

"But tell me what I missed," Fiona repeated. "I canna remember when a Campbell last came to visit, let alone *Gavin* Campbell."

"Do you fancy him?" Lorelei asked.

"Fancy…? Och, nae!" Fiona laughed. "I have listened to

him tell too many lasses they are beautiful as Venus herself and sweet as roses in the spring and other such nonsense."

Juliana gave Emily a direct look. "I hope you remember that."

Fiona furrowed her brows. "Why should she remember… Oh! Did the mon flirt with ye already?"

Emily waved a hand. "He asked leave to call on me. That is all."

Her eyes widened. "He did?"

"Yes, but I suspect he did so to have an excuse to come over to rile your brothers." Emily smiled. "They do not seem to be on the best of terms."

"'Tis true there has been bad blood between us."

"So I gathered." Emily paused. "I probably should explain to you why I granted Mr. Campbell leave to call." When she finished, Fiona's face looked stormy.

"My brothers expect to use ye?"

"They were not very subtle about it," Juliana said.

"I canna believe Ian would agree to such a thing." Fiona gave Emily a sideways glance. "I thought he might be sweet on ye."

Emily felt her cheeks warm and prayed she wasn't blushing. The idea was preposterous, given how he felt about his land. Just because she thought him attractive—she couldn't deny that her senses were heightened around him, but she tried to check those feelings—didn't mean he reciprocated. Just because their exchange of words reminded her of a well-played game of chess didn't mean anything, either. They were engaged in a war of sorts and both of them knew it.

"Your brother has been very kind in tolerating us. And, actually, I agreed to the scheme. I would like to see the clan name restored."

"Ye would? But—" Fiona stopped abruptly. "Ye really wouldna mind Gavin paying ye court?"

"I would not go so far as that," Emily answered. "As a widow, I can allow a bit of flirtation if it will help your family accept me, but I have no intention of allowing anything beyond that."

Fiona tilted her head. "Ye loved your husband so much, then?"

Juliana snorted. "Hardly."

"Juliana..." Emily warned.

Her sister frowned. "There is no harm in telling Fiona you were not happy with an old man who—"

"That is *enough*." Emily turned to Fiona. "My marriage was one of convenience. Let us leave it at that."

"I never liked the earl, either," Lorelei declared before switching the subject. "So tell us why you said you were surprised that Gavin would come here."

"'Tis just that he spends little time in the country. He prefers Glasgow or Edinburgh and, of course, London." Fiona looked wistful. "I wish I could go to London sometime."

"Well, you can come with me when I go back," Lorelei said.

Fiona frowned. "Ye are returning to London?"

"Not yet, but Emily promised me a Season next spring."

"A Season..." Fiona's eyes sparkled. "I would so like to attend a real ball, and go to the theater, and see an opera and all those things that Gavin has talked about..." She sighed. "But Ian would never let me."

Lorelei lifted her chin. "Well, then we will have to figure out a plan to make him let you."

Fiona smiled. "Do ye think we could?"

"Of course!" Lorelei looked at Emily. "We can come up with something."

Emily smiled back, not wanting to burst any bubbles. She still hadn't looked at any reports beyond what she already knew. Providing a Season for Lorelei—and Juliana if she could be persuaded—would be costly. She would have to rent a townhouse as well, if she needed to chaperone. But…if the funds proved to be there—and they would be *her* funds—she would certainly offer to include Fiona. It might set off another battle in the war she and Ian were engaged in, but it would be one more challenge to win.

• • •

Neither of the uncles looked overly pleased to see her two mornings later when she appeared in the doorway of the distillery. Ian and his brothers had gone to check on the barley fields to determine which ones were ripe for harvest, and she'd decided to use the opportunity to ride over.

The sweet-sour smell of damp barley germinating filled her nose as she walked into the malting room where Broderick and Donovan were turning the wet grain over with wooden shovels so it wouldn't clump. They both straightened, and Donovan looked over her shoulder.

"Did Ian bring ye? I thought he was checking the fields."

"He is. I came by myself."

Broderick raised a brow. "Did we nae answer your questions the last time ye were here?"

The only time…she'd been there once. But she didn't correct him. "Yes, you were quite thorough in explaining the process. How this"—she gestured to the grain on the stone floor—"will next be dried in a kiln, then put in a mash tun to produce sugar, which will then be fermented and eventually distilled. And," she added, "that the whisky is put in used oak barrels only so it does not gather too much wood flavor."

"It seems ye listened closely," Donovan said.

"I think the process interesting. You both explained it very well."

"Then why are ye here?" Broderick asked.

"Actually, I wanted to look at the ledgers. Ian said you kept them here."

"We do, but why would they interest ye?"

He already sounded defensive, so Emily smiled at him, hoping to defuse the situation. "I involved myself with the running of my husband's estate and want to do the same here." No need to mention she'd involved herself out of necessity. "Working with numbers is mentally challenging." No need, either, to say the challenge was how to keep herself and her sisters from being put out on the streets of London. "I am sure everything is in order, so do not worry on that account."

"'Tis nothing for us to fash about," Broderick said. "Ian kens we keep a clean record."

"I am sure you do." Emily smiled again, not wanting to demand the ledgers, but determined that she would. "I am truly interested in seeing what your production is, the cost of it, how much you sell to Glasgow and at what price, and also how much you retain for personal use."

"That is all?" Donovan asked in a dry voice.

She chose to ignore his tone and nodded pleasantly. "That is all."

Broderick frowned. "If we show ye the ledgers, what good will it do ye?"

"I learned how to cut costs while studying the earl's books." Again, no need to say that it was a matter of survival. "I want to see if there is a way we can increase profit."

"We make enough profit without taking advantage of the public-house owners who buy from us."

"I understand," Emily said, "but if there is a way to earn more money—without hurting your current customers—would you not want to do it?"

"What do ye mean?" Donovan asked.

"Your whisky is excellent." For the first time, both of the

men smiled slightly. "I know that the gentlemen's clubs in London would snatch up all you could send them once they have tried it."

The uncles exchanged glances and then Donovan shrugged. "It will nae hurt anything to let her have a look."

Broderick hesitated, then shrugged, too. "I suppose it willna."

Following him to the small office to the side of the malting room, Emily felt like she'd just won a huge victory.

The feeling of winning was short-lived once she arrived back at Strae Castle that afternoon. Ian's face looked like a thundercloud as he met her at the entrance.

"Where have ye been?"

"I rode over to the distillery."

"By yerself?"

He sounded indignant, although she wasn't sure if he was angry or upset. Probably both. "It is only a mile."

"Maggie said ye left this morning," Rory said as he and Devon came out of the Great Hall to stand beside Ian. "Were ye sampling too many drams and fell asleep?"

He probably meant that as a jest, but before she could answer, Devon spoke up. "Or did ye ride off somewhere to meet the Campbell?"

"Why would I…" Her voice trailed off as she realized Ian was staring at her with suspicion. "You think that I would chase after Mr. Campbell?"

Devon didn't give Ian time to answer, either. "Ye are a Sassenach. Who kens what ye might do? We doona need—"

"*Sguir dheth.*"

Ian didn't raise his voice, but his tone was hard. Emily didn't need to understand Gaelic to realize that the command had its effect. Devon gave him a surly look but grew quiet. Ian turned back to her.

"What did keep ye away all day?"

"I was going through the ledgers. You can ask either of your uncles to vouch for my presence," she answered.

Rory gave her an incredulous look. "Why would a woman spend hours looking at numbers?"

Emily gave an exasperated sigh. No wonder Juliana found the man so annoying. "As much as it may surprise you, some women are actually good with numbers." He started to retort, but she went on. "I want to send some of the whisky that is mature to London to establish a market there."

"And what did Donovan and Broderick have to say about that?" Ian asked.

"They were not that terribly excited about it," Emily admitted. "I gather they are quite loyal to the Glasgow men they sell to."

"As they should be," Rory said. "Scots need to take care of their own first."

"I do not disagree," Emily replied, "but I intend to improve the lot here at Strae Castle. How can anyone not want that?"

"Bloody English." Devon stomped off before Ian could admonish him.

She sighed once more as she watched him leave. "I do hope I can get him to change his mind about us."

"Nae likely," Rory said with no trace of sarcasm in his voice. "Devon was captured by dragoons a number of years ago, and they tortured him."

Emily's hand flew to her mouth. "I am so sorry. I did not know."

"'Tis a tale for another time," Ian said grimly. "Meanwhile, I will speak to him."

"Please do."

As he and Rory left to find Devon, Emily made her way to her bedchamber to change her clothes, but the thought of what Devon must have gone through stayed with her throughout the evening meal and lingered as she prepared for bed.

She lay for a long time staring at the ceiling, wondering what she could do, before finally drifting off into a fitful sleep, filled with odd pieces of dreams.

And then, the dreams shifted, and she saw the man again. Once again, he stood in the shadows near her bed watching her, knife in hand. Her skin chilled as a cool breeze swept over her and she opened her eyes slowly.

No one was there, but the room definitely felt chilly. Emily glanced at the window to see if it had been left open, but it was tightly closed. She knew the door was bolted, since she'd taken to barring it after the last "dream." Still shivering, she drew the blankets to her chin.

She did not believe in ghosts, but where had that cool air suddenly come from?

Chapter Ten

The next morning, her sisters looked up from the round table in the smaller dining room as Emily entered.

"Heavens! You look like something one of those wolfhounds might have dragged through the woods," Juliana said.

"Good morning to you, too," Emily answered as she walked to the sideboard and poured herself a cup of tea that she hoped was as strong as the Scot whisky. Foregoing cream and sugar, she carried it back to the table. Luckily, they were the only ones there.

Lorelei swallowed a mouthful of poached egg. "You did not sleep well?"

"No." She debated on whether to admit she was worried about the resistance she felt from the MacGregors or to mention that the dream—both times—had terrified her. She opted for neither.

"My head was spinning with all the accounting ledgers I looked at yesterday. It took me a while to calm my thoughts."

Juliana gave her a speculative look. "I never saw you

agitated when you were going over old Albert's accounts. And, Lord knows, *those* were something to be disturbed about."

"I remember, too. We were in such dire straits that I had to make do with last year's gowns." Lorelei held up her hand before either of her sisters could retort. "I am not complaining. I understood. My point is that, even with our finances in such a dreadful state, you never seemed upset."

"Were the distillery ledgers in such a mess that you could not find your way through them?" Juliana asked. "Or the profit only marginal?"

"Neither. The uncles, or at least one of them, kept very orderly books," Emily answered. "And, while I think I can certainly increase profits if I can sell to London, the amount of money taken in was adequate."

Lorelei frowned. "Then why could you not sleep?"

She must really look worse than she felt for her sisters to persist in their questioning. Maybe she should have just stayed in bed and asked for a tray to be sent up. The thought no more than entered her mind when she dismissed it. Maggie would take the request for a tray as typical *English* self-indulgence and she wanted—needed—to somehow get on the housekeeper's good side. And her sisters, instead of interrogating her at the table, would have been in her room with questions as to why she was abed...especially since she never allowed herself to act sick.

Emily took another sip of fortifying tea and forced a smile. "This is going to sound silly, but I dreamed about that ghost Lorelei mentioned."

"*What?*"

She started, for the question had not come from her sisters, but from Ian who now stepped through the doorway. Closing her eyes briefly, she wished he hadn't heard.

"What is this about a ghost?" he asked as he pulled out

a chair and sat.

"Fiona told us about your father," Lorelei replied. "Actually, it was about your mother. Your stepmother, I mean."

A wary expression crossed Ian's face. "My stepmother?"

"Yes. Fiona said she was murdered in her bed and that your father found her—"

"Lorelei." Emily frowned at her sister. "This is hardly a topic for conversation at the table."

"I…I am sorry." She didn't look all that contrite, though. "You said you dreamed about it."

"Never mind. It was just a silly dream."

Lorelei shook her head stubbornly. "But you said it kept you awake."

Ian turned toward Emily, his gaze a slow perusal from her hair to her face and to her hands which, either from fatigue or the effects of the tea, had begun to shake. She gripped her cup to still them and lifted her chin. "It was nothing."

"Tell me about it."

She *really* should have stayed in bed, regardless of what the housekeeper would have thought. At least, she would have been spared having to explain a dream to Ian who would probably think her addle-brained. "I dreamed there was a man in my room."

Lorelei gaped at her and Juliana looked up from the toast she was buttering. One of Ian's brows lifted and she suddenly realized how that must have sounded. Merciful heavens! Did he think her one of those wanton widows who welcomed men to their beds?

She suddenly felt overly warm and prayed she wasn't blushing. What if he thought she was hinting that he would be welcome? The thought of his body—his hard, muscular, *naked* body—next to her in bed shot a heat wave to her face. Good Lord. She'd long ago closed off such thoughts. Why were they flitting through her mind now?

"Of course, there was no one there," she said and added for emphasis, "I keep my door bolted."

That made Ian draw his brows together. "Do ye nae feel safe?"

"I..." Good Lord! She couldn't tell him she'd had this strange dream before. "I...just got used to doing that in London."

"In yer own home?"

She supposed that didn't sound good, either. "I... My husband was gone a great deal..." Between the devil's dens and the gambling hells that much was true, thankfully. "I just took precautions."

Juliana choked on her toast and reached for her tea. Emily hoped she wouldn't blurt out the real reason that it was necessary to lock Albert out when he'd smoked too much opium. Or that Ian might not wonder why she hadn't had any servants about. "Really, the dream wasn't important. You should have something to eat while the food is still hot."

"What did this man look like?"

She sighed inwardly. Obviously, Ian wasn't going to let this go. "I do not know. His face was in shadow. He was just standing there... Well, not really. As I said, there was no one in the room."

"Did the man have a weapon?"

Really. The man should work for the Bow Street Runners. "I..." For a moment, she contemplated lying, but she wasn't good at it. "I...thought...maybe...there was something shiny in his hand. I am not sure."

"Oooh! Like a knife?" Lorelei asked and turned to Ian. "Maybe Emily saw the ghost who murdered your stepmother!"

"Did Fiona not say the *ghost* was supposed to be her father? And that he walks to *find* the murderer? Not to *commit* murder?" Juliana grimaced. "Not that we believe in ghosts."

"Of course there are no ghosts," Emily said. "As I said earlier, I tossed and turned last night because I had a lot of things to think about. Somehow, Fiona's story must have gotten mixed up in my mind. *Really*. It was just a *dream*. Nothing more." She plastered a smile on her face and rose, motioning for Ian to stay seated. "If you will excuse me, I need to discuss some things with the housekeeper."

And she swept out, hoping Ian wouldn't follow her.

• • •

He didn't. Instead, he went in search of his brothers, particularly Devon. It took a bit to round them all up, but thirty minutes later they were gathered in the library.

"What's this all about?" Carr asked.

"It seems the countess had a nightmare last night—"

"What?" Rory gave him an incredulous look. "Ye called us in here for that?"

"At least, that is what she called it," Ian continued.

"Daft English eejits. Scared of a dream," Devon muttered.

"She said she dreamed a man was standing in her room, watching her."

"I think I can clear this up," Alasdair said. "Fiona said she'd told the women the myth about our father supposedly roaming the halls looking for our stepmother's murderer. That probably caused Lady Woodhaven to dream about it."

Carr frowned. "That happened eleven years ago. Fiona really should stop spreading those rumors."

Rory shrugged. "Ye have to admit it makes a good story what with all the strange noises an old castle makes."

"And an *Englishwoman* would be stupid enough to believe it," Devon added.

"The countess doesna strike me as stupid," Ian said.

"I agree." Carr nodded. "But what about the dream frightened her so much? That someone might have gotten into her room?"

"The man in the dream was holding a knife," Ian answered.

There was a moment of silence as the brothers looked at one another. Ian knew they were probably all remembering the bloody scene from eleven years ago. The piercing, keening sound that had rent the air before their father's roar of anger had made everyone leap from their beds in the predawn light. The convergence at the door of their stepmother's bedchamber, the blood-spattered sheets…

Alasdair gave him a cautious look. "Ye doona think the killer has returned, do ye?"

Ian shook his head. "Emily—Lady Woodhaven—said there was no one there when she woke. Besides, she bolts the door."

Carr knit his brows. "Why would she lock it?"

"I asked her that," Ian replied. "She said something about it being a habit, but I didna get the sense that was the whole of it."

"She thinks someone wants to harm her?" Alasdair asked.

"I doona think it's come to that." Ian looked at Devon. "But someone may want to scare her, mayhap enough into leaving."

Devon scowled. "Ye think I have something to do with this?"

"I doona want to, but ye hate the English—"

"And ye ken why!" Devon balled his fists. "Ye were nae the ones tortured by the bloody dragoons."

"I ken that." Ian gentled his voice. The lad had been only six and ten when he'd been dragged away. It had taken Rory three days to track them down. Three days and nights of hell for Devon. "But ye also ken about the secret passageway that lies behind the wall of that chamber."

Rory stepped closer to Devon. "All five of us ken about that passage."

"Aye." The hidden passage ran between the walls of their stepmother's chamber and the one Emily currently occupied. The backs of the armoires had panels that opened into the small space and a few paces away was a narrow, spiraling iron staircase that led to the cellars and a postern gate.

Devon shook with anger. "But ye are blaming me!"

"I am nae blaming ye." Ian kept his voice calm, knowing how explosive Devon could get. Carr put a hand on Devon's shoulder, but he shook it off.

"Then why did ye bring it up?"

Ian sighed. Originally, the passageway had been a means of escape should the castle be besieged. Their father had shown it to them after the murder and after he'd searched it for any clue of the intruder. "Ye have nae hidden your feelings about the Sassenachs. We had discussed nae making life pleasant here for them, so I thought ye might want to frighten them a bit."

"Ye ken Devon doesna like the passageway," Carr said quietly.

Damn it. He *had* forgotten. His brother had been only eight when it happened and one day had decided to explore the passage after the midday meal. The panel had snapped shut and the candle he'd taken with him had snuffed out, leaving him in pitch black. No one had realized he was missing until suppertime.

"I am sorry," he said.

Devon strode to the door, still furious. "Ye should be." Not waiting for a response, he opened it and then slammed it behind him.

"I will follow him," Rory said and left.

Ian looked at Carr and Alasdair. "I shouldna have brought this up."

Carr shook his head. "Ye had to ask."

"Aye, better than to doubt," Alasdair added.

Ian didn't want to admit he still had doubt. Devon had, after all, matured and was no longer afraid of the dark. He'd also endured torture at the hands of the English, and his temper was explosive. But would he truly want to harm the women?

Ian prayed not, but there was one thing he could do to ensure no more "dreams," real or imagined, intruded in that room again. He would move Emily to the new part of the castle whether she liked it or not.

• • •

Emily walked to the stables shortly after the noon meal, wondering why Ian had offered to show her more of the property. She hoped he wasn't going to continue to question her about the dream, but she didn't want to turn down a chance to see more of his—*her*—holdings, either.

To her pleased surprise, Muirne was saddled and waiting for her. She hadn't been sure if Ian would continue to let her ride the filly, even though she'd shown him she could hand the young horse. Jamie led the animal to the mounting block as Ian exited a stall with Paden.

"Allow me," he said, dropping the stallion's reins. Before she could fathom what he was up to, his hands had circled her waist and he'd lifted her into the saddle as though she weighed no more than a sack of feathers. The feel of those strong hands, even though momentary, seared through her jacket like fire, causing an odd sensation to flare throughout. The filly must have sensed her unsettled emotion for she sidestepped and tossed her head.

Ian grabbed a rein. "Are ye sure ye want to ride this one? She has nae had exercise lately."

"That is all the more reason I should." Emily gently tugged the rein loose. "I am quite looking forward to a ride."

He hesitated a moment, then swung up on Paden's back. Soon they crossed the drawbridge and put the horses to a brisk trot. They rode in silence for a few minutes before he glanced her way.

"I was thinking ye should take a chamber in the newer section of the castle."

Ah. So he *was* going to go on about that dream. "I like being in the old part. I try to imagine your ancestors building it and living there before they… Well, before the proclamation was made."

Ian grimaced slightly. "Which proclamation would that be? The original one from Mary, Queen of Scots, the one by James VI, Charles I, or William III?"

Perhaps not the best question to have asked, but it did divert the conversation. "I had no idea there were so many."

He shrugged. "And those doona take into account the feud with the Duke of Montrose or the '15 Rebellion."

"Did your clansmen ever try to negotiate a peace treaty?"

Ian looked at her as though she had suddenly sprung a Medusa head. "We are *MacGregors*."

"Yes, but—"

"We were the ones who were wronged, lass." He waved his arm in a far-flung gesture. "We held lands far beyond what ye can see here. Nae only was Glen Strae ours but Glenorchy, Glenartney, and also Glen Fruin for a time. Some of the lands extended west into Perthshire as well." His hand settled on a muscled thigh. "We were the ones robbed."

"I had no idea," Emily said quietly. "I guess that explains why my sisters and I are resented."

He gave her a quick glance. "Did ye really expect to be welcomed?"

The words stung, but at least he was being truthful. "I suppose not." She flicked a fly from Muirne's mane. "Though I had hoped we could coexist peacefully."

"I doona ken if that will happen," he answered, "but I think ye should consider changing your quarters to be nearer to your sisters."

So they were back to that. "Do you think I am in danger?"

He shook his head, maybe a little too quickly. "'Tis just that the old part of the castle is drafty and the timbers creak and groan, which can lead to nightmares."

She gave him a curious look. "You do not believe the ghost is real, do you?"

"I have nae seen him."

"Do you believe in ghosts?"

He smiled noncommittally. "Ye are in Scotland. All of our castles are haunted."

Emily tried another tack. "Has *anyone* seen your father's ghost?"

"I doona ken for sure. There have been reports of strange noises, but as I said, the castle is old." He hesitated. "Shortly after the incident happened, we had a terrified maid insist she heard screams, but she was a girl come up from the village to clean."

"A vivid imagination probably, especially if she were cleaning…that room."

"Aye, but…" Again, he paused. "The sounds were coming from the room ye are in. The lass ran screaming from the castle. By the time we checked the rooms, there was nae one there."

She tilted her head to study him. "Is that why you gave me that room when I first arrived? Hoping to scare me and my sisters away?"

Ian had the grace to look sheepish. "'I canna deny it."

Somehow, she refrained from rolling her eyes. "Well, if I hear screams, I will let you know."

He frowned. "Ye still want to stay in that chamber?"

"Oh, yes." She certainly wasn't going to let him "scare" her with silly stories about ghosts. To move to the newer section of the castle would make her seem weak. "I will not be moving."

"As ye wish then." He pointed to a cottage in the distance. "We can make our first stop there."

She nodded and they rode on in silence. In spite of what she'd just said, she felt a chill run down her spine.

Chapter Eleven

They spent the next several hours visiting various crofters who, although they looked a bit wary, acknowledged Emily cordially enough. Ian was glad he'd made these rounds earlier, when she'd first arrived. It had given his clansmen time to mull the situation.

Now there was only one other person that he felt needed an introduction. And he had no idea how it would go. Old Gwendolyn took no council but her own. Some claimed she had the Sight. He wasn't sure he believed that, any more than his father's ghost roaming the halls, but the healer did have an uncanny sense of whom to trust. More than once, she'd warned of someone about to turn coat on the MacGregors.

"Whose place is this?" Emily asked as they neared the small, whitewashed cottage with its thatched roof.

"'Tis where the MacGregor healer lives."

"Old Gwendolyn?"

He looked at Emily in surprise. "Ye have already heard of her?"

She smiled. "Fiona told us."

"Och, aye." He wondered just what his talkative sister had said. Hopefully, she hadn't mentioned the Sight or worse, the rumors from those who feared the healer and called her a witch. It was bad enough Fiona had talked about the ghost. Emily certainly didn't need her head filled with the possibilities of witchcraft among the clan.

"What did my sister say?"

"Not much, just that she was a healer." When he looked askance at her, she shrugged. "Fiona said she had taken one of the housekeeper's tisanes to a neighbor, and I asked if Maggie had healing skills."

"Ah." Good, then. Emily would not have formed an opinion. Old Gwendolyn's crone-like appearance could be startling—with her long white hair, gnarled hands, and stooped shoulders. That, and the fact that her eyes were black as ebony, had probably led to the onset of witch rumors more than the herbs she used.

Emily looked around. "All the squares of ground laid out with different plants make a very decorative effect."

"I doubt a single plant is for decoration. These are all part of her herbal garden."

She gave him a quizzical glance. "Most of the crofters we visited had their gardens in the back."

Ian smiled. "Gwendolyn does, too, but what she grows back there are the plants that need soggy ground as she is nae far from the peat bog."

"Ah, yes! The bog. I want to…"

Just then the front door to the cottage opened and a huge wolfhound that looked almost identical to the two at the castle bounded out.

"I see Cedric is home." Ian pointed to the dog. "That means Gwendolyn is, too. The animal accompanies her everywhere."

Before she could reply, the healer appeared in the

doorway. Dressed in her usual plain homespun gown of dark wool, she hobbled forward. Ian watched Emily covertly to gauge her reaction, but she simply smiled at the woman with what appeared to be genuine friendliness.

Ian made the introductions, careful to say only that the dowager countess would be spending some time with them, but Gwendolyn gave him a sharp look.

"Do ye think I doona ken who this woman is?"

He blinked. "Well, I—"

"Ye may be the laird, but doona think an old woman like me doesna hear what is being said."

"Said? Has someone visited ye lately then?" he asked.

Old Gwendolyn smiled, revealing a full set of white teeth. "I have all sorts of visitors, but ye probably wouldna recognize them."

Fae? Ian hid a smile. The healer—however old she actually was—did like to embellish a good tale. Perhaps she was trying to impress Emily. A certain amount of mystique was sometimes necessary for a healer to be accepted. He glanced at Emily again, but her pleasant expression had not changed.

But he'd almost forgotten the history of this location. There was a menhir behind her cottage with Pictish engravings. Such stones were not that unusual, although most were found much farther north and on the Isles. Gwendolyn had planted a circle of primroses around it, probably to enhance the myth that faeries used it as a portal to the otherworld. Oddly, the flowers seemed to thrive like heather. For a brief moment he wondered if perhaps she *did* possess some otherworldly qualities. Then he gave himself an inward shake.

"I doubt the creatures of the forest or the bog would have told ye," he said with a smile.

Her eyes suddenly burned like hot coals. "Ye would do well to avoid the bog."

"Why?" Emily asked, curiosity plain on her face.

Gwendolyn turned to her. "Danger lies there, lass. Mark my words."

• • •

Those words still lingered in Emily's mind as they rode away from the healer's cottage an hour later. "Old" Gwendolyn had not at all been what she expected. True, when she'd first walked out of her cottage she had looked old, but after conversing with her over delicious sweet cakes and an aromatic tea—that she had to get the recipe for—the healer had seemed younger, somehow. Her face was not as lined and she hadn't hobbled when she'd walked them to the door. She had also been remarkably up-to-date on Emily's arrival.

She said as much to Ian. "For someone living alone, your healer seems to know what is going on."

"Well, it is nae because she has 'creatures' talking to her, as she might like ye to believe. Old Gwendolyn travels about the countryside..." He pointed to a mountain in the distance. "Even to Ben Cruachan where she picks the mountain laurel berries."

Emily widened her eyes. "She walks that far, by herself?"

"She has a nag that she rides, and Cedric is always with her," Ian answered. "Besides, 'tis nae that far, only two miles or so. Shorter if ye cut through the bog."

"But didn't she say it was dangerous?"

"Aye, if ye doona have a care where ye walk."

"I am not sure I understand."

"I will show ye. The bog is on our way back to the castle."

A few minutes later, they rounded a bend in the road and Emily saw a flattish span of land with what looked like dug-up dirt around the edges. Ian reined in Paden and the filly stopped of her own accord.

"This is the bog. Decayed matter mixes with the mud of the soggy ground under it." He gestured to the upturned earth. "We let this dry and then use the peat for fuel."

"So what is dangerous about it?"

"Ye have to ken how far ye can go. As I mentioned, the ground is like a marsh. Where the peat has nae been cut, a man can sink down into it. The more ye try to free yourself, the deeper ye sink." He glanced at Emily. "'Tis what the healer meant."

It had sounded more ominous than that to her, but she didn't want Ian thinking she was given to superstition. *Especially* after all that talk about the ghost.

"Has anyone been lost to it?"

"Nae recently, although a man or two has disappeared on his way home from Taynuilt after drinking too much."

"Taynuilt?"

"'Tis the village beyond the hill. The road winds, so sometimes the local folk cut through the bog, since 'tis shorter."

Emily felt a shiver. "And if they are tipsy, they might get lost."

"Aye. At night, 'tis nae easy to see where the soil gives way."

"I suppose the men who cut the peat know what they are doing?"

Ian nodded. "Once the ground has been turned up, it allows water to seep out from the marshy part, which then allows the cutters to move farther in. But, to make sure they are safe…" He pointed. "Do ye see the boards over there?"

Emily followed his direction and could barely make out something that looked lighter than the dirt lying flat over it. "Yes."

"When the cutters are determining how far to go, they place the boards atop the bog. If they have nae sunk the next morning, then they do another test by stepping on them. If there is little give, 'tis safe to start digging."

"I had no idea it could be so dangerous to dig up something we use for heat. Are you sure you should endanger your men?"

Ian looked at her. "'Tis nae more dangerous than the English sending men into mines for coal."

"I had not thought of it like that." Emily frowned. "You must think me the epitome of a spoiled aristocrat."

Something in his eyes changed as he continued to gaze at her. She couldn't quite decipher what it was. A strange sensation shot through her that was part anticipation and part dread.

"I think—"

"Never mind. It was rude of me to say that." Suddenly, she didn't want to know what he was going to say. She didn't want to be told that Scots thought all English aristocrats were spoiled and used to luxury. She didn't want to be told—maybe not in words—that Scots would never consider the English friends. "It is getting late. We should be getting home."

Picking up her reins, she nudged Muirne into a canter. She heard a Gaelic curse and then hoofbeats drumming behind her.

• • •

Ian decided not to try to catch up to Emily, even though his stallion could easily keep pace with the filly. One reason was because he wasn't sure if she was angry and, in time-honored male tradition, it was much wiser to give an angry woman time to calm down. He wasn't sure *why* she would be upset, but she had abruptly taken off… It was another female mystery mere mortal men had trouble understanding.

But his second reason for staying behind was more

important, even if he'd been trying not to think about it. If they arrived in the bailey together, he would have the opportunity to assist her in dismounting. He'd probably look like a fool flying off his horse before a groom could help her, but his hands *itched* to be around her waist again. To hold her just a wee bit too long and a wee bit too close... *Lucifer's horns! I truly am an eejit.*

So he held Paden back, giving Emily time to reach the bailey and dismount without his help. When he walked into the castle a short time later, he heard voices—male and female—coming from the library. Turning down the hall, he made his way there.

To his surprise, both his uncles and his brothers, sans Devon who'd gone off by himself again, were gathered around Emily, who held a letter in her hand.

"I really did not expect an answer so soon," she said.

"To what?" Ian asked as he walked through the door.

Emily waved the paper at him. "To this."

"She went ahead and wrote to someone in London about the distillery," Broderick said.

"Not just *somebody.* The owner of White's Gentlemen's Club. It is the most exclusive in all of London." Emily beamed at Ian. "I sent a post the day after I tasted that first dram. I knew it was excellent...and now White's is interested in buying MacGregor whisky!"

He took the letter and scanned it. "They are sending a man up here?"

She nodded. "Their procurator. If he likes what he hears and sees—and tastes—he can offer a contract immediately." She turned to Broderick and Donovan. "I know we will have to step up production, but the barley is ready to be harvested, so this is a perfect time!"

"To add more grain to the malting and mashing phases means longer working hours for the men," Donovan said.

"Can you not just hire more men?"

"Nae for those two processes. They both require careful watching."

"Aye," Ian broke in. "'Tis much like a cook who serves a fine meal. The kitchen maids doona have a hand in it."

"Well, from what you told me, that part takes only several weeks at most. And do not worry about the extra time needed with the bookkeeping," Emily went on. "I can take care of that."

Broderick frowned. "Ye want to be personally involved?"

"Of course. I intend to make the distillery very profitable."

"And what will ye do with the profits?" This came from Rory.

Emily frowned slightly. "Share them, naturally. Whatever the distillery earned last year, you will keep. I will retain the profits above that." She looked around at the suddenly silent men. "That seems fair, does it not?"

A loud crash came from outside the door before anyone could answer. Turning, Ian saw a small table in the hallway had been overturned and a broken vase lay on the floor. Angry footsteps faded away. Ian sighed.

Evidently, Devon had returned.

Chapter Twelve

"That damn Campbell is back." Rory burst into the smaller dining room where Ian, Carr, and Alasdair, along with Emily and her sisters, had gathered to take the noonday meal. Now that harvesting was officially underway, the men and women who normally ate in the Great Hall had taken knapsacks with food so they wouldn't have to waste time returning to the castle from the fields.

Ian arched a brow. "I'm surprised he has nae shown up sooner. It's been near a fortnight."

"Where is he?" Emily rose. "We should not keep him waiting."

Rory snorted. "It would nae hurt to keep a Campbell waiting."

Juliana glared at him as she stood, too. "He might have news of our stolen sheep."

He glared back. "He dinna say anything about sheep."

Emily sighed as her sister strode out. Juliana and Rory squabbled like children. She was never quite sure which one of them started the arguments, but neither of them ever wanted to give way. Lorelei gave her a helpless shrug as she walked past.

At least Ian's other brothers were polite. Except for Devon, of course. He was an angry, troubled man, and she was concerned about him. She kept meaning to ask Ian about what had happened while Devon had been a captive, but the timing never seemed right. For now, though, it was probably better that he wasn't here.

Gavin was seated in the small room across from the Great Hall that would be called a parlor were it in London. She paused for a second before approaching the door, remembering the original battle she'd fought with the housekeeper.

The room had been closed when she'd first arrived and obviously not used, by the amount of dust on everything. She'd asked for the room to be cleaned, the carpets beaten, the furniture uncovered, and the silver candelabra, nearly black with tarnish, polished. Maggie had said it would be put on a list of things to do. When nothing had happened over the course of three days, she'd gone to the housekeeper and asked for a polishing cloth, much to the startled surprise of several maids who were being given orders. Then Emily had marched into the room, taken the covers off the chairs, pulled out the carpet, and had begun polishing the silver. There had been some whispers at the door and scuffling feet. After several minutes, two maids appeared, saying they'd been sent to help. Emily suspected Maggie had done so grudgingly, but she wasn't about to argue.

Now the room looked as a proper sitting room should. The hearth had been swept clean, the soot removed from the stone. The candlesticks on the mantel gleamed and the wood on the tables had been waxed until it shone. Even the chairs had been brushed until the texture of the seats looked soft and inviting.

Gavin rose from an armchair as the ladies entered. And—to the MacGregors' annoyance, she was sure—bowed to her sisters, taking their hands and brushing a kiss in the air over each. For once, Juliana looked disconcerted and Emily heard Rory mutter something in Gaelic under his breath. Lorelei dropped a curtsy and batted her lashes, which brought a frown to Alasdair's face. When Gavin turned to her, Ian stepped between them.

"Have ye news on the sheep?"

For a moment, Gavin seemed to contemplate him, and Emily thought he looked almost amused. Then he took a step back and shook his head.

"I've asked about and no one has seen your sheep."

"Ye doona think someone would admit to reiving, do ye?" Ian asked.

Gavin shrugged. "I've ridden to our near pastures myself. I have not seen an increase to any flock."

"That is so disappointing," Emily said before the sparring could turn into a full argument. "Whatever do you think could have become of them?"

"My guess is that they were carted off to Loch Awe and shipped out."

Rory narrowed his eyes. "Who told ye they were *carted* away?"

Emily felt her eyes widen. When he'd been summoned to Strae Castle, no one had said anything about the cart tracks Rory had found. She waited to see what the answer would be.

But Gavin just smiled easily. "It hardly takes a genius to deduce that two dozen sheep cannot just disappear. Either carts or wagons would have been waiting."

She supposed he had a point, since she knew Ian had directed men to search for the sheep as well.

"Then why are ye here?" Alasdair asked.

Emily winced at the curt tone, but Gavin seemed to take

it in stride.

"As I said the last time I was here, I planned to call on Lady Woodhaven."

Ian took a step closer. "The countess is in mourning and nae receiving such calls."

Her mouth dropped open and she closed it quickly, not sure if she should be angry that Ian would presume to dictate what she could do or that he was aware of Society's custom of widow's weeds. Not that she was wearing them.

Which apparently Gavin had noted as well. "Lady Woodhaven is not wearing black, if I might point that out."

A soft sound, suspiciously like a growl, came from Ian. "'Tis nae always practical."

"That is true," Emily said quickly. "I needed to limit the wardrobe I brought."

"And I would compliment you on doing so," Gavin said. "The blue of your gown matches not only your eyes, but also the skies."

Ian made that sound again. "Do ye want to throw in the loch as well? Her eyes are the same color as it."

Emily blinked at him. He thought her eyes were blue as Loch Awe?

"*Touche*, MacGregor. I should have added that," Gavin said, then gazed around the room. "Actually, I have come at my father's behest. As a gesture of good will between our clans, he would like to invite all of you to a ball at Kilchurn once the harvest is in."

"Oh! A *ball*! That would be lovely!" Lorelei clapped her hands happily and turned to Emily. "We can go, can't we? Say that we can!"

"Well, I..." She looked at the MacGregor brothers quickly. Perhaps it was better that she make the decision. Not looking at Ian, she answered. "Of course. We would be delighted."

"Good," Gavin replied. "Then that is settled."

But judging from the expressions on the MacGregor faces, which ranged from surprised to surly, she was pretty sure nothing was settled.

• • •

Over the next two weeks, Emily hardly saw Ian. Or, to be more precise, she *saw* him as he was leaving each morning. With the harvesting of the barley under way, the brothers and both uncles rode out shortly after the sun rose and didn't return until well after dusk.

Timing was critical, so they all worked alongside the crofters and clansmen. Emily tried to imagine a single aristocrat she knew who would actually help his groundskeeper at a country estate, let alone get his hands dirty working with the farmers who leased land. Even the "country gentry," a notch below the aristocracy, weren't inclined to do more than issue orders. Since she thought of herself as a practical, no-nonsense type of person, she was accumulating a great deal of respect for the independence of Scots.

Of course, no one had been inclined to invite her to accompany them—and she probably would have been more of a hindrance than a help, if she were honest with herself—but that didn't stop her from following and observing from a distance.

She'd already learned the process of harvesting barley, having dragged the information from Donovan and Broderick. Once the barley turned golden and the peeled kernels hard to indent with a fingernail, the grain was ready to be cut. Then the stalks were arranged in small bundles, with ten bundles tied together to create sheaths that were erected to stand and dry.

For the past week, she had watched from a distance as

Ian swung his sickle, cutting cleanly through the fibrous stems as he walked along a row. The work was labor-intensive and the early autumn days unusually warm. It hadn't taken long for him to remove his shirt, leaving him clad only in doeskin breeches. Watching his back muscles work and his biceps bulge with each swing was endlessly fascinating, even if she did feel a bit like a wanton for enjoying it.

She hadn't known a man could look so perfectly sculpted, like a Greek statue in motion. Albert had always kept his nightshirt on when he'd come to her bed, although what she could feel of his weight had been soft and pudgy. Luckily, those episodes had been few and quickly over, and she'd been thankful—the Lord forgive her—when he'd passed away and she never had to experience the humiliation again.

Now, watching Ian move with practiced precision, his black hair glistening nearly blue in the sunlight, she was reminded of a black panther she'd once seen in a traveling zoo. The animal had paced his cage with graceful agility, exuding power with every stride.

An odd tingle coursed through her as she wondered what it would be like to have such an animal—the human one—in her bed.

She felt her face heat at the thought, not even knowing where it had come from. As far as she was from her goal of being *accepted* by the MacGregors, to think—no, to fantasize—about anything more was ludicrous. Keeping that thought firmly in mind, she turned Muirne back to the castle.

As she rode into the bailey, she noticed a carriage parked in the yard. No crest was attached to the door, but it looked well-made, the wood varnished, and the brass lanterns polished.

"Have we a visitor?" she asked Hamish as she entered.

The castellan gave her a dubious look. "A Mr. Everard. He says he's from White's, in London."

"Ah! The procurator! Wonderful," Emily said. "Is he in the parlor?"

"Aye. I have sent for Broderick."

"Broderick?" She frowned. "Whatever for?"

He lifted his chin ever so slightly. "He handles the distillery business."

"But I am the one…" Emily let her voice trail off. There was no use arguing with the castellan. Meanwhile, she would take matters into her own hands. "Please bring a bottle of the MacGregor whisky to the parlor…and two glasses."

His eyes widened, although she wasn't sure whether it was because she was requesting whisky in the middle of the afternoon or whether she'd asked for two glasses. For a moment he hesitated and she wondered if he'd refuse—she thought there was a bottle in the library that she could get—but then he gave a terse nod and walked away.

She shook her head at his retreating back before she turned to greet her guest…and, hopefully, new business partner.

"Mr. Everard. I am Lady Woodhaven," she said as he rose from his chair. "We were not sure when to expect you. Did you have an easy journey?"

He gave her an incredulous look. "Traveling a week, over roads that grow increasingly more like a deer trail and as deeply rutted as a dry stream, can hardly be called easy." He lifted one shoulder in a slight shrug. "But that is of no significance. I am here to taste the whisky and decide whether it is good enough for White's."

"You will soon have a sample and be assured that it is." Emily smiled and gestured for him to be seated. "I look forward to working with you."

His look turned condescending. "I was told by the butler that the man in charge of the distillery had been sent for."

She managed to keep her smile in place, even when

Hamish—she didn't bother to correct his status—came in with a bottle and *one* glass. If she had excelled in one thing while being Albert's wife, it was to hide her true feelings.

"Would you be so kind as to pour a dram for our guest?"

Hamish started to smirk at his little victory, but bootsteps were heard in the hall. In a moment, both Broderick and Donovan came through the parlor door. Emily leveled a look at the castellan.

"It seems we will need *three* more glasses, Hamish."

"Aye. Three," Donovan said.

She wasn't sure if he'd noticed that Mr. Everard already had one or if he was really including her. Whichever it was, Hamish's mouth tightened, but he nodded and left, soon to return with—thankfully—three glasses.

Emily watched covertly as the procurator took his first sip. She kept her smile hidden at his look of astonishment. "What do you think?"

He swirled the remaining contents gently, inhaled the aroma, and took another sip. He held it on his tongue like a fine wine before he swallowed. Then he smiled. "This is excellent. I think it will be in high demand at White's." He turned to the uncles. "Gentlemen. A toast to our future endeavor."

Broderick and Donovan both grinned, held up their glasses, and in true Scot's fashion, downed their drams. Emily pushed her irritability out of mind.

"This will truly be a joint adventure," she said. "As I was about to tell you, I am planning to be a full participant in the distillery business."

Mr. Everard eyed her. "That is totally unheard of. Women have no head for business."

She bit back a retort, silently cursing the stupidity of some men. "When my husband was…indisposed, I had no choice but to look into our business matters. I did not find it that difficult to understand profit and loss." The Lord knew she'd learned all about loss—and debt—in abundance. Thankfully, Albert had not favored White's, so perhaps the procurator was not aware of how badly off the earldom had been.

"Even so, I prefer to work with the owner of the distillery. It makes things simpler," Mr. Everard said.

"It certainly does," Emily agreed. "As it happens, I am the owner." She would have laughed at the look of bafflement on his face except for the fact that Donovan was frowning and Broderick scowling.

"I was told the owners were Murrays," he said.

"We are," Broderick said. "My brother took over the business more than thirty years ago and I joined him two decades past. Ye can count on us."

Mr. Everard looked relieved. "Good. Then that is settled."

"Actually…" Emily somehow managed to keep her voice calm. "It is not settled. I have been given title, in my own right, to Strae Castle and its holdings. And, while I agree that the Murrays may see to the daily managing of the distillery, I will be involved with negotiations, as well as any legal matters that arise." Ignoring the piqued expressions on Donovan's and Broderick's faces, as well as the annoyed look on the procurator's, she set down her glass. "If you do not wish to work with me, I am sure there are several other gentlemen's clubs in London that would be glad to offer White's some competition."

For a moment there was silence. Emily kept her expression impassive, hoping she hadn't gone too far. She had no idea whether any other London clubs would be willing to work with a woman, either, but she did know that, if she wasn't firm, she wouldn't be taken seriously. And she wasn't about to let that happen.

Finally, Mr. Everard nodded. "It is most unusual, but I agree to your terms."

Inwardly, Emily wanted to leap and shout with joy. She had won a battle, if not the war. Instead, she offered a slight smile. "I think you will discover you have made a good decision." She glanced at Broderick and Donovan. "I will count on your help, since your expertise will be invaluable." She picked up the bottle that Hamish had left and began to pour. "Shall we have another toast? To success?"

As they drank, she was confident the endeavor would work. She just hoped Donovan and Broderick saw it that way as well.

• • •

The procurator left the following morning. The Murray brothers followed him out of the Great Hall when he was through breaking his fast, leaving Emily behind. She had really wanted to follow his uncles out to ensure there were no "private" arrangements being made with Mr. Everard, but Ian hadn't come in until very late last night and this morning he'd been irate. If it had to do with her—and it probably did—she needed to find out what it was before he left again for the day. Although Devon had gone, the other three brothers still remained in the room, along with a few older men who weren't working in the fields, so she would have to wait. A few minutes later she heard Broderick and Donovan return. Whatever had transpired had certainly not taken long. After what seemed like an endless amount of time finishing their plates, Carr, Rory, and Alasdair took their leave as did the others. She looked across the table at Ian.

"Are you not happy with the agreement that was reached?"

He put down the piece of toast he was about to bite. "I have nae seen the contract, but if my uncles thought it solid—"

"They did." That much was true, at least. After a certain

amount of haggling, they had agreed that the money offered was acceptable. "We will turn a tidy profit."

"Even so, it would be better if ye let Broderick and Donovan handle everything."

Emily bristled. *What is it with men?* "I am perfectly capable of understanding the business."

"I didna say ye could nae understand it." Ian sighed. "The clansmen doona want ye to be involved."

She stared at him. "How would they even know?"

"This isna London, but that doesna mean people doona gossip. Besides, ye were seen at the distillery several times."

"That does not mean anything."

"Ye were probably overheard talking to my uncles." Ian shrugged. "However the news got out, it did. I spent hours last night trying to convince the clansmen that the local supply of whisky wouldna be interrupted because we would be shipping to London."

So that's why he had not come home. He'd been putting out the proverbial fires…or trying to contain them, at least. "So you are not angry with me?"

He shook his head. "Nae angry. I just think 'twould be better if ye let my uncles handle this."

She raised her eyes heavenward in exasperation. "You do not think me capable?"

A corner of his mouth quirked. "I have nae doubt ye are."

"Then why should I not be involved with the business?"

"Because ye have been here a little over a month, and ye are English." He held up a hand before she could protest. "Ye canna help that, but many older Scots remember Culloden, nae to mention *MacGregors* still have good reason nae to trust the English."

She couldn't argue the point. "I understand that, but if your kinspeople do not see me about, or interact with me, they will never learn to trust that I am not against them."

"Ye ask a lot."

"If I am to *live* here—and I *am*—it is crucial that I be accepted." Emily raised her chin defiantly, expecting Ian to rebut, but he remained silent. Something flickered in his eyes, though. "One of the reasons I want to be active with the whisky trade is to *prove* that I am capable of working hard… that I have earned a part of the profits we will be making."

Another flicker. It passed so suddenly she didn't have time to interpret it, but his unusual golden eyes were trained on her like a hawk. Well, she certainly was not going to be a mouse. "Not all Englishwomen are vain, self-indulgent creatures. And," she added for emphasis, "I do intend to make Strae Castle my home."

He studied her, the sharpness of his gaze not changing. "Ye have had a chance to see the property and examine the ledgers. The harvest is nearly in. Ye ken we will do well this year." He paused. "I thought ye'd want to return to London before the weather turns cold. Winters are bitter in the Highlands."

"You think you can scare me off because of the weather? It will take more than that." She rose, motioning for him to stay seated. "I am not leaving…except for the moment. I need to remove the sheets from my bed and take them to the laundry."

He frowned. "Maggie can send a girl up to do that."

"There is no need." Emily smiled. "As I said, not all Englishwomen are spoiled. I intend to prove myself to your clan."

• • •

Ian watched her leave, mulling over what she'd said. Emily was certainly unlike any English woman he'd met and certainly not like his stepmother. Isobel hadn't been much older than

Emily when his father had married her. The daughter of a dragoon officer, she'd *acted* like she were a princess, insisting she have a personal maid—one from England, properly trained—as well as expecting his father's household servants to do her bidding. And his father, infatuated as he'd been with his young, beautiful bride, had quietly commanded them all to obey. It had been a fraught-filled two years before she'd met her demise and the servants had been able to resume their regular routines.

Unfortunately, Emily had the same fair coloring as Isobel. That their appearances were similar was just another reason for the MacGregors who remembered Isobel to dislike Emily. Or, at least, not trust her.

Trust her. That's what she wanted his clan to do. He grimaced, thinking how unlikely that was to happen, even if she *didn't* assume airs and *did* work hard to prove herself. Even he resented that she held the deed to Strae Castle and the MacGregor lands. It was a barrier that was nigh unsurmountable. Especially more so if their clan name was reinstated, giving them the right to reclaim their lands. As head of the clan, he would have to defend their rights, even if King George did not agree. That possibility was only too real and, with Gavin Campbell sniffing around Emily's skirts, she would have a ready ally and clan war could very well break out.

Ian rubbed his temple, feeling the onset of a headache. His brothers had not been exaggerating when they'd had their earlier discussion. War with the *Campbells* who, more often than not, sided with the Crown, could quickly put an end to the MacGregors' reinstatement. History had proved how many times that had happened before.

The whole thing was a quagmire more treacherous than any peat bog.

But fashing about it would do no good. Emily said she

intended to make Strae Castle her home, and he already recognized the tone of her voice when she wasn't about to be deterred. Somehow, this situation needed to be reconciled, but he had no idea how to do it. Maybe he should…

A female scream rent the air, suddenly halted in mid-screech. *Emily*? Ian pushed back his chair, knocking it over, and rushed to the door.

Chapter Thirteen

Ian ran out of the empty Great Hall to find Emily lying in a heap at the bottom of the spiral stairs, crumpled bedsheets on the floor beside her. She wasn't moving and her eyes were closed. Rushing over, he knelt down, his fingers searching for a pulse along her neck. He breathed a sigh of relief when he felt a faint but steady beat.

His hand lingered there for a moment, savoring the satiny softness of her skin, before he noticed the bump on her forehead that was already beginning to swell. He touched it gingerly and she moaned slightly, but her eyes remained closed. He looked at the winding stairs. She must have tripped on the sheets coming down and, with no railing, had pitched off them. Guilt washed over him and he chastised himself for allowing her to stay in the old part of the castle. He should have insisted that she move closer to her sisters. At least he could remedy that right now by taking her to one of those bedchambers.

As he started to slide his arms beneath her shoulders, he paused, looking down at her face. Long eyelashes, darker than her hair, rested against the delicate curve of her cheekbones. Her lush, full lips were slightly parted. A sudden urge to kiss them jolted him like a lightning bolt. He had no business kissing Emily, especially since she was unconscious. Taking advantage of a woman was not something he did, but the urge was nearly irresistible. He couldn't remember the last time he'd so desperately wanted to taste a woman's mouth. Certainly not the occasional tavern wench who slaked his lust in exchange for coin.

Ian looked around. The foyer in front of the Great Hall was entirely empty, workers having gone to the fields and the other servants busy in the newer part of the castle with their daily routines. He was alone with Emily. He glanced down at her once more. There was more color to her cheeks and her breathing was even. She would no doubt stir in a moment or two. What harm could come from stealing a wee kiss before she did? No one would be the wiser…

He bent his head and brushed his lips across hers. The softness and warmth nearly undid him, and he wanted more. Wanted to tease and nibble and take. Wanted to wake her with dozens of kisses. Somehow he managed to lift his head, although his eyes lingered on her delectable mouth. With a sigh, he slid his arms beneath her shoulders and knees and lifted her. As he did, her head fell against his shoulder and, although he knew it was because she was unconscious, it felt right—like she belonged in his arms.

He gave himself an inward shake. Such thinking would only lead to trouble. His clan was depending on him to help restore their lands, not conspire with the enemy. He looked down at Emily once more. She didn't seem so much like the enemy anymore, even if she was English.

More foolish thinking.

"*Cad a tharla*?" Fiona rushed from the solar as he strode past it. "What happened?"

Juliana appeared behind her. "What's wrong?"

"Is Emily hurt?" Lorelei crowded behind them.

Down the hall, Ian kicked the door open to an empty bedchamber. "She fell off the stairs while carrying some bedsheets."

"*A Mhuire Mhàthair!*" Fiona exclaimed. "And damnation!"

Ian lifted an eyebrow at his sister. "Calling on the virgin and cursing at the same time might nae get results."

"Ye ken what I mean! 'Tis time ye talk to Maggie about taking the servants to task for nae treating Emily proper."

"That is not entirely your housekeeper's fault," Juliana said before he could respond. "Emily likes to be independent."

Yes, she does. Ian lowered her carefully to the bed. She probably—most certainly?—would not have agreed to the kiss had she been awake, but he couldn't truly regret the small pleasure.

Emily moaned again, her eyes fluttered, then opened. She blinked up at them and tried to sit up but fell back. She raised a hand to her temple and winced. "I guess I took a nasty fall."

"Ye did," Fiona said, fluffing a pillow and stuffing it behind her to help her sit.

"'Tis good ye remember," Ian said, "but I will send for Old Gwendolyn just to make sure ye are all right."

"Is that necessary?" Emily asked. "I hate to be a bother."

"'Tis nae bother." Fiona glared at Ian. "If my eejit brother had ordered the servants to help ye, ye would nae have fallen."

"Ye already made that point." Ian turned to Emily. "'Tis better our healer look at ye, since ye were unconscious for a few minutes."

She gave him a puzzled look, and he hoped she hadn't been more seriously hurt, but then she nodded, stopping at once.

"Ouch."

"That settles it then," Fiona said. "I will ride over myself and fetch Gwendolyn."

"And send Maggie up," Ian said.

A few minutes later his housekeeper arrived, a contrite look on her face. Ian had no doubt Fiona had already let her feelings be known, but he wasn't going to admonish Maggie in front of the Englishwomen.

"I've sent for the healer, but do what ye can until she gets here."

She nodded and less than a minute later Ian found himself on the other side of a closed door while maids bustled by with cool water and cloths. He could hear female voices engaged in conversation, and he hoped they weren't wearing Emily out with their questions about what happened.

He was glad she remembered going down the stairs and falling, but equally glad she would have no memory of what else had taken place. That would be his little secret.

• • •

Ian MacGregor had *kissed* her. At first, Emily thought she'd dreamed it, drifting in some sort of hazy trance, feeling the lightest brushing of his lips across hers. And then, as she floated toward consciousness, she realized what she'd felt was real. His mouth, gentle as a zephyr breeze, had slowly stroked across her own, lingering for just a moment, teasing her senses before he broke the contact. And, in some foggy, recessed area of her mind, she'd wanted more...a sensation she couldn't remember *ever* having. Still, she had been too befuddled to open her eyes or even make a sound. The last thing she remembered was him picking her up and tucking her close. She'd experienced another strange sensation as she'd nestled against him and allowed herself to drift away once more. She had felt *safe*.

The bedchamber he'd taken her to suddenly felt empty as he was shooed out the door, even though it was crowded with her sisters, the housekeeper, and what seemed like a dozen maids, coming and going.

"I am sure I am quite all right," she said as Lorelei dipped a cloth in cold water and pressed it to the bump on her head. "Oh, that does feel wonderful."

"Which just proves you might not be as 'all right' as you think," Juliana said, wringing out a second cloth.

"We will see when Gwendolyn gets here." The housekeeper looked around the room as if to make sure all was in order. "I will go downstairs and make ye a fresh pot of tea with some honey. 'Tis always good for what ails ye."

Emily wasn't sure if Maggie was making the overture because Ian had given orders or because she was sincere. Either way, perhaps it was a start to a reconciliation.

As she bustled out, Emily could hear male voices in the hallway, probably Ian's brothers or uncles come to find out what all the ruckus was about, since so many servants had congregated. It didn't take long for the voices to fade, and she wondered if Ian had left as well. It was rather nice knowing he'd lingered.

A short time later, Fiona returned with the healer in tow. She promptly dismissed the maids, although Juliana and Lorelei insisted on staying. Nodding once, Gwendolyn then poked and prodded Emily to make sure the only injury she had was the bump on her head. She *tsked* when she examined it.

"Ye might as well let the laird in," she said, without turning around. "He will want to ken what I say and I doona like repeating myself."

Emily exchanged a surprised look with her sisters. There had been no noise, not even boots shuffling, outside the door.

How had the healer known Ian was there?

But he was. When Juliana opened the door, he nearly fell through, like some small boy listening at a keyhole.

"Is Em—the countess—going to be all right?" he asked.

The healer straightened with surprising agility and, as a sunbeam from the window lit her face, she seemed younger somehow. Odd. Usually sunlight made people look older.

"Fiona told me that the lady was nae conscious when ye brought her to the room. Do ye have any idea how long she was such?"

"Just a few minutes," Ian answered. "I was still in the Great Hall when I heard her scream and fall. I brought her directly here."

Not directly, Emily thought and tried not to smile. There had been the kiss…

The healer studied him and, as Emily watched, a slight flush crossed his face. For a moment, she wondered if he was thinking the same thing.

"Just a few minutes," he reaffirmed.

"'Tis good, then. Even so, 'tis hard to ken how hard she hit her head when she fell." The healer rummaged in the knapsack she'd brought and pulled out two small bags of herbs. "I will make a poultice of comfrey and foxglove to help with the swelling, but ye must be sure the lady stays awake for the rest of the day." She looked at Emily. "Just last year I treated a young man with a blow to his head. I cautioned his father to keep him awake, but he didna listen. The lad didna wake up."

The words had a chilling effect, which was probably just what Old Gwendolyn had intended. "I will stay awake."

"I will make sure she does," Ian added.

Lorelei pointed to her sister. "We will sit with her, too."

"Aye. See that ye do." The healer looked satisfied that she'd instilled enough fear into them. "I will go then and make the poultice."

After she left, Ian pulled up a chair by the window. Fiona gave him a curious look. "'Tis sheaving day. Are ye nae going to go check on the fields?"

"My brothers can handle it. I doona think they've left yet, so ye can tell them."

As much as Emily liked the fact that he wanted to stay, she also didn't want his clansmen thinking he was neglecting his duties because of her. "Really, if you have matters to attend to—"

"I am staying."

Lorelei stared at him. "This is not proper."

He raised a brow. "'Tis my home. I say what is proper."

Juliana pursed her mouth. "You are almost as arrogant as your brother."

His brow went slightly higher. "I assume ye mean Rory?"

Surprisingly, Emily saw a faint blush on her sister's cheeks. Of course, it could have been anger, since Juliana tossed her head. "He would be the one."

A corner of his mouth quirked, but before he could answer, someone knocked. Fiona opened the door to find Hamish standing there.

"What is it?" Ian asked.

"'Tis a problem at the distillery. One of the wash backs has developed a crack. Broderick asks that ye come at once."

"Damnation." Ian rose. The wash backs were where the fermenting of the sweet syrup extracted from the mash tuns was turned into alcohol. If the pine vat had a crack and the liquid started leaking, it would mean they would have less whisky to distill. Not good when they'd just signed a contract to sell a good amount to White's. And, with the harvesting coming to a finish, he couldn't afford to call in hands to help repair it.

"Go." Even as she spoke, a maid appeared with the

poultice and tea. "As you can see, I will be fine."

He hesitated, then finally nodded. "I will be back as soon as I can."

A warm feeling enveloped her as she leaned against the headboard and sipped the strong tea, poultice balanced on her head. Even if Ian couldn't stay, it was his intention that was important. And, besides, they couldn't afford to lose a batch of whisky.

She sipped more tea contentedly. It really was quite good.

• • •

It was a good thing Broderick had sent for him, after all, Ian thought as he started to ride home a little over an hour later. The crack in the pine had been fresh, not completely gone through the thickness of the wood, and they had been able to repair it without wasting any of the fermenting barley.

He had barely crossed the old drawbridge and entered the bailey when the heavy wooden door to the castle flew open and Fiona bounded down the steps. From the expression on her face, he knew something was wrong. He reined in and slid off the stallion at the same time.

"What is it? What's wrong?"

"'Tis Emily…we canna keep her awake!"

She'd hardly finished the sentence when he ran past her into the castle and hurried to the bedchamber where he'd left Emily. He pushed the door open without fanfare and then stopped dead in his tracks.

Juliana and Lorelei each had one of Emily's arms around their shoulders while she hung like dead weight between them. They were attempting to walk with her, but her feet dragged and her head lolled.

He reached them in three strides. "Let me take her." Not waiting for affirmation from either of them, he disengaged

Lorelei, tugging Emily's arm around his neck while his hand slid round her waist. Holding her against him, he managed to shuffle forward. Since the chamber wasn't large, it was more like a macabre dance of three steps forward, turn—while Emily slipped down his side and he propped her up—before taking three steps back. Then repeating. She mumbled to herself and her eyelids fluttered, but she didn't wake up.

"Have ye sent for the healer?"

"Yes, but—"

"I am already here." Old Gwendolyn entered the room, followed by Fiona. In her hand she held a bag of herbs. "I was going to leave these with the comfrey and foxglove but forgot." She squinted at Emily and squeezed her cheeks. "Mayhap 'twas nae a mistake after all. It seems the faeries kenned I was needed."

"Do ye ken what is wrong with her?"

"I doona work magic, laird. I need to examine her first. Place her in the chair."

"Shouldna I keep her moving?"

The healer gave him a chiding look. "'Tis nae helping, is it? And I canna see what is wrong if yer prancing about."

Ian clamped his mouth shut and carefully set Emily down, then stepped back. "Hurry," he said when the healer simply stood there, observing.

Gwendolyn ignored his command and turned to Fiona. "How long has she been like this?"

"I am nae sure." Fiona shrugged. "Mayhap less than an hour?"

Ian glared at her, then at Emily's sisters. "Were ye nae in the room?"

"We were," Fiona shot back. "We were all sitting here, talking and sipping tea. Emily was a bit quiet, but 'tis to be expected when her head hurt."

"Then she started to get sleepy," Juliana said. "We tried

to get her to stand up, but she just fell back on the bed—"

"And then she was out," Lorelei finished. "We tried to wake her, but Fiona said not to shake her."

"Fiona was right." The healer gently squeezed Emily's cheeks again. "'Tis dangerous with a blow to the head." Emily mumbled something incoherent and her eyes slowly opened.

Ian frowned when he saw how bloodshot they were. "What is wrong with her? Why are her eyes like that? Is she bleeding inside?"

Old Gwendolyn squinted, then leaned forward to sniff her breath and looked up. "Did ye put whisky in the tea?"

"No, of course not," Juliana said. "It was just tea, with a little sugar."

Ian eyed the tea service sitting on the small table by the window. "Did ye all drink from the same pot?"

"Yes," Lorelei said. "One of the maids brought it up shortly after you left."

"But..." Fiona paused. "Emily was already drinking a cup when the pot of tea arrived, remember? Another maid had brought it with the poultice."

Ian reached for the pewter mug sitting on the bedside chest. "Was this her cup?" When Fiona nodded, he bent his head. He blinked as his eyes smarted. "'Tis whisky all right."

The healer frowned. "Whisky could make her sleepy."

He remembered how Emily had drunk that dram when she'd first arrived. "I doona think a bit of whisky would cause her to pass out." He bent and sniffed again. The strong fumes of alcohol assailed him again along with a sweet smell. Could someone have put something else in the tea?

Emily mumbled and attempted to sit straighter, although she was not very successful. Still, he breathed a sigh of relief that she was at least awake.

"Find the maid who brought this," he said to Fiona. "And take her to the library."

His sister's eyes widened, but she merely nodded and left. He turned to the healer. "Ye will stay with Emily?"

"Aye, laird."

By the time he got to the library, Fiona was there with a defiant-looking Maggie and a trembling maid. Apparently, Fiona had told them what had transpired. Ian tried to rein in his temper and turned to his housekeeper.

"Did ye prepare a special cup of tea for Lady Woodhaven?"

"Aye." She lifted her chin. "The blend I use with rose hips and mint. I mixed it with honey."

That would explain the sweet smell. "Did ye add whisky?"

She frowned. "Nae. Why would I do that?"

"Whisky was found in the cup." He turned to the maid who looked on the verge of tears. "Did ye add whisky?"

"Nae! Nae!" She started to cry.

Maggie put a hand on the girl's shoulder. "How would she have access to spirits?"

It was a logical question, but he had to ask the maid anyway. "I doona ken, but someone put whisky in that cup. It made Emily—the countess—drowsy and she fell asleep, which was very dangerous." He took a deep breath and gentled his voice. "Effie," he said to the maid. "Did ye by any chance leave the cup standing somewhere before ye took it to the bedchamber?"

She shook her head, snuffling into the back of her hand.

Maggie looked speculative. "I set the cup on the counter to steep a bit, then I walked to the door with Gwendolyn in case she had any more instructions. As I was returning, I asked Effie to take the tea up to Lady Woodhaven."

At least she was addressing Emily by her title instead of Sassenach, but Ian hadn't time for niceties right now. "So the cup was unattended for a few minutes?"

Fiona frowned. "Ye think someone else put whisky in it?"

"Someone else had to," he replied.

"But who would want to do that?"

"'Tis a good question." Who would have access to whisky, as well as not draw attention to himself or herself by being in the kitchen? Any number of clansmen might have come through to take a bit of bread and cheese with them to the fields, but none would be carrying a whisky bottle at that time of day. His brothers... He couldn't picture any of them—even Devon—stealthily pouring whisky into a teacup meant for Emily. Probably *especially* not Devon... He would just say it was a waste of good Scots whisky on a Sassenach. That thought relieved Ian a little, but he still grimaced.

"'Tis a good question," he said again, "and I intend to find out."

...

As Ian made his way back to Emily's chamber, he pondered whether or not whoever had added the whisky to the tea had done it deliberately so Emily would fall asleep or because the person thought it might ease the pain. Scots did use whisky as a remedy for a lot of ills. There might have been no malicious intent at all.

He pushed the question to the back of his mind as he entered her room. Emily was sitting in the armchair by the window and, although still pale, she was alert. He winced as she turned her head and he saw the swollen bump already turning purple.

"Does it hurt overmuch?"

"Of course it does." Juliana gave him a look that made clear she thought he was daft. "Did you expect it would not?"

"The poultices help." Lorelei placed another on her sister's injury and held it there. "And we have all been keeping an eye on her."

"I am right here," Emily said. "I can speak for myself."

"But you are not to exert yourself." Lorelei looked at the healer. "Is that not what you said?"

"Aye," Old Gwendolyn answered, "but answering a few questions should nae harm her."

"And I have a few questions," Ian said.

"Do ye have any for me?" the healer asked. "If nae, I will be leaving. The lass should make a full recovery now that she is awake."

"Thank ye." Ian turned to Fiona. "Will ye see Gwendolyn to the door?"

Fiona nodded and looked at Juliana and Lorelei. "Mayhap we should let my brother ask his questions in private?"

Juliana frowned, but Lorelei tugged her sleeve. "I, for one, could use some fresh air."

"An excellent idea," Ian said, "and, Fiona, please bring some broth back in a few minutes." He paused to give her an unspoken message. "Bring it yerself."

Emily gave him a curious look when they left. "Did the maid confess to adding whisky to my tea?"

He shook his head and told her what had transpired. "Well," she said when he finished, "it is hardly a crime to add liquor to tea."

"'Tis close when 'tis enough to make ye pass out."

She frowned slightly, laying the poultice down. "If that much was added, funny I did not taste it."

Ian narrowed his eyes in thought. She had a point, especially since he'd seen her drain a dram without repercussions. If two or more drams had been put in, she would surely have noticed the smell, honey-infused or not. The pewter mug wasn't big enough for that much whisky *and* tea. "Ye tasted nothing?"

She started to shake her head, then stopped. "No. The tea just tasted strong."

"Hmmm." There was no need to prolong the conversation until he could further investigate. "At least, ye will nae have to fash about tripping on the stairs again."

"Oh?"

"I am having yer things moved in here. Ye will stay with the rest of us from now on."

"But I liked that room. It had… I don't know… A *castle-ish* feel to it."

He lifted a brow. "A castle-*ish* feel?"

"Yes…very medieval, like it is a part of history."

"Aye, 'tis that," Ian said. "Complete with a ghost that gives ye nightmares."

Her eyes widened. "You do not believe in ghosts, do you?"

He didn't, but he hadn't dismissed the possibility that someone had used the passageway to access her room to scare her. "'Tis nae the point. After Isobel was killed, that part of the castle was nae used for years because the maids were scared to go up there. 'Tis why ye were having to carry the sheets down yourself probably." He pointed to the bump on her head. "I'll nae have ye falling again."

"But I have walked those steps at least a hundred times by now."

"And ye could have gotten tangled in the sheets carrying them down before."

She furrowed her brows. "I had the sheets folded over my arm. I did not get tangled in them."

"Then why did ye stumble?"

"I do not really know." Her frown deepened. "My foot slipped on one of the boards, I guess. I just remember losing my balance."

Ian stared at her. "How far up were ye when ye fell?"

"Near the top. I had just taken a few steps down. Why?"

The hair at his nape began to rise, a warning signal, but

he didn't want to worry Emily yet. "The stairs are old and probably need repair. All the more reason to stay in this room."

Before she could argue with him, Fiona reappeared, a tray with broth and bread in hand. "The bread just came out of the oven," she said, letting Ian know silently that she had supervised putting together the tray. "I thought Emily would like some to go with the broth that I skimmed from the stewpot."

He nodded. "Then I will leave ye to it."

His sister gave him a curious look, but he didn't acknowledge it. Instead, he forced himself to walk out at a casual pace, as though his mind weren't in turmoil. Every nerve ending was on edge, and he hadn't felt this wary since the days after his stepmother had been killed.

Thankfully, the Great Hall and large foyer were empty, the clansmen still in the fields. Ian picked up the sheets where they'd fallen and shook them, but nothing fell out, which was expected. Then he searched the ground below and around the staircase, but the stone floor was kept clean and there was nothing there, either. He looked up the stairs and began climbing.

It didn't take long before he discovered the loose board. It stood out at an angle now, no doubt caused when Emily had slipped. Ian bent down, rubbing his thumb across the holes where nails had been. The openings showed fresh wood as though the nails had just been removed. But he hadn't found any nails on the floor.

His nape hair stood nearly on end. Had someone deliberately loosened the board? Had someone wanted Emily to fall? Maybe to her death?

Chapter Fourteen

"I am going to join the rest of you for the evening meal." Emily picked a simple gown from the wardrobe in the bedchamber. "I have been stuck in this room for nearly three days."

Fiona looked up from the half-burned log she'd just turned in the small hearth. "The healer said ye should rest."

"I have been resting. For *three* days."

"Ian wants ye to wait until Old Gwendolyn checks ye again."

"And when is she coming?" Emily tried not to sound grumpy. The first day she truly had not minded staying abed. Her head had hurt and her side was bruised from the fall. Yesterday had been somewhat tolerable, although her sisters had kept up a nonstop conversation and Fiona had hovered over her like she were truly an invalid. But today… She'd had all she could take of being confined to four walls.

"I doona ken. She has rounds she makes. 'Tis better ye wait." Fiona replaced the poker in its stand. "Is there anything else I can do for ye?"

Emily gave her a wary look. Ian's sister was trying to

change the subject, a tactic she was all too familiar with, having used it herself to steer Juliana and Lorelei away from things they could not have when they were younger. She wasn't about to be led off her topic.

"Yes. You can walk with me up to the ramparts so I can get some fresh air…and a change of scenery."

Fiona shook her head. "Ian wouldna like ye going up there."

Emily frowned. "Why not? Does he think that I cannot climb stairs just because I slipped and fell?"

"The steps are uneven… Besides," she continued quickly as if she'd just had a revelation. "They are strenuous. Gwendolyn said ye are nae to strain yourself. So…I canna let ye climb them."

Emily eyed her suspiciously. Fiona had been acting very much the watchdog since the accident. As soon as Ian left in the mornings for the fields, she would appear. She didn't leave the room unless Juliana and Lorelei were there and even then, she didn't stay away long. It wasn't until Ian returned, usually well after dark, that Fiona left for the night. A thought struck her.

"Did Ian tell you to keep me prisoner in this room?"

Fiona's eyes widened slightly and Emily realized that he must have told his sister to not let her out of her sight. "He did, didn't he?"

"Nae!" She denied it a bit too fast. "Ye are nae a prisoner."

Emily shrugged. "Perhaps that was a poor choice of words. A *confined guest*, then?"

His sister didn't answer directly. Instead, she looked around. "Ye doona like this room? We have others that are empty."

She was changing the subject again. "The room is fine." And it was. Emily had to admit the windows allowing the morning sun in made it a more cheerful room than her former one. The walls were paneled in wood, which kept the cold from seeping through the stone, and there were rugs on the floor to keep her feet warm.

Fiona waved her hand about. "We've brought the things from the old room, too. Are ye missing something?"

"No." She was making another attempt at keeping Emily from leaving the room. "Everything is here." Not that she had much. Apart from her clothing, she had few personal items…a simple hairbrush and hand mirror, a few inexpensive baubles that hadn't been worth selling, and a picture of her parents. "But that is not the point. I am bored sitting here."

Fiona brightened. "I can get ye a book from the library. What would ye like to read?"

Emily narrowed her eyes slightly. She might as well test a theory that was beginning to form in her head. "That is an excellent idea, but, since I have not had an opportunity to look over your selection, I will accompany you and choose something myself."

"Oh, I doona think—"

"What? That I am incapable of choosing a book? Or that I might stumble and fall in the hallway? There are not even any steps to climb, since this chamber is on the first floor and so is the library."

"'Tis nae that—"

"Good. Then it's settled." Emily looked at the gown she'd intended to wear. She didn't have time to change into it lest Fiona come up with yet another excuse for her to stay in her chamber. The wrapper she wore around her night rail would have to do. No one, except a few servants, was in the castle at this time of day anyway. She marched to the door. "Are you coming with me?"

Fiona actually looked distressed, and momentary guilt swept over Emily. She didn't mean to cause the girl discomfort. Ian had no doubt left orders for his sister, and she suspected Fiona didn't want to face his wrath at being *disobeyed*—men!—but she needed to get out, if only to the library. "If Ian is upset, he needs to be upset with me, not you."

She nodded reluctantly and pointed to the gown on the bed. "Do ye want to change first?"

Emily shook her head. "This will be fine."

"Then let me make sure nae one is about."

"I will be fine." Emily opened the door and stepped out in the hallway. To her surprise, Hamish was standing only a few feet away. He glanced over her shoulder at Fiona and some unspoken message must have taken place for he nodded briskly before he turned to walk away.

Emily gazed after him. Why was the castellan standing outside her door? Was he eavesdropping? Or…had he been told to guard her door? But why?

• • •

"I thought I told ye to keep the countess occupied." Ian tried to keep the ire out of his voice as he looked at Fiona, seated across the desk from him in the library late that evening. Hamish had told him about the afternoon excursion.

"I tried!" She didn't bother to hide the annoyance in her own voice. "Emily is feeling better and she doesna want to be stuck in a room. I doona blame her."

"The cook has instructions to send a tray up with Effie." After her tearful response to his questioning, Maggie had suggested she be personally responsible for keeping an eye on whatever was served to Emily. The maid had been only too happy to prove herself. "Did that, at least, get done?"

"Aye, but Emily was nae happy about that, either."

He supposed she wasn't. He hated feeling confined, too, so he understood her agitation, but until he had a chance to do some more investigating, Emily was safer in her room.

"She asked me today if ye were keeping her a prisoner." Fiona gave him an accusatory look. "Mayhap ye should tell her the truth."

"I doona ken what the truth is. Yet," he added.

"That ye think someone loosened that board on the steps on purpose." Fiona glared at him. "That it was nae accident. Ye said so yerself."

He probably should nae have told his sister that, but he hadn't known any other way to convince her how important it was to keep an eye on Emily. Or, rather, on anyone who came near her.

"And ye ken why I told ye."

That seemed to mollify her somewhat. "Aye. And I will protect her." Fiona patted her boot. "I've got my *sgian dubh* right here."

"Hopefully, ye will nae have to use it."

"Still." Fiona frowned. "Do ye nae think Emily should ken she is in danger?"

"I doona want to alarm her," Ian replied, "nor do I want her being suspicious of our brothers."

"Ye mean Devon."

Ian winced slightly. He didn't want to think his brother was responsible for inflicting harm and danger on Emily, regardless of his anger at the English in general. He'd insisted he'd nothing to do with using the passageway to her room. And, in spite of his surliness, Ian had never known Devon to lie to him.

"'Tis nae fair to accuse him without proof," Ian said.

"True." Fiona studied him. "Is that why ye have nae told our other brothers about the stairs?"

"Partly." While they knew someone had put whisky in the tea, because Emily fell asleep, they had already left for the fields when the fall from the stairs had happened. Devon didn't need his brothers thinking he was guilty. Besides, they were all needed for the barley harvest. "I doona want a lot of questions being asked right now. I doona want to give the true culprit any reason to think we suspect the fall was anything more than an accident."

"That makes sense, I suppose."

"There was enough talk about the whisky," Ian said. "'Tis better that just ye and Hamish ken about the stairs for now."

"Why did ye even tell Hamish then? I told ye I would protect Emily." She patted her boot again. "He is nae as skilled with a blade as I am."

Ian couldn't help but smile. Fiona was proud of how accurate she was with a knife. "I doubt he would dispute that." Nor would anyone else who'd seen her practice, but that was neither here nor there. "As castellan, he hears and sees things we doona. Servants talk. I had to tell him so he'll ken what to listen for." And, Ian wanted the castellan to provide protection for Fiona, although that was something best left unsaid.

"Hmmm. Well, ye need to think what ye'll say to Emily. She caught Hamish standing outside her door this afternoon. She dinna ask me why, but I could see she was thinking on it."

"Could ye nae have made an excuse?"

She glowered at him. "I tried to get to the door first so I could wave him away, but Emily was closer. She had it open before I could get there."

He sighed. "It was nae yer fault. I'm sorry."

Her expression softened. "Keeping Emily in the dark is nae going to solve matters."

"I suppose ye are right." Ian rubbed his eyes, which burned from lack of sleep. The clansmen were working from dawn to dusk to harvest the barley, and he worked alongside them as any worthy laird would. He spent his nights thinking about who would hate Emily so much as to attempt to kill her. Unfortunately, there were scores of his clan who hated Sassenachs.

"Ye need to talk to her."

"I ken." He sighed again. Not all of his tossing and turning at night was because of the accident. A large part of his restlessness was due to recalling the kiss he'd given Emily. A kiss she was unaware of, but would live in his mind for months, if not longer. He suspected the memory might be permanently embedded in his brain. The warmth of her mouth, the soft fullness of her lips, the silky texture of her skin… When he finally slept, his body reacted like that of a green lad with his first maid. One lustful dream followed another, like tumbles in the hay. He'd managed not to see her since the first day, determined to get his reaction to her under control. Yet, he couldn't avoid the situation forever. And, as Fiona pointed out, Emily could not be confined to her room forever, either.

He took a deep breath. It was time to confront his fantasy.

• • •

Emily managed to escape her sickroom the following morning, although perhaps "escape" was too fanciful a term, since Fiona had, for some reason, left her alone and the castellan was not standing out in the hallway. Actually, she had just opened the door and walked out.

She *felt* like she'd escaped, though, which was somewhat ridiculous considering she'd been confined for only three days in a very comfortable room, and Strae Castle was her home.

Passing the Great Hall that was empty now, since the workers had already left for the fields, she made her way to the smaller dining room. She doubted her sisters would be there. Juliana generally forewent breakfast and Lorelei tried to keep London hours, albeit Emily made a point of making her rise before nine o'clock. Since she'd been stuck in her room, Lorelei had probably taken full advantage and was still sound asleep.

Emily expected Fiona to be in the room. Instead, Ian sat alone at the table, half turned away from her, looking out the window. Sunlight glinted off his raven hair, the strong outline of his jaw made prominent by a shadow beard. He was dressed simply in doeskin breeches and a white linen shirt, open at the throat and its sleeves rolled up. No doubt he was getting ready to leave for the fields, yet the informal attire and his rather tousled look seemed almost intimate.

She paused just outside the doorway, unsure what to say to him. He'd left her room that first day while she had still been somewhat groggy, although she recalled every detail of his kiss. Even now, three days later, the memory was strong enough to send a quiver to her stomach, as though a bevy of quail had taken wing. For a wicked moment she wondered what he'd do if she confronted him with the fact that she was aware of it? Would he kiss her again? She *tsked* at herself. When had she become a romantic ninny?

He must have heard the sound, for he turned away from the window to look at her. He rose, his whisky-colored eyes turning slightly darker. Or maybe they looked that way only because he'd moved away from the sunlight. She gave him a tentative smile.

"Good morning. Do not blame Fiona for letting me out," she said quickly. "I was about to go stark raving mad."

He smiled. "I willna have Fiona flogged then."

Emily felt her eyes round before she realized he was teasing. Or, at least, she thought he was. He must have sensed her hesitance, because the smile widened into a grin. "Ye need nae fear that will happen, lass. If any fool were to attempt to try, my sister would likely turn the whip on the man. And I am nae a fool."

He'd called her *lass*. She knew it was a common term, but she'd heard it used only to describe Scottish women. Did that mean he was beginning to accept her presence here? Maybe one day, she'd no longer hear *Sassenach*? The more she learned about his people, the more she wanted to be a part of them.

He sobered. "Do ye think me a fool?"

"What?" She blinked, aware that she'd been woolgathering and felt warmth flood her cheeks. "Of course not."

"Well, 'tis good then." He pulled out a chair. "Would ye sit?"

She took the chair and watched as he drew his own to the table. "Are you not going to the fields today?"

"Aye, but a bit later." As if he'd rung some invisible bell, Effie and another maid appeared in the doorway with two covered trays. As they set them down, the fragrant aroma of cinnamon porridge wafted up along with the smoky-sweet smell of roasted boar dribbled with honey.

"This smells delicious!"

"'Tis a hearty meal." Ian picked up the basket of freshly baked bannocks, their still warm scent assailing her nose as well, and offered her one. "'Twill strengthen ye now that ye are up and about."

She gave him a wary look. "Then I am not going to be sent back upstairs?"

He swallowed the bite of bread he'd taken before he spoke. "Fiona told me ye felt like a prisoner there."

Not exactly a direct answer, but she was determined not to be confined. "I did. One can lie abed for only so long without anything to do." Something sparked in his eyes and she realized how that might have sounded. She felt heat sweep across her face and chewed her lip. Dear Lord! How had that slipped out? "I…I mean…it is quite boring to be confined.

By myself." Goodness! That didn't sound much better. She worried her lip again, willing herself to remain silent, lest she babble some other wanton-sounding thing. Ian contemplated her for a moment, and she wondered what he was thinking. And prayed she wasn't blushing again. He rattled her even when she didn't think he was trying to.

His voice was noncommittal when he spoke. "I doona want ye to feel like a prisoner, but I do want ye to take care, lass."

There was that word again! It gave her a rather warm, cozy feeling. And it took another moment before she realized what he'd said. "Take care? What do you mean?" When he looked uncomfortable, she added, "I am not usually clumsy and I have never fallen down stairs before, but thank you for your concern." When he frowned slightly, she widened her eyes. "Do you think someone meant me harm?" It looked to her like he actually squirmed in his chair.

"I doona ken for sure. The board came loose somehow."

"That is fairly common in old houses," Emily answered, "and, I would think, especially in old *castles*."

"Mayhap." He didn't appear convinced. "I dinna like finding that someone put whisky in your tea as well."

She frowned. "That is fairly common, too. Someone may have thought they were doing a good thing."

Ian looked as though he wanted to say more, but then he shook his head as if to clear it. "I hope ye are right, but until I can do a bit more checking around, which will be when the harvest is done, I want ye to stay close to Fiona."

So she had been right. Ian had instructed his sister not to let her out of sight. That probably meant he'd told Hamish to stand guard as well.

She clasped her hands to keep them from shaking while a chill slithered down her spine. She was still a Sassenach surrounded by Scots—one of whom didn't like her. At all.

Chapter Fifteen

"Thank you for granting my request," Emily told Ian as they prepared to enter the Great Hall to break their fast the next morning. She'd taken a tray in her room last evening, but only as a compromise.

"I still doona think this is a good idea," he grumbled.

Fiona gave him a poke with her elbow. "I thought ye said we needed to provide a united front."

He moved out of range. "I ken that." Turning to Emily, he exaggerated a bow, then offered his arm. "Allow me to escort ye, my lady."

Behind them, Lorelei giggled. Emily could only imagine Juliana rolling her eyes at such a grand gesture. She gave both sisters a warning look over her shoulder, then smiled at Ian. "There really is no need to be so formal."

"Aye, there is," Fiona whispered. "Remember… It shows the clan ye are under their laird's protection."

In England, she'd legally been under her husband's "protection," too, although that really meant she was chattel… the personal property of an earl. No one had asked questions when that property had a bruise. Fiona had explained, though, that in Scotland "protection" meant something else entirely. A laird—even though the Crown had outlawed the term, Scots were defiant—didn't inherit his title because of bloodline. He was *chosen* to lead his clan by his people. As their leader, he had a responsibility to protect and keep each of them safe. His word was also law, at least to his clan. A show of his support would go a long way to deter whomever—if there was someone—had tried to injure her.

"Well?" Ian tilted his head in question and she realized she'd been woolgathering again. She tucked her hand into his proffered arm, rather than laying her fingers on top as would have been proper. If this was going to be a show of solidarity, then she'd make sure everyone who watched them realized it.

Besides, she rather liked the feel of his solid muscle beneath her hand. That should shock her, but somehow it didn't.

Conversation halted as they entered the hall, then soft murmuring began as they proceeded toward the dais where Ian's brothers and uncles were already seated. The first thing she noticed when they got closer was that the smaller table where she and her sisters usually sat had been removed. She gave Ian a questioning look.

"Ye will sit beside me tonight."

She widened her eyes. "Beside you?"

"Aye. 'Tis time."

She had hoped he would finally seat her on the dais on one of the ends, but she hadn't expected the place of honor *beside* him. His brothers, ranked by age, always sat to his right and his uncles to his left. She glanced at the high table. Were they willing to finally accept her? Carr's and Alasdair's expressions were neutral, Rory was staring pointedly, although she realized he was looking past her, probably at Juliana, and wondered what her sister had possibly done to irritate him this time. Devon looked sulky, but that wasn't unusual. She slipped her gaze to the uncles, but they were conversing and not paying attention to them. His ward Glenda was at her usual place below the dais, watching with the same wooden expression she usually wore.

The crowd went silent once more as Ian pulled the chair out beside him and seated her. For a brief moment, she almost wished he'd let her sit with her sisters and Fiona near the end of the table. Having nearly one hundred pairs of eyes trained on her was disconcerting, especially when one or more of those sets might truly resent her. She folded her hands in her lap and gave Ian an anxious, sideways glance.

"Are you sure this is a good idea? Perhaps I should sit—"

"Exactly where ye are." His hand slipped under the table and on top of hers. He gave it a gentle squeeze. The gesture was probably meant to be reassuring, but she was instantly aware of how close his fingers were to the very intimate part of her. An odd, thrumming sensation began at that juncture, and the room suddenly felt very warm. Almost as if he read her thoughts—Dear Lord! She hoped not!—he released her hand quickly. His eyes darkened for a brief moment.

He started to speak but was interrupted as a clansman burst through the door at the far end and ran down the length of the room toward the dais, out of breath when he got there.

"Dragoons!" he managed to wheeze, although as deadly quiet as the room had gotten, the word carried. "They are coming!"

• • •

"What the bloody hell are the damn dragoons doing on our land?" An hour later, Devon paced back and forth in front of the library's hearth—at a rate that was making everyone slightly dizzy.

None of the brothers had asked him to stop, and Emily realized movement was probably the way he let out his anger. She remembered that dragoons had captured Devon years before and made a mental note to ask Ian about that later.

"We canna be sure they are coming for us," Carr said. "Our kinsman said they were marching south from Fort William."

"And that message was relayed several times," Alasdair said. "Ye ken how easy it is for one of the riders to put his opinion on it."

Emily knew well how gossip could start and grow into devastating rumors that had only an element of truth in them. The MacGregors—as well as most of the other clans, from what she'd been told—used a system of relay riders that they kept posted at strategic locations. Fiona had said originally it was to spy on the other clans, but after Culloden, Scots wanted to keep an eye on whatever the English were doing at Forts William, Augustus, and George, since those were the three that controlled Scotland.

"'Tis possible they are replacements for ones on patrol," Ian said.

Devon snorted. "The last company was replaced just this summer. I tell ye, they are coming for MacGregor lands!"

"Legally, there are no MacGregor lands," Carr reminded him. "Our kinsmen who hold lands have different surnames—approved by the king—so the Crown canna just take them."

"Nae?" Devon stopped pacing. "Our grandfather was given 'approval' by the damn king to live *on our own lands* because we dinna fight at Prestonpans..." He leveled a look at Emily. "...and yet *she* comes here with the deed to our property—"

"This is nae her fault," Ian said sharply.

Devon glowered at him. "Damn King George went back on his word."

Carr sighed. "'Twas his grandfather who granted our grandfather the right—"

"What difference does that make?"

Rory nodded. "Devon is right. It shouldna make a difference."

Juliana narrowed her eyes and Emily shook her head subtly, hoping her sister would understand and not blurt out something that was going to make this situation even worse. Thankfully, Lorelei noticed and gave her sister a poke.

"If the dragoons carry orders from the Crown, taking away our rights, I will fight it." Devon looked at each of his brothers. "Even if it means killing."

"Think, brother," Carr said "That would mean an end to our hopes of restoring our name when Parliament meets next month."

"And we doona ken why they are marching," Alasdair added. "It may have nothing to do with us."

"Why else would the dragoons be coming?" Devon demanded.

Emily took a deep breath. "I understand how you feel—"

"Do ye?" Devon asked. "Ye are English, a—"

"*Enough*," Ian warned.

Devon clenched his fists as he stared at his brother, his anger nearly palpable. Ian stared back. She saw his brothers start to tense, and even his uncles straightened. She hoped the argument wouldn't lead to a full-out brawl. Evidently, Fiona sensed the tension, too, because she rose swiftly from her chair near the hearth and placed a hand on Devon's arm.

"The past is over. We must wait and see what they want this time."

He frowned but didn't jerk away.

"Fiona is right, Devon," Carr said. "Ye ken it, too."

He hesitated, then unclenched his fists. "'Tis hard to—"

"We ken," Alasdair said, "we ken."

Emily really needed to find out what had happened to Devon. As horrid as it might have been, she wanted to understand Ian's brother. Maybe she could offer a bit of reassurance right now.

"I would like to finish what I started to say."

"I am nae sure that is a good idea, right now," Ian said.

Donovan shrugged. "We might as well hear what the countess has to say."

"She has plans for the distillery," Broderick added. "Mayhap she has a plan to waylay the dragoons, too."

Emily wasn't sure if he was being sarcastic or not, since his expression was neutral, but it almost always was. She decided to continue.

"First, I want to reassure you, as I did when I first arrived, that I have no intention of asking any of you to leave. I may hold the deed, but I want us to work together." She repressed a sigh when all she got was wary looks. "And, while I do not have a *reason* regarding the dragoons, I find it illogical to think that King George would be sending them to take away property that—as you pointed out—either belongs to your kinsmen who took other surnames or to me. For once, my being English might be a benefit to you."

She looked around, making a point to smile at Devon, who didn't return the gesture. Instead, he drew his brows together. "Ye will never understand. MacGregors have been hunted *by the English Crown* for no greater sin than bearing our name for more than two centuries. We are nae animals, even if ye Sassenachs think so!"

"I do not think…" She sighed, not finishing the sentence, for Devon had stormed out the door.

• • •

Ian caught up with Emily, her sisters, and Fiona as they left the library and headed for the solar. "Might I have a word with ye, Lady Woodhaven?"

"Of course." She turned to the others. "I will be along shortly." As they continued on, she turned to Ian. "Why the formal address? Everyone else goes by their Christian names."

"I was nae sure ye would take kindly to that after Devon's behavior. I apologize for my brother."

She tilted her head. "Perhaps we could stroll in the garden?"

He gave her a wary look. Nothing was blooming in the garden this late in the season except a few wild clumps of heather. The day was overcast and damp, so she was certainly not seeking the warmth of the sun. However, the garden was both a place where they could publicly be seen and yet have privacy from servants. Which meant that Emily wanted to *talk*… An event that most men looked forward to with as much enthusiasm as having a tooth pulled. Still. He owed her that much for not creating a scene in the library where a fracas had nearly broken out after Devon's hasty departure.

He turned toward a hallway that led to a rear entrance. "This way."

She followed him silently until they neared a folly in the middle of the garden. It wasn't especially extravagant or fanciful, simply a small rounded structure with five steps that led to an open-arched entrance. The whole thing was no more than a story high and made of sandstone that had been brought from the Borders. On a sunny day, the little building had a golden glow.

Ian mounted the steps and gestured to a cushioned oak bench inside. Square windows placed at seated eye level every few feet gave a circular view of the garden.

"This is lovely," Emily said as she sat down. "I have wanted to come here, but it seemed like a special place to which one needed to be invited."

"In a way, it is." Ian sat beside her, leaving a proper space between them, since he doubted she'd planned a tryst. His ever-lusty groin tightened at the idea and he pushed the randy thought aside. "My father built it for my mother. She liked to come here for peace and quiet when the daily clan troubles boiled over."

Emily gave him a sideways glance. "Like today?"

He nodded. "I apologize again."

"Thank you, but there is no need. It is just going to take longer than I expected for your family to accept the circumstances…to accept me." She paused. "Well, except for Devon." She turned to Ian. "I know he was captured by dragoons and that must certainly have been horrible, but what else can you tell me about him? He seems so angry."

Ian sighed. "Devon is three years younger than me, yet older than the others. Even as bairns, he seemed to feel things more deeply than the rest of us."

"Then he must have taken your mother's death hard?"

"Aye. He was a lad of ten. 'Twas the last time I saw him cry. And," he added, "the first time he ran away."

"Did someone go after him?"

Ian shook his head. "Da was too devastated to even notice he was gone, I think. And, with the others too young to leave alone, I didna follow him, either."

"I understand," Emily said. "When my parents were killed, my sisters had only me to take care of them."

"And how old were ye?"

"Nine and ten…Juliana was three and ten and Lorelei only eleven."

He hesitated a moment. "'Twas the reason ye married?"

"Yes." She took a deep breath. "My father was certain one of his inventions would result in great fortune. Sadly, none of them did, so there was little money for a dowry."

Emily looked down at her folded hands. "The earl agreed to take in my sisters if I married him."

Something that felt very akin to a knife blade sliced through Ian. He had thought—at least when she'd arrived—that she'd married the elderly Woodhaven for his money. In a sense, she had, but for the right reason. As laird, he understood the responsibility of taking care of not only his family, but also his clan. He reached over to tip her chin up with his fingers.

"Did he treat ye well?" The question was no more out his mouth when he saw a flash of pain in her eyes and knew the damn earl had not. But the look vanished almost instantly.

"I had no expectations," she said. "It was…a convenient marriage."

The invisible knife twisted in his gut once more. What she'd left unspoken was clearer to him than the words he'd heard. He had a thousand questions he wanted to ask, but no right to. Still, he couldn't resist asking one.

"Did ye come up here to escape…memories? Mayhap some that were nae so good?"

She made a little scoffing sound. "I suppose one could say that." For a moment, she gazed out to the garden, then she turned to him. "You might as well know the truth. My sisters and I are here because we have no place else to go."

Ian started. "What about the earl's country estate? And the London townhouse?"

"His cousin claimed the estate and it did not have a dowager house." She shrugged. "I sold the townhouse to pay off creditors."

Lucifer's horns! This was worse than he'd expected and it also made clear why she was so desperate to live at Strae Castle. She had to.

She gave him a wry smile. "So you see, *that* is why you are stuck with me."

Being stuck with her didn't seem so terrible, although he was well aware his clan expected him to fight when the time came and their name and lands were cleared. Rage built at the earl who'd squandered his money and left no provisions for his wife, and along with the anger, a desire to protect her surged through him.

He leaned forward, cradled her head, and brushed his lips over hers. "This will be yer home then, lass—"

"God Almighty! I kenned the Sassenach would get to ye!" Devon stood in the archway, staring at both of them. "I kenned it!"

Before Ian could react, Devon turned and stomped off. Ian started to go after him, but Emily held him back. "He needs time."

"He is a grown man, not a bairn."

"That may be..." She hesitated, then smiled. "But I would rather continue where we left off. If you do not mind."

He blinked, not sure he'd heard correctly. If he did not mind? *Mind*? All his *mind* could think of was kissing her.

With a groan, he pulled her close and covered her mouth with his.

Chapter Sixteen

Pure pleasure washed over Emily like warm water as Ian's mouth claimed hers. This was nothing like the tentative brushing he'd just done or the measured kiss he'd given her when she'd fallen. This was a kiss demanding more, and somewhere deep within her, a need emerged.

His lips were soft yet firm, teasing, pressing, yielding. He sucked her lower lip between his, gently nibbling before releasing it. The sensation had her quivering, wanting more. Was she actually doing this? Participating even? As if invisible floodgates had suddenly opened? Angling her head, he positioned her to deepen the kiss, his tongue seeking entrance. Her arms curled around his neck as she opened to him, her body melting into his.

"Emily! Where are you? Emily!"

Lorelei's shouting brought her out of her reverie and Ian's head snapped up. Before they could untangle, her sister appeared in the open doorway. Her sister's eyes widened and her mouth formed a perfect open circle as her face turned pink. Emily was probably just as flushed. She certainly felt like it, although from embarrassment or her surprising reaction to Ian, she wasn't sure. Lord, her body still thrummed, like a finely tuned harp. There was hardly a point in trying to deny what had taken place. She dropped her arms and folded her hands in her lap.

"What is it?" she asked, hoping she sounded as nonchalant as Ian looked. He appeared calm, as though he'd just been interrupted reading a book.

Lorelei glanced from one to the other, her eyes still round. Finally, she found her voice. "Devon just came charging through the castle, shouting something about—sorry, I should not use this word, but he did—the *bloody* English and history repeating itself." She frowned. "Fiona went after him and Juliana is looking for you in the old part of the castle."

Ian sighed and straightened. "I had best go find him before he has a full-blown explosion. He will be hard to control if that happens."

Emily wanted to ask—desperately—why his brother would react so violently to finding them kissing. Granted, Devon wasn't fond of her. He'd made quite clear what he thought of *Sassenachs*. But even disproving of Ian's affection for her—and she wasn't really clear if it was affection or a sympathetic reaction to her tale in an opportunistic setting—it didn't involve Devon. And, as Ian had pointed out, his brother was an adult, not a child, or even an adolescent. So why would he fly into a rage?

Emily gave Ian a questioning look as they both rose, but he shook his head subtly and she understood this was not the time to ask. Lorelei's expression had changed from shocked to inquisitive and the less said right now, the better.

They followed Ian into the castle where Juliana and Rory were arguing.

"You are going to run after your brother when we do not know where my sister is? We need to find her!"

"And I have to find Devon," he nearly shouted.

Juliana glared at him. "Fiona's gone after him."

"Ye doona understand! She will nae be able to handle him if he—"

"I am right here," Emily interrupted as they approached. "And I am fine."

Ian gestured to Rory. "Go. He should be easy to track."

Rory turned, muttering under his breath about daft females.

Carr appeared from the hallway that led to the library. He gave Emily a brief glance before he turned to Ian. "I think 'tis time for a family conference."

Squaring his shoulders, Ian gave a curt nod. "Ye are right about that."

Emily made no attempt to follow him as he left. Lorelei frowned.

"I guess we are not invited."

"We are not family." Emily suspected the "conference" was going to be about her, but she could hardly demand to attend.

Juliana gave her a curious look. "Do you know what happened to make Devon so angry?"

"I..." What could she say? "I..."

Lorelei suddenly giggled. "I think I know."

Emily shot her a warning look, but it was too late.

"What?" Juliana asked.

"I think Devon saw his brother kissing Emily."

Juliana's mouth dropped open and she closed it with a snap as she turned to Emily. "You were *kissing* Mr. MacGregor?" And then, before Emily could reply, she continued. "Are you mad?"

"Oh, yes," Lorelei chirped. "I saw them myself."

Emily could cheerfully throttle her sister but resisted the urge. From the look on Juliana's face, her other sister wanted to throttle *her*.

She sighed. Obviously, it wasn't only MacGregors who didn't approve a match.

• • •

Ian closed the library door, not particularly surprised to see that his uncles were still here. It had been quite the morning with the outrider delivering his message, the turmoil it had caused the clan—to say nothing of the turmoil kissing Emily caused *him*—to another of Devon's angry outbursts. Hopefully, Fiona and Rory would catch up to him before a dragoon did. Ian wasn't sure his brother could survive another capture.

He looked from his uncles to Carr and Alasdair. He thought he knew what they wanted to discuss—or rather, *tell* him—but he asked anyway. "What is the subject of this family conference?"

"The Sassenachs," Donovan said. "Especially the dowager countess."

He had been right about the subject then. "What, in particular, is the problem?"

"The problem is that she is *here*, where she does nae belong."

"I doona see what can be done about that," Ian answered. "Carr said the deed she showed us is authentic, which means she has a legal right to be here."

His uncle frowned. "I thought ye were going to persuade her to return to London once ye convinced her that everything was in order here."

That had been his intention, although with what Emily had just told him about her circumstances, that had changed. He grimaced. If he were honest with himself, he'd been attracted to her since she arrived, although he'd done his best to ignore those feelings. Then, he'd actually begun to enjoy her company—her wit, her straightforwardness, her determination—and their kiss had told him she was not immune to him, either. But looking at his brothers' and uncles' faces, this was not the time to announce his feelings. Nor could he reveal what Emily had told him without her permission.

"I canna order her to leave."

"Ye are willing to let her have Strae Castle?" Broderick asked. "Ye are willing to put her above yer clan?"

"Nae! That willna happen." At least, he prayed it wouldn't. That wasn't a choice he wanted to make.

"And what of the distillery?" Broderick went on. "I have been running it for years. I..." He looked at his brother. "*We* have made it profitable."

Carr intervened. "It will continue to be. The contract that was drawn up still gives ye the same profit margin ye have now. And even more in three years when the bottles we're distilling this year will be ready."

"But the excess goes to the countess."

"That seems fair." Alasdair shrugged. "She was the one who got the London agent to come up here and agree to buy our whisky."

"However, business is nae the reason we are all in here," Carr said. "We are worried about Devon and his reaction to Lady Woodhaven."

Ian sighed. He was worried about his reaction, too. "I will have a talk with him when he returns."

"I doona think that will help," Alasdair replied. "He canna even accept the sisters... Lorelei, especially, has done nothing to insult him. But..." He paused. "Ye ken the reason Devon feels the way he does."

"We doona ken for sure."

Carr studied him, then said softly, "Lady Woodhaven

looks like Isobel."

"I will grant that their coloring is the same," Ian replied, "but ye canna compare the countess to our father's wife." Lucifer's horns! Two women couldn't be more opposite in integrity and honor.

"We doona," Alasdair said, "but Devon is a different matter."

Ian sighed again. Devon had been twelve when their father had married Isobel. He had been the most vocal of all of them when their father had told them of his plans. He'd resented, quickly and hard, that his father got married only two years after their mother's death. "Aye, he is."

"It didna help that Isobel received…visitors…when Da was away," Carr said.

"Ye might as well just say it." Ian felt a muscle twitch in his jaw. "Our lovely stepmother was promiscuous."

"Yer father—our brother—didna deserve that," Donovan said.

There was no doubt in Ian's mind that their father had loved their mother with his whole heart. Had, in fact, wandered about like a lost soul, hardly speaking or taking an interest in anything, for a whole year. And then, at an event in Glasgow, Isobel had come into his life. "Nae, he didna."

"Isobel betrayed the man who loved her," Broderick said.

Ian nodded his agreement. Vivacious, free-spirited, lighthearted, and bubbly, Isobel had brought their father out of his melancholy, and he'd fancied himself in love once more. Grateful that such a young and pretty woman would agree to become his wife, he'd turned a deaf ear to whatever whisperings arose about her.

But Devon hadn't. Young and untried, innocent of the nuances that took place between men and women, he blamed Isobel's behavior on the fact that she was English…and the English had always been the enemy.

• • •

Emily didn't see Ian again until the noon meal was served. Since the workers stayed in the fields throughout the day, they were eating in the smaller room near the kitchens. Normally, Ian and his brothers would be out as well, but with everything that had happened this morning—not to mention their "family" conference—they were still at the castle.

She watched him covertly as they sat at the round table, wondering how the talk had gone in the library. Ian appeared calm and collected as did Carr and Alasdair, although they usually did. Rory was the hothead and Devon the rogue, but neither of them had returned. Still, the conversation felt strained, as though everyone were behaving with the best manners.

"Might I have a word with ye?" Ian asked her when the meal was finally over. "'Twill just take a moment."

Emily had the strangest sensation that his family was hesitant to leave, as were her sisters. All of them seemed to be hovering. Did her sisters think she needed a chaperone? For that matter, did Ian's brothers know what had transpired in the folly? She felt her cheeks warm as she recalled, in precise detail, exactly what had happened. She glanced sideways at Ian. Had he felt the impact as strongly as she did? Her cheeks grew hot and she pushed the thought away.

"If ye will all excuse us?" he asked. The question seemed to break whatever collective lingering they were doing, for Carr nodded and headed for the door with Alasdair.

Juliana and Lorelei slanted looks at her. "We will be in the solar."

"Follow me," Ian said when everyone left. For a moment she hoped he'd take her back to the folly, but instead, he led her to the sitting room across from the Great Hall. He left the door open, but perhaps that was just as well. At least no one could accuse them of improprieties. She felt disappointed, although she knew that was silly.

"What did you want to tell me?" she asked when she'd settled in a chair. Ian remained standing and began to pace, his expression troubled. For a moment, she wondered if he was going to tell her that the kiss had been all wrong, and her heart slithered to her feet. It was the first time in her life that she'd felt passion and she didn't want him to ruin it. She clasped her hands to keep them from shaking.

"I think ye should ken about Devon."

Emily blinked. This certainly wasn't what she'd been expecting, although it was better than what she'd been thinking. Then again, since he hadn't mentioned the kiss, maybe it hadn't meant that much to him. She gave herself a mental shake. *First I don't want him to talk about it and now I do?* It wasn't like her to bibble-babble. "Yes?"

When Ian finished explaining the circumstances of his father and stepmother's marriage, she nodded. "I think I understand. I resemble Isobel and I am English, so he associates me with her."

"True, but that is nae all of it." He began pacing again. "I told ye Devon was captured by dragoons when he was but six and ten… The officer in charge of the company was Isobel's father. He'd never approved of his daughter eloping with a Scot. *Especially* a MacGregor, since we had been proscribed for so long." Ian paused. "Ye can imagine how it went when the man found out Devon was nae only a MacGregor, but the son of the man who'd married his daughter. They probably would have ransomed him in return for Isobel, but she was already dead. So, instead…" His voice trailed off.

Emily gave an involuntary shudder. "You mentioned he was tortured?"

Ian looked grim. "They used him for target practice."

She felt the blood drain from her face. "Oh, no," she

whispered.

"Aye. They took him to a field and gave him a head start running. Then they shot after him."

Her hand flew to her mouth as she gasped. "They could have killed him!"

"'Twas nae the intent." Ian resumed pacing. "They wanted to scare him into thinking that. I think they made a game of who could fire the closest shot. When Rory brought him home, he was wild, as though he'd lost his mind."

"It is no wonder he hates the English then." Emily was quiet for a moment. "Will he ever be quite right?"

"I doona ken. Our father had been murdered but three months before, and Devon took that hard."

"Murdered?" Emily widened her eyes. "By whom?"

Ian shook his head. "The killer was never found, but an English dagger was stuck in his back."

A chill slid down her spine. "Dragoons?"

"We are nae sure, but 'tis the reason Devon was snooping around their camp. He thought he might find the killer." Ian clenched his jaw. "I dinna ken he'd gone until it was too late."

"You cannot blame yourself for that."

He grimaced. "I was the oldest. I was in charge."

Emily frowned. "You were but eight and ten."

"Old enough to watch over my brothers."

"Where were your uncles? Why did they not help you?"

"They were nae here. Donovan was living in Inverness at the time, and Broderick had moved to Glasgow shortly after Isobel's murder to start selling our whisky."

"So there was no one to help you…or Devon."

"Well, Cory was four and ten, Alasdair a year younger, and Rory ten. Among us, we managed to keep Devon in control." He forced a half smile. "Most of the time."

"It explains a lot," Emily said. "Thank you for telling me."

"I thought ye should ken."

She nodded. "And now that I do, one way or another, I am going to make Devon my friend."

Whether he liked her or hated her, Devon had become her mission.

Chapter Seventeen

When Ian woke the next morning, sunlight was streaming in his window. He must have finally fallen asleep. He'd tossed and turned most of the night, partly because neither Rory nor Fiona had returned home with Devon, and his *other* reason—and he wasn't sure if this was the *real* reason he hadn't been able to sleep—was Emily.

The kiss they'd shared in the folly had given him an inkling of how passionate she could be under the missish guise she wore, and his wayward cock was only too eager to explore those possibilities. But also, after hearing her plight, he realized how similar their backgrounds were. She'd lost her parents five years ago and had to take care of her younger sisters, like he did with his brothers when his father had been killed. She'd done the practical thing, sacrificing herself to an old man, who sounded as if he'd not cared one wit for her, in order to provide a home for Juliana and Lorelei. He could understand why Strae Castle was as important to her as it was to the MacGregors, not that his clansmen would understand. Scots were still pitted against the English.

And now, Emily wanted to make Devon her friend. Ian wasn't sure that was even possible.

He threw off the covers, dressed quickly, and made his way to the small dining room, expecting to find it empty this late in the morning. To his surprise, Fiona was at the table with Emily and her sisters, breaking her fast. He breathed a sigh of relief.

"Ye are back! Did Rory and Devon return as well?"

"Nae," she replied.

He frowned. "Did Rory nae catch up to ye? And ye dinna find Devon, either?"

"Aye to both your questions." She buttered a piece of toast. "Rory found me and we both found Devon."

"Where are they then?"

She started to take a bite, then put the bread down. "They are following the dragoons."

"*What*?" Ian resisted an urge to pull at his own hair. Emily sent him a worried look and he sensed she was thinking about what would happen if they got caught. He was thinking the same thing. "Are they both daft?"

"Aye, probably." Fiona scooped up some shirred eggs, apparently not concerned that her brothers might be in grave danger.

"Will ye stop eating for a minute and tell me the story?"

"I'm hungry. I have nae eaten since yesterday morning." Fiona eyed the eggs on her plate, then reluctantly put her fork down. "Devon wanted to find out what the dragoons were up to, so we hid in the trees and waited—"

"Ye are all daft!"

"If ye are going to interrupt, I will finish my food."

Ian sighed. "Go on then."

"'Twas nae long before we heard them marching along the road." She turned to Emily. "There were only twenty of them and the eejits dinna even look right or left. If we'd had more men with us—"

"Doona speculate. Just finish telling me what happened." Ian tried not to let his annoyance show.

Fiona glowered at him and cut a piece of ham, which she thoroughly chewed, no doubt chastising him by making him wait. Irritating as it was, he was pretty sure his brothers were safe or she'd not be drawing this out. He forced a smile.

She swallowed. "As it happens, the dragoons marched right on past us and stayed on the road to Inveraray."

That surprised him. "They are headed to the Campbells?"

"'Twould seem so. They dinna turn and head this way, at least." She picked up her toast. "But Rory and Devon are trailing them to make sure."

That made sense. Ian trusted Rory to stay far enough behind—and to watch his back—to avoid getting caught. But another question remained. "I wonder why the dragoons are going there?"

"That is what Rory and Devon intend to find out," Fiona said.

Emily cast him another worried look, and Ian groaned inwardly. Following the dragoons to make sure they didn't double back was one thing. Snooping around the Campbell lair was quite another. As much as he had an urge to saddle his horse and ride after his foolish brothers, he had no plausible excuse for simply appearing in Inveraray.

So for now, all he could do was wait.

• • •

Rory returned with Devon as they were sitting down to the evening meal a day later, again in the small dining room, since Ian and his other brothers hadn't come in until well after the clansmen had eaten in the Great Hall.

Emily watched covertly as the two took their seats.

Devon hadn't spared her a glance, but he didn't seem angry. Perhaps Rory had been able to calm him down, or maybe just being away had served its purpose. Ian had said Devon was given to disappearing for several days at a time. She just hoped she would be able to break through those barriers he'd erected against everyone English.

"What were ye able to find out?" Ian asked.

"The dragoons did go all the way to Inveraray," Rory said.

"'Tis good then," Ian replied. "We doona need dragoons spying on how abundant our harvest is."

"We doona need them around to steal the peat we cut after the harvest, either," Alasdair said. "But I wonder why they went to Inveraray?"

Rory shook his head. "We didna want to breach the castle—"

"Speak for yerself, brother," Devon growled. "I was nae afraid to try."

"It would have been foolish of ye," Ian said sharply, causing Devon to glare at him.

"I dinna say ye were afraid." Rory gave his brother an empathetic look. "But taking the chance of getting caught was nae worth it."

A muscle clenched in Devon's jaw, and Emily wondered if he really would have tried to sneak into the Campbell castle or if part of his defiance was trying to prove something to himself. She suspected the latter and filed it away for future reflection.

"Were ye able to find out anything?" Carr asked.

Rory shrugged. "We saw the ducal carriage in the driveway, so Argyll was home from London. I suspect the dragoons were delivering a message from Kilchurn Castle or receiving one from Inveraray."

"Kilchurn Castle?" Emily asked. "Where Gavin

Campbell and his father live?"

"Aye," Rory answered. "Chances are, neither are up to any good. I still think they stole MacGregor sheep."

Juliana narrowed her eyes. "Would those not be Emily's sheep?"

He gave her an annoyed glance, but to ward off an ensuing argument—Devon's face was already looking like a thundercloud—Emily intervened.

"Those were *our* sheep." She smiled at the brothers. "We are united now."

Devon snorted. Ian gave him a warning look.

"Back to the matter at hand," Carr said. "Did ye discover anything else?"

"Aye," Rory answered. "They dinna stay long. Half of them rode back toward Kilchurn—"

"We followed to make sure they dinna detour toward us," Devon added.

Ian nodded. "And the other half?"

Rory frowned. "They rode south."

"South?" Carr knit his brow. "Ye think they were delivering a message to somewhere else as well as Kilchurn?"

"I wanted to follow them." Devon cast Rory a baleful look. "But my brother threatened to bash my head in and tie me to a tree."

Rory shrugged. "Only until the riders were gone."

Emily felt her eyes widen. Rory sounded so nonchalant as though he'd actually *do* that. None of the other brothers looked overly concerned, though. "You really would not hurt your own brother, would you?"

Devon gave her a quick glance before he looked away. Rory grinned. "Och, aye. 'Tis nae like we have nae sparred before."

Sparred? Is that what they called bashing someone's head in here in Scotland?

"It wouldna have been wise of ye to split up," Carr said, "and if we hadna heard from ye, we would have had to send riders out searching."

"Aye," Fiona agreed. "'Tis just as well ye didna follow them."

"But I could have found out where they went," Devon said stubbornly.

"I suspect I ken," Ian said grimly. All eyes turned to him. He sighed. "Bute lies south of Inveraray. Argyll must have sent the earl a message."

The brothers exchanged glances.

"And it would have come from London—"

"Parliament is nearly ready to convene—"

"Which means something is in the wind—"

Emily frowned. "What are all of you talking about?"

They all paused. Finally, Ian spoke. "Since the Earl of Bute is the former prime minister—"

"Yes, I know," Emily said. "I have met him on several occasions." That caused the brothers to exchange glances. "What of it? His son is in Parliament and I am sure he likes to stay informed as to what is happening." She looked around. "Why would that be important to you?"

Ian hesitated. "Lord Mount Stuart is sponsoring a petition to reinstate the MacGregor name and restore our rights."

"You have mentioned that." Emily lifted her hands, palms up. "There could be any number of reasons why the Duke of Argyll sent a message to the earl."

"True, but why would the duke also send a message to Kilchurn? Or mayhap receive one from his brother?" Carr asked. "The Campbells could be planning to protest the petition. They have never favored our clan rising again."

"Then that makes them the enemy, does it not?" Juliana asked.

"No!" Lorelei exclaimed. "We are invited to their ball." She gave Emily a wistful look. "I had so wanted to go to a ball."

"And ye will." Alasdair smiled at her. "And I'll be looking forward to dancing with ye, before I have to leave for Ireland."

Lorelei brightened. "I would enjoy that."

Emily frowned at her sister, then looked at Ian. "Do you think it wise that we attend if they are plotting something?"

His brothers burst out laughing and even Devon smiled.

"Did I say something humorous?"

Ian grinned. "In a way, ye did."

"I do not understand."

"Battles are won by kenning what your opponent is planning," he said. "And what better way to do it than by entering their own lair?"

Carr nodded. "Where we will have several sets of eyes and ears. If something is amiss, we might be able to find out what it is."

"Then that means we are going to the ball?" Lorelei asked. "For sure?"

Emily sighed, even as Alasdair assured her sister they would attend. Her sister had a kind heart, but sometimes, she wondered if Lorelei would ever grow up.

• • •

"I doona think it wise to take the Sassenachs to Kilchurn's celebration this weekend," Broderick told Ian the next afternoon as he came in from the fields.

The last thing he wanted to discuss was Campbell's ball. He was dirty and itching from stacking barley sheaves all day. He needed a bath—and a dram of whisky—but both his uncles and Devon had been waiting for him near the door to the Great Hall. He was too filthy to suggest the sitting room directly across the way—Maggie would chastise him like a bairn—so he motioned for the three of them to follow him down the hall to the library. At least the chairs in there were leather and cleanable.

"I am guessing this has something to do with the dragoons?" he asked after he'd closed the door.

"Aye," Broderick answered. "Devon rode over to the distillery this morning to tell us what he'd learned."

Ian wasn't surprised. His uncles hadn't been around for the last few days, since the grain was at the fermentation stage and needed to be watched closely in order to know when to separate the wash and start distilling it. They'd basically been sleeping in the office of the distillery so they could keep checking.

"'Tis likely Henry Campbell is hatching something with his brother the duke," Donovan said, "else why would the dragoons have gone in separate directions?"

"And leave so soon after arriving at Inveraray?" Broderick added.

"I agree with ye," Ian said, "but we doona ken why."

Devon snorted. "The Campbells doona want us to have our name back."

"We doona ken that for certain."

"Nae, but Argyll spends more time in London than he does at Inveraray or Kilchurn. He tends to side with the English more than the Scots." Broderick looked at each of them. "And the Countess of Woodhaven is English. What if she's in cahoots with him?"

Ian grimaced. If only he could tell them what he knew. That her situation was as dire as theirs, but he was pretty sure the irony of that would be lost on his uncles and certainly on Devon. Besides, it was not his story to tell. "Lady Woodhaven has never given any indication that she's acquainted with the

Campbells," he said. "In fact, Gavin Campbell was expecting an elderly dowager the day he came here."

"She did say she'd met the Earl of Bute, though," Devon said.

"Aye and that 'tis the reason we came over," Donovan said. "If she mentions that to Henry or even the duke, if he's at the ball, she could easily say she'd prefer the earl nae petition Parliament this fall. Argyll would listen to an English countess's opinion."

"Even worse, 'tis possible Bute himself might be at the ball. The dragoons rode in that direction." Devon narrowed his eyes. "She could put the word in his ear directly."

After what she'd told him, Ian doubted very much that she would. "The countess could have put us all out if she'd had a mind to when she first arrived, but she didna." He grew thoughtful. "Since she *has* met Lord Bute, mayhap she could even put a word in his ear to encourage the petition."

Devon gave him an arched look. For a moment, he wondered if his brother was going to bring up the kissing in the folly. Ian was fairly sure he hadn't told their uncles or one of them would have mentioned it. He met his brother's gaze steadily until Devon finally looked away.

"When she arrived, she needed us," Broderick said. "Ye said yourself she had questions on everything, and Donovan and I can testify to her getting involved in the distillery, even though we dinna want her to."

"And we've already discussed that she will be bringing in more profit." Ian tried to keep the testiness out of his voice. "We doona need to keep hammering at it."

"Aye, the woman is smart and sly," Donovan said. "Much like Isobel was."

"And ye ken how that turned out," Broderick added. "She made a fool of all of us..." He paused, then shrugged. "Well, for certain, your father."

"Lady Woodhaven is *nothing* like Isobel." Ian didn't bother to keep the edge off his voice. "And I willna have ye comparing her to that bitch."

Broderick frowned, Devon lifted his eyebrow again, and Donovan gave him a long look before he nodded.

"Aye, I suppose ye are right," his uncle said, "but it would still be wise that she nae attend the ball, just to make sure she doesn't put a word in Campbell's ear, instead of Lord Bute's."

He didn't want Emily attending the ball, either, but for entirely different reasons. The Campbells had been busy with their own harvesting, and Gavin had not returned to call on Emily, but Ian hadn't forgotten the sly insinuation that he might want to pay court. If he had his way, he would keep them miles apart. He sighed.

"Unfortunately, the invitation has already been issued. 'Tis nae we can do to prevent the countess from going."

Devon lifted a corner of his mouth in a slight smirk. "Then ye will have to keep a close eye on her, won't ye?"

He wasn't sure if his brother was being sarcastic or reminding him about what he'd witnessed. It didn't really matter, because Ian intended to keep a very close eye on Emily at the Campbell ball.

• • •

"I think dinner went surprisingly well," Emily said as she and her sisters retired to the solar after the evening meal. She sighed as she sank into one of the comfortable, stuffed armchairs. The room had been built to let in the sunlight during the day and the walls, accordingly, were papered in gold damask with trailing vines to give the impression of being outdoors. She'd found, though, that pulling the green velvet drapes at night and having the brazier lit gave the room a warm, cozy feel, more like she was deep within a forest with the sun's rays setting. The room made an excellent place to retreat from the men—and servants—in the castle as well.

"Yes!" Lorelei clapped her hands excitedly. "And we are definitely going to the ball at Kilchurn!"

Juliana rolled her eyes and Emily almost joined her. That admission had been made without much enthusiasm from Ian after Lorelei had brought up the subject. Again. His uncles and his brothers—save for Alasdair, who seemed amused—had given her disdainful looks. She'd wanted to remind them that Lorelei was young…just six and ten, but doing so would only reinforce their opinions that Englishwomen were shallow.

"What I meant was, the conversation was quite cordial," Emily said.

Juliana nodded. "Rory actually did not insult me, either."

"Maybe if you treated him nicer, he would stop," Lorelei said.

"*Me*?" Juliana frowned at her sister. "It is not I who starts the arguments."

"That is debatable." Emily smiled to take the sting off her words. "It seems you and Rory are like oil and water. But," she added before Juliana could argue with *her*, "tonight went very well. Even Devon acted civilly."

"Do you think he will ever come around to accepting us?" Lorelei asked.

"I hope so," Emily answered. "But he has had some very bad experiences with the English."

"But he should not blame *us*," Juliana retorted. "We—you—are nothing like his stepmother, who sounds like she was a hoyden."

"And we certainly are not dragoons." Lorelei drew her brows together. "Although I am sorry for what happened to him."

"So am I." Emily had told her sisters what Ian had

relayed to her. "All we can do is be kind and hope Devon will eventually realize we are who we are."

"But for now"—Lorelei changed the subject—"can we discuss the ball? I am so excited!"

Juliana somehow refrained from looking heavenward again and Emily sighed inwardly, even as for the next half hour they indulged their sister in conversation about all sorts of speculation about a Scottish ball.

Emily was tired when she finally retired to her bedchamber. Thankfully, one of the maids had been in to turn the sheets down and a small fire burned in the brazier. She saw this as a small step in her goal to being accepted by the MacGregors. When she and her sisters had first arrived, none of the servants had attended them. Now, Maggie answered questions in full sentences and Hamish even smiled on occasion.

She noticed then that a glass of mulled wine had been set on the bedside stand, along with a small plate of marzipan squares. Emily smiled. That was probably Fiona's doing, since she'd made known she loved marzipan. She'd stayed downstairs to talk to Ian and probably brought this up before she went to bed.

Quickly, Emily took care of her ablutions, donned her night rail, and slipped between the sheets. There was nothing quite as decadent as sipping wine and eating dessert in bed. She took several sips of the strong-tasting wine. Perhaps a bit too much apple cider had been added, but it helped to counter the sweet marzipan.

Mmmm. The tastes of both were intense. In a few minutes she was having difficulty keeping her eyes open. She must be more tired than she thought…as the glass slipped from her hand.

Chapter Eighteen

"Is your sister still abed?" Ian asked Juliana and Lorelei the next morning as he entered the dining room to break his fast. Normally, he'd take the morning meal in the Great Hall with the rest of the clansmen, but he'd overslept, having been awake most of the night thinking about the conversation he'd had with his brothers and uncles. Emily was usually an early riser, so he'd expected to find her here.

Juliana shook her head. "I have not seen her this morning."

"She is probably with Fiona on the battlements," Lorelei said. "They both like to watch the sun rise."

Juliana frowned. "I saw Fiona a few minutes ago walking toward the stables. Emily was not with her."

"Besides, the sun has been up for well over an hour." Ian felt some apprehension. "Mayhap one of ye should go and check on her."

Lorelei's eyes widened. "You think something may have happened to her?"

He didn't want to alarm the ladies, but an increasing

sense of uneasiness was nagging at him. "She is probably just tired and still sleeping but, since she said she didna need a maid to wake her, we should check."

Juliana stared at him for a moment, then put her napkin down and stood. "Come along, Lorelei."

"But I have not finished eating..."

"You can finish later." She gave Ian a measured look, then tugged at her sister's chair. "How many times have we been chastised for sleeping late? We will have something to hold over her now."

Lorelei grinned at that. "True."

Ian fidgeted in his chair as the two left the room, then decided to follow them. He was halfway to the door when he heard a blood-curdling scream. He bolted down the hallway and up the stairs as though the hounds of hell were on his heels.

Lorelei was slumped on the floor outside Emily's bedchamber, holding her head in her hands. "I think she is dead!"

Terror struck him. He flung open the door so hard it banged against the wall and nearly hit him in the face on its rebound. He paid it no mind, his focus on the bed. Emily lay pale and still, a crimson stain spread across the white sheets.

"Is she—"

"She breathes," Juliana said, holding her sister's hand. "Barely."

Ian hurried to Emily's other side, noticing for the first time the empty wine glass half hidden in the folds of the sheet. He picked it up and sniffed, detecting a musty odor that he couldn't identify.

"Laird?"

He turned, seeing Maggie at the door, Hamish behind her. "Send for Old Gwendolyn. Quickly!"

Hamish nodded. "Aye, laird."

"What has happened?" Maggie asked, stepping inside the room, then she stopped upon seeing the stain. "Dear God! Do we need the physician, too?"

Ian shook his head. If Emily had been poisoned, the healer would know what to do. He looked at the plate of half-eaten marzipan and narrowed his eyes. "I want every servant who was in the castle last night to assemble in the Great Hall. And make sure everyone is accounted for."

Her eyes grew round, but she didn't ask any questions.

Ian turned back to Emily and put a hand to her forehead. Her skin was cold and clammy. He took hold of her shoulders and shook gently.

"Wake up, *mo cridhe!* Wake up!"

"Let me."

Juliana brushed his hands away and then slapped her sister sharply on both cheeks. Ian started to grab her, but Emily's eyes fluttered open. For a moment, she looked confused, then her face twisted into a grimace and she rolled suddenly, retching over the side of the bed. Instinctively, Ian wrapped his arms around her waist, hauling her from the bed and dangling her in front of him.

"I doona ken what ye drank or ate, but ye need to get it out of ye."

She retched again, the foul odor wafting upward. He paid no heed.

"Please…" Emily managed to get the word out before spewing again.

"Air do shocair… Hush, now."

"Leave…me…"

"Nae, I canna."

"You are embarrassing her by witnessing this." Juliana put a hand on his arm. "I can hold her until she is through." She motioned with her head toward the door. "Please leave."

"Please…"

It was the last thing he wanted to do, but Emily sounded suspiciously like she was crying. He couldn't tell for sure, since she was still hanging half upside down. She made a choking sound, and Juliana all but knocked him over with the force of her push. "You are not helping!"

Ian backed off, realizing how mortified he would be if the situation were reversed. Besides, it would only make matters worse if she started to cry while she was casting up the dregs of her stomach. He frowned at Juliana. "I will be right outside that door."

"Fine. Just *go*. And close the door."

He stepped outside, contemplating whether to follow Juliana's order, then decided privacy was probably best.

"Is she going to be all right?" Lorelei was still sitting on the floor and looking like she might become ill herself.

"I doona ken. I pray so."

It seemed like an eternity before Old Gwendolyn arrived, although in truth, her cottage was only a ten minute walk at most. Quickly, he started to tell her what had taken place, but she didn't wait for him to finish.

"Wait here," she said and stepped into the room, closing the door firmly behind her.

He was tempted to ignore her order. When had women suddenly started telling him what to do in his own castle? He'd taken only a step forward, when Lorelei grabbed his ankle, causing him to lurch sideways against the wall. He frowned at her. "Are ye trying to kill me, lass?"

"No." She rose slowly, leaning against the opposite wall. "But from the sounds I heard out here, Emily would not want you in the room."

That was the second time he'd been admonished. His frown deepened. Then he finally nodded. It did sound like the upheaval was still going on. After what seemed like yet a second eternity—and the sounds quieted—the door opened and Gwendolyn stepped out, her face grim. She put down her bag and handed him the glass.

"Hemlock."

He stared at her. "Are ye sure?"

She gave him a look that instantly reduced him to a lad in knee breeches. "I recognize hemlock when I smell it."

"I dinna mean—"

"Nae matter." She waved off his apology. "Ye did the best thing possible, making her purge her insides."

He breathed a silent prayer of thanks. "She will be all right then?"

"She should be. I gave her mashed mandrake root to make sure her belly was empty. I left another dose to clean her insides." She eyed Lorelei. "Ye and your sister need to make sure she drinks warm water with salt every hour as well… 'Twill make her retch again, but 'tis the only way to make sure all the poison is gone." She picked up her bag. "I will come by tomorrow."

He turned to the door after the healer left, but Lorelei stopped him once more. "You cannot think Emily wants to see you in her condition?" She ignored his glower and instead patted his cheek as though he were a bairn. "Juliana and I will take care of her. That is what sisters are for."

With that, she slipped through the door, leaving him standing in the hallway. He sighed and turned away. Emily's sisters stuck together like his brothers did. That made his thoughts turn to Devon. He hoped his brother had nothing to do with this, but he could not deny that Devon hated the English…and he'd resented Isobel as well.

The vivid dream that Emily had about the man with a knife *might* have just been a nightmare based on Fiona's stories. The alcohol in the tea *could* have been a coincidence. It was possible the board on the steps had accidently come loose. But he couldn't deny this fourth incident. Someone was trying to kill Emily.

"I suppose ye are going to blame me for the poison." Devon made the statement without much inflection as he looked at his brothers gathered in the library once more, late that afternoon. "I mean, who else is there?"

The question definitely held a note of sarcasm. Ian winced. The last thing he wanted to do was think Devon actually capable of murdering a woman. From the looks on the faces of his other brothers—and Fiona's—he knew they felt the same. Their very silence spoke volumes. Evidently, Devon sensed it, too. He slumped in his chair.

"Go ahead and call the magistrate then."

"We'll nae be calling the magistrate," Ian replied. "And we are nae accusing ye."

Devon raised an eyebrow but didn't answer.

"We aren't," Carr said quietly, "but we need to get to the bottom of this."

"True," Alasdair said. "Ian's questioned the servants—"

"Aye," Ian interrupted. "Effie said she turned down the covers on the bed about half past eight o'clock, but she did nae leave wine or marzipan. The other maids were busy in the kitchen and Hall. They all vouched for one another."

Rory gave him a skeptical glance. "Of course they would."

"But would they lie?" Carr asked. "Especially to Ian?"

"That is a point," Alasdair said. "Any MacGregor kens lying to the laird would mean banishment."

"Once upon a time, it would have," Rory retorted. "But ye do remember the English took away a laird's power?"

"But nae loyalty," Alasdair said. "The English may assert their laws, but it doesna stop any clan from keeping to our old ways."

Fiona spoke up. "What if it was nae a maid?"

"Hamish said the men were all accounted for," Ian replied.

"It might nae have been a servant, though. The Great Hall was full."

Rory smirked. "I doubt one of our clansmen would have sneaked upstairs with wine and marzipan."

Fiona narrowed her eyes at him. "Doona act like I'm daft. The maids stay on the top floor. Would anyone question a man walking out with wine and sweets to tryst with one of them?"

"*Hmmm.*" Carr turned to Ian. "Mayhap we should question Maggie as to whether one of the maids has a lover?"

"She would probably box my ears." Ian gave him a grim look. "Besides, Emily said she arrived at her chamber just past nine o'clock. The maids would still have been busy cleaning up for at least another hour. The wine had to have been left in the thirty minutes after Effie was in the room and Emily got there." He shook his head. "Any supposed swain leaving that early for a tumble—carrying wine and a plate—would have been noticed."

Devon stirred. "So it comes back to me then."

Ian frowned at him. "Nae one is saying that."

"Ye doona have to. My feelings about Sassenachs are well known to all." Devon shrugged. "Nae one would question one of us carrying a glass of wine and a plate of marzipan away. And..." He grimaced slightly. "Nae one can account for my whereabouts."

"Ye always go straight to your bedchamber." His brother liked to read, a fact Ian had discovered one night when he'd barged in without knocking. Devon's interest was the classics, no less, which was why he tended to keep his hobby a secret. Ian also suspected it was a form of escape. He'd never shared the information. And now, Devon was giving him a knowing look.

"I canna prove it."

"Well, ye doona have to," Rory said. "At least, nae to us. We are family."

And they were, Ian thought. But so were Emily and her sisters. He didn't want to have to make a choice between them. It was his responsibility, now, to protect both.

But could he?

• • •

Emily startled at the knock on her door, praying that it would not be Ian. Even though the room had been cleaned, the floor scrubbed and fresh sheets put on the bed, she wasn't ready to face him. She'd spent most of the afternoon forcing herself to swallow the mashed mandrake and drink that horrible concoction of warm, salty water. Consequently, she'd also spent much of her time hovering over the chamber pot.

"I will see who it is." Lorelei rose from her chair.

Juliana gave Emily a quick look, evidently reading her thoughts. "Do not let any man in."

But it was Fiona at the door, holding a cup of broth. "Gwendolyn said ye are nae to eat anything for twenty-four hours, but I thought ye could use this."

Emily accepted the warm cup eagerly. She felt weak as a kitten after her ordeal, to say nothing of the purging. She started to take a sip, but Juliana stayed her hand.

"Did you pour this yourself?" she asked Fiona.

"Aye. There is mutton stew for tonight. I stirred the pot and scooped the liquid out myself." She drew her lips into a tight line. "If there is poison in that, we will all be eating it."

Juliana relaxed her hold. "I just wanted to make sure."

"I doona blame ye," Fiona answered. "Ian has given orders anything Emily eats has to be tasted by someone else first."

Emily stared at her. "Does he think that is really necessary?"

"I just came from a meeting with my brothers," she answered. "Until we find out who the culprit is, Ian is nae taking any chances."

Juliana studied her, then opened her mouth to speak and closed it again. She furrowed her brows.

"I think I ken what ye want to ask." Fiona looked from her to Emily, then back. "Ye are thinking Devon may be a suspect."

"*May* be?"

"Juliana!" Emily exclaimed, nearly spilling her broth. "Fiona is his sister!"

"I know, but..." Juliana hesitated, then lifted her chin. "I am sorry, but we all know Devon hates us. Who else—"

"Devon said the same thing himself," Fiona broke in. "And he has nae excuse for his whereabouts." She looked at each of them. "I canna believe my brother would stoop to murder."

"Of course you cannot," Lorelei said. "I would not believe anyone who accused my sisters of a crime, either."

"'Tis nae just family loyalty," Fiona said. "Devon has always been honorable. 'Tis unmanly to kill a woman."

"Especially with poison," Emily said thoughtfully. "That is a method women have used for eons."

"Aye," Fiona agreed, "and Devon is also very smart. Do ye nae think he would make sure he had an excuse of some sort to cover such a deed? Instead..." She gave each of them a deliberate look. "He was alone in his bedchamber during the time Ian figured out this happened."

"That would make sense, I suppose," Juliana admitted.

"What about Glenda?" Lorelei asked. "If she heard about Ian kissing Emily—"

Emily felt her cheeks warm. "Let's not go into that right now."

"Glenda always acts jealous of you. She might have done it," Lorelei went on. "And you said poison is a woman's choice of weapon."

"I did not mean—"

"'Tis possible," Fiona said thoughtfully. "Glenda is nae a servant, so she wouldna have been questioned. I will speak to Ian about it."

"I wish you would not…"

"She *must*." Juliana squeezed Emily's hand. "This person must be caught."

Emily put her cup down, her hand trembling as reality finally set in. She'd made excuses for the other incidents, because she hadn't wanted to admit someone actually hated her. And she'd been too weak and tired today to consider much of anything, but the broth had revived her somewhat.

Someone truly wanted her dead.

Chapter Nineteen

Emily still felt a bit wobbly the next evening when she went down to the dining room. Ian had made her promise to stay in her room that day while he finished up with the harvest. Her first inclination had been to resist, but by the time she finished her ablutions and donned a fresh gown, she realized how weak she still felt. Fiona had brought breakfast and lunch to her, and her sisters had stayed with her throughout the day. She suspected that if she lurched into the hall unexpectedly, she'd probably find a guard lurking there, too.

But she couldn't hide in her bedchamber forever. As far as she knew, the clansmen had not been told what had transpired, but she would have preferred taking the meal in the Great Hall where Ian's people could see she was alive and well as a warning to the...culprit. She still had trouble believing someone would deliberately put hemlock in her wine. However, Fiona said Ian had requested they all meet in the smaller dining room tonight. She suspected he was going to make some kind of announcement to his family about what had happened.

Now she took a deep breath to steady herself and walked through the door, Juliana and Lorelei trailing behind her. The room was crowded with Ian's brothers and uncles and a new "guest." Glenda was sitting next to Fiona. Generally, she ate in the Great Hall with the others, so her presence tonight must mean that Fiona had relayed her concerns to Ian after all. The girl looked pleased, though, so he probably hadn't told her exactly why she was here.

Ian rose and pulled a chair for her. He nodded to Hamish who'd been standing at the door. The castellan disappeared only to return a moment later with Maggie and two young lads carrying platters of food. The housekeeper did not look particularly happy, and Emily had never seen the two boys before. Normally, women worked in the kitchen and served the meals. She glanced at Ian. Had he taken to heart that poison was usually a woman's weapon and dismissed the maids from the kitchen? That would certainly account for Maggie's demeanor. Emily just hoped he hadn't dismissed the cook, too.

"Set everything down in the middle of the table," Ian said.

The lads' eyes widened, but they moved quickly, one spilling some of the soup from the tureen and the other nearly causing a leg of lamb to slide off its server. Maggie scowled at both of them and they skittered out.

Hamish placed two bottles of wine on the table. "I uncorked them myself."

Ian nodded. "If ye and Maggie will wait, I want ye to hear what I have to say."

Devon looked wary, the other brothers resigned.

"Has something happened?" Broderick asked.

"Aye. Someone tried to kill Lady Woodhaven the night before last."

His uncle frowned. "Kill her? What do ye mean?"

"I mean, someone put a glass of wine along with some marzipan on Em…Lady Woodhaven's nightstand." He looked around the room. "The wine had been laced with hemlock."

Emily watched the group through lowered lashes. Donovan looked shocked, Devon sullen, and Glenda's face had gone white. Which could have been from Ian's brusque tone or the seriousness of the proclamation, Emily reminded herself. It didn't mean the young girl was guilty.

Broderick raised an eyebrow. "Are ye certain? We harbor no witches here."

"Old Gwendolyn confirmed it was hemlock," Ian said grimly.

"I suppose she would ken, since she probably has some medical use for it," Donovan said.

"Oh, she does!" Glenda burst out. All eyes turned to her and she flushed.

"What would that be?" Fiona asked.

The girl's face reddened further. "I've heard some of the maids say they ask her for a potion to…" She hesitated, the color growing to the shade of a beet. "To stave off men's attentions… So they would not get with child." When everyone stared at her, she stammered on. "Sometimes the maids pick it themselves and take it to Old Gwendolyn to fix."

Ian's face looked like a thundercloud. "And how many maids ken where to find it?"

Glenda looked at him wide-eyed. "I doona ken, but it grows in the fields. 'Tis nae hard to find."

Emily tried to keep her expression impassive. If the plant was that common, it meant nearly anyone could have picked it and made a tincture to put drops in the wine. She looked directly at Glenda. The girl wouldn't meet her gaze. *Had she done it?*

If Ian suspected as much, Emily couldn't tell. His face

had become a rigid mask, hiding whatever he was feeling. "I will look into that. Meanwhile…" He looked around the table. "Until I can get to the bottom of this, we will all be eating from the same platters and drinking from the same bottles."

Broderick's brow rose again. "Do ye suspect one of us?"

"I accuse nae one." Ian glanced at Devon. "Nae one. And, for now, I want to keep this attempt within these walls. But we also have to make a point. We will be taking our meals in the Great Hall after tonight. If we are seen taking food from the same platters, whoever is responsible for this will have to think twice."

Carr nodded slowly. "'Tis a good idea. I canna think of a single MacGregor who would want to kill one of their own."

As opposed to killing a Sassenach, Emily thought.

Ian's mouth tightened, but he nodded. "To make sure that doesna happen, either Maggie and Cook will supervise the food preparation and Hamish will keep an eye out for whoever enters the kitchen." A muscle twitched in his jaw. "I will not have another murder take place at Strae Castle."

Emily felt a chill slide down her spine. He meant *her* murder. Bless him, he was doing everything he could to protect her. She prayed that it would be enough.

• • •

Ian wished he hadn't been so blunt, since no one seemed to have an appetite now. He hoped it was because of his harsh words and not because they feared the food in front of them was tainted.

"We will nae insult Cook by leaving the food untouched." He ladled soup into a bowl for Emily and placed it in front of her before handing off the huge spoon to Fiona. Then he broke one of the loaves of bread Maggie had carried in and handed half to Emily, keeping the other half for himself. Tomorrow night he planned to do the same thing in the Great Hall to show one and all that Emily was under his personal protection.

He was aware of Glenda watching his solicitous movements from beneath her lashes, mouth drawn down. Her expression gave him cause to reflect on his earlier conversation with Fiona. Poison was a female's preferred weapon, since most didn't know how to handle a knife or shoot a musket. It would have been easy enough to put whisky into the tea after Emily fell and hit her head, but would a slight girl, barely four and ten, have had the strength to loosen a board on the steps?

Ian knew his ward was somewhat infatuated with him, that she saw him as a hero when he'd done only what any other man would have done, given the same circumstances. She was at a vulnerable age, just coming into womanhood, so he'd walked a fine line between not completely squelching her awkward flirtations and keeping a distance. Mayhap he should have been firmer, but even if Glenda were jealous, would she actually try to murder Emily? The idea seemed as preposterous as Devon trying to kill her.

And yet, someone at Strae Castle had tried.

"Do ye nae agree?"

Ian blinked, suddenly aware that Donovan had asked him a question and that everyone, especially the ladies, was watching him. "I doona ken—"

"Ye have nae heard a word I said, have ye?"

"Sorry. I was pondering."

"Understandable," Carr said, "but I think we should consider changing our plans."

"*No!*"

The plaintive wail came from Lorelei, Fiona, and Glenda at the same time. Ian blinked again. "Plans?"

Donovan sighed. "I suggested that we doona take the

women with us to Campbell's ball."

Ian frowned. "We already discussed this."

"Aye, but that was before the…incident…happened," his uncle answered. "Ye canna oversee the serving of food or drink at Kilchurn Castle. Whoever put the tincture into the wine may have more left. If that person were to put a few drops into the wrong drink at the ball and someone took ill, the result might very well be clan war. We doona need to be at odds with the Campbells this close to Parliament starting up and Lord Mount Stuart's petition considered."

"But that is exactly why we should go! *All* of us, nae just ye men," Fiona said.

"Nobody is going to try to poison one of us," Alasdair pointed out.

"We are MacGregors," Rory added.

"So is Fiona," Juliana retorted, "and Glenda as well."

He glowered at her. "Fine. We will take them with us then."

"If the Sassenachs stay away, our sister and Glenda should be safe," Devon said.

"Aye." Broderick nodded. "Nae a soul would harm them."

Fiona gave each of them an annoyed look. "Are ye all daft? Have ye nae considered that if Emily and her sisters stay behind, it will be a clear insult to the Campbells?" She looked at Ian. "I doubt we would have been invited at all had it nae been that Emily is an English countess. I am sure Gavin Campbell will be expecting her and her sisters to attend."

Ian didn't need to be reminded about Gavin. He remembered all too well the interested look in the man's eyes and his remarks about coming to call. Thank God he hadn't made a habit of it. Yet. But his sister was right. Not bringing them would be seen as an offense. Even worse, speculation might start rumors about the attempted murder. Rumors had a vicious way of escalating. Someone else might try to do the same. Instead of having one traitor to flush out, he would have more.

"If I might interject?" Emily asked. "Fiona is quite right on two counts. First, if I do not attend, your clansmen will wonder why. If we hope to keep the attempt to...harm me a secret, then they will assume that I consider myself above them. I will not have that. Secondly, if Lord Bute is in attendance, or the Duke of Argyll himself, either will wonder why I am not present." She looked at Ian's brothers. "And, unfortunately, in aristocratic circles, that would indeed be an insult."

Ian held up a hand before anyone could argue. What Emily said made sense. They couldn't afford to insult either the earl or the duke. "We are all going," he said, "and I expect each of ye"—he looked around the room slowly, making sure each one understood his meaning—"to protect our lady."

"She is nae our lady," Devon muttered. "Nae a MacGregor—"

"Enough!" Ian glared at him. Must his brother always make a point of that? He didn't want to be forced into a position where he had to make a choice between Emily and his family. And yet, he felt he was being pushed into doing just that.

• • •

After Emily finished breakfast the next morning—she'd managed to get from her chamber to the small dining room without a guard, or at least not one whom she saw, although she thought she'd heard footsteps behind her—Ian escorted her, her sisters, and Fiona to the solar.

"At least two of ye need to stay with Em—the countess—at all times," he said, the tone of his voice brooking no argument. "Do ye understand?"

Fiona looked heavenward. "We are nae daft, brother."

He nodded curtly. "I will depend on ye, sister."

She shook her head after he left. "I wonder why he thinks he needs to call ye "countess" or "Lady Woodhaven" when we all ken he kissed ye."

Lorelei giggled and Emily felt her face heat as though she'd just gotten too close to the hearth. Ian had not mentioned the kiss since, nor had he attempted to find a bit of privacy for them to indulge again. She was beginning to think she actually was a ninny. Men were always willing to steal a kiss, especially if the lady was willing. And she had been willing. Her cheeks warmed further. She had even *encouraged* him, but she didn't regret it. Even now, she could recall every minute detail. How soft, yet firm, his lips were and how warm. How strong, yet gentle, his hands had been as they'd cradled her head. How he had tasted slightly of buttery toast and how the faint, fresh scent of soap clung to him. Still, the kiss had probably meant much more to her. Given her hapless marriage and lack of prior experience, Ian's kiss had been the first to arouse her. He was probably quite used to that effect on women. She frowned. That idea was not appealing at all.

"Doona fash." Fiona apparently misread her grumpy expression. "My brother will get to the bottom of this."

"I am sure he will."

Fiona went to the door, opened it a crack, then closed it again. "Just as I thought. He posted a guard in the hall." She smiled at Emily. "Ye will be fine."

For a brief, fleeting moment while she was lost in her woolgathering, she hadn't thought about reality. *Ninny*, she chided herself. Ian was seeing to her safety while she was indulging in silly fantasies. Those footsteps she'd thought she heard earlier had probably been this guard. "I wonder what he told the man? We are trying to keep the news of the incident from spreading."

"Doona fash about that, either," Fiona said as she took her seat again. "'Tis Hamish's younger brother, John. He'll have been sworn to silence."

Juliana gave her a skeptical look. "But will an armed man following Emily around not draw attention?"

"He will nae appear armed." Fiona grinned. "But he usually carries a half-dozen knives hidden about his person."

Juliana blinked and Lorelei stared at her wide-eyed. "Why?"

"He likes knives." Fiona shrugged. "All Highlanders carry at least one, if nae more."

Emily immediately began to wonder where Ian might have stashed his on his person and then felt her face warm once more. What had gotten into her thinking this morning? Was she feeling some odd, long-lasting effect of the hemlock?

Juliana persisted with her train of thought. "But having a man follow Emily around will still cause suspicion."

"Nae so much," Fiona answered. "Some years back, the Duke and Duchess of York passed through on their way to Kilchurn. John was smitten with the lady's maid and followed them back to England. The duchess took pity on him and made him her personal footman." She shrugged again. "So it will nae seem so odd to have him assigned to Emily."

"What made him return?" she asked.

A bleak expression flitted across Fiona's face. "His wife—he married the maid—died in childbirth six months ago. The bairn didna survive, so John came back."

"I am sorry," Emily said. "Has he been living here at the castle?"

She shook her head. "In Dalmally. Hamish must have sent for him."

"*Hmmm,*" Juliana said. "If John married an English maid, perhaps he does not hate us."

"We doona hate ye."

Juliana gave her an arched look. "Obviously, someone does."

"Ian will find out who that is." Fiona looked earnestly at each of them. "I would wager one of the reasons he brought John in was so he could accompany us to the ball. He kens how to blend in and nae be noticed."

Emily nodded. "People do tend to talk in front of servants as though they have no ears."

"Aye. And he'll be able to talk with the Campbells' servants to see the way the wind blows there."

"Well, I am just glad we are going to the ball," Lorelei said.

"I am, too," Fiona answered. "With the Duke of Argyll spending so much time in England, it will feel almost like a London ball."

"Oh, I hope so!" Lorelei nearly bounced in her seat. "I cannot wait!"

Emily smiled at her sister, wondering if she had ever felt so young. She hadn't had a Season and, given her lack of dowry, no serious suitors. She'd married the Earl of Woodhaven out of necessity and had simply endured.

And now, someone here wanted her gone. She could leave, but that would mean Lorelei would not have her Season nor would she be able to help Juliana. Emily lifted her chin. Her sisters were not going to be put in the same predicament she had been.

She would survive this. Attending the ball would be the first step in flushing out the villain. So be it.

Chapter Twenty

Ian paced the entryway by the door in the old part of the castle, waiting for the ladies to make their appearance. Outside, the carriages waited to take them all to Kilchurn Castle for the ball, saddle horses tied behind the conveyances, stamping their hooves impatiently. He tried to avoid looking any of his brothers in the eye, for they probably felt as uncomfortable as he did.

He tugged at the damned neckcloth that felt like it was choking him and pulled at the sleeves of the frock coat that felt too tight across his shoulders. At least the material was wool, not velvet or some equally impractical material, and he'd torn the lace frippery from the linen shirt as well. He longed for a proper jabot and kilt with its freedom of movement, but the damn Crown had banned the tartan. Not that it mattered, he supposed, since the MacGregors were still proscribed anyway, but the formal English attire felt like foppery. He ran a hand through his hair, and a smile started to form. He and his brothers refused to wear powdered wigs. It was only a wee bit of rebellion, but one the king could not punish them for.

The smile stopped midway as a rustle of skirts announced the arrival of the women and Emily came into sight. He nearly let his mouth gape like a halfwit at what she was wearing. He was accustomed to seeing her in practical day gowns of subdued colors that fit loosely and were very properly buttoned to her neck and covering her arms. Even when she wore breeches to go riding, she had a long cape that pretty much hid her femininity. But now, it was all he could do to keep from ogling.

The gown was a deep sea-blue silk the same color as her eyes and enhanced the honey-gold tones of her hair, which was piled on top of her head in a mass of curls instead of the usual simple knot she wore. A few tendrils had escaped to frame her face enticingly, making his fingers twitch to touch them. But then his gaze dropped and he frowned.

The neckline of her gown was cut *much* too low. He wondered who had laced her stays so tightly that the plump fullness of her breasts pressed against the fitted bodice—the swell of ivory mounds just visible and tempting to any sighted man under ninety. He clenched his jaw. Gavin Campbell was only one-third that age and not blind.

"Have ye a shawl?" His voice sounded a little husky, and he heard a couple of his brothers chuckle, but he ignored them. "It will get cool." That sounded hapless even to him and he heard another chortle, but he couldn't seem to stop. "Mayhap a cape?"

Emily gave him a puzzled look and then held up her hand, showing him the matching wrap that she'd been holding, only he hadn't noticed. More sniggering behind him ensued. This time, he turned to glare at his brothers, who stopped guffawing abruptly. He gave a satisfied grunt, then realized that they hadn't stopped because of him. They were all staring over his shoulder. Slowly, he turned around.

Emily's sisters and Fiona had joined them. Lorelei was

attired in pastel pink that complemented her pale hair and Juliana in yellow that brightened hers, but Ian knew his brothers' attentions were riveted on their sister. They were all used to seeing her in her customary breeches and the overly large tunics she favored or, at a clan gathering, in simple, woolen gowns like most of the women wore. He swallowed. Somehow, recently, his sister had developed curves.

Her gown was some shimmery material that changed from white to silvery gray when she moved, and she must have been wearing a corset, too—he didn't know she'd owned one—for her waist was cinched and the bodice left no doubt she'd grown into a woman.

"Where did ye get that gown?"

"It is one of mine," Lorelei answered. "Well, actually, it was our dear cousin Anne's."

Behind him, Rory snorted. "She is nae planning to come to Scotland, too, is she?"

Juliana shot him a look. "She might if I wrote and asked her."

"Shut yer *beul*!" Devon muttered to Rory.

"Aye! Be quiet, both of ye," Ian said.

Lorelei gave them a puzzled glance, then shrugged. "Anyway, is the gown not beautiful on Fiona? It sets off her gray eyes and makes her hair look raven black. I am sure she will catch the eye of a lot of young men this evening."

He was pretty sure Fiona would and not because of her eyes or hair. The neckline on this gown was also low, but she had some sort of frilly lace thing stuck in it, thank God.

"What is that thing?"

Lorelei giggled. "A fichu."

That sounded French, but at least it provided a degree of modesty. He drew his brows together. "See that it does nae fall out."

This time he heard a chorus of "ayes" behind him. Fiona

gave them all an annoyed look. "I doona plan to wave it about."

"See that ye doona," he all but growled.

Fiona tossed her head at him and started for the door, the others trailing after her. Emily was still not wearing her shawl.

He grimaced as he followed them out. It seemed he'd have two problems this evening. He could make sure one of his brothers was always near Fiona all night, but how was he going to get Emily to keep that wrap on?

• • •

The tension in the carriage was so thick, Emily thought it might cut off the air. Lorelei and Juliana were in the second carriage with Glenda, Alasdair, and Carr, but Fiona had elected to ride with her, Ian, and Rory. At the moment, no one was speaking. Fiona was obviously put out with Ian, although she had the good sense not to stir the waters when his face looked like a storm about to unleash its fury.

At least Rory and Juliana were separated so everyone would arrive intact. They'd managed to exchange several more barbs before getting into their respective carriages. Emily sometimes wondered what the outcome would be if her sister and Ian's brother were lost in the woods and they'd have to cooperate with each other to find a way out. Or maybe they should just be locked in a room until they could be civil to each other. She sighed. They weren't children and she couldn't make them play nice together.

As the carriage rolled along, she hoped all would go well. They'd already had to leave John, her guard, behind, since a horse had kicked him two days ago and broken his leg. Not that she thought she needed a guard with Ian and his brothers around. Her thoughts turned to Devon. He had elected to ride his own horse, which didn't surprise her. He probably was not planning to stay overly long. Apart from being angry much of the time, she sensed he was somewhat of a loner by nature. She started to smile. How ironic it would be if he actually met Anne.

Rory lifted an eyebrow. "Is something funny?"

Considering that Fiona was staring out the window with her arms crossed, Ian was glowering at nothing in particular, and Rory seemed annoyed, there was nothing hilarious about the situation at all. And, for some reason, that made her laugh.

Fiona turned, Ian studied her as though she'd taken leave of her senses—maybe she had—and Rory raised both brows.

"I was…just…thinking," she said when she managed to gain control of herself, "of what would happen if our cousin Anne actually did come to Scotland and met Devon." Nobody's expression changed, so she went on. "She gave Lorelei that gown because she was sure there would not be a dressmaker anywhere north of the border."

"So she thinks we are barbaric?" Rory asked.

"Yes." She stifled another urge to laugh. "Anne is quite sure Scots—Highlanders in particular—are as wild and dangerous as those Indians in the Colonies that we read about."

Ian gave her a skeptical look. "Then 'tis best she never meets Devon."

"That is just the point." Emily sobered. "Devon is as much misconstrued about the English as my cousin is about the Scots. Just imagine if they both found out they were wrong."

Rory grunted and leaned back against the squab. "That has as much chance of happening as yer sister and I getting along."

Emily smiled at him. "You do not believe in miracles?"

He grunted again. "I think the Lord has better things to do."

Emily sat back as well. *The Lord might very well have better things to do, but do I? Hmmm.*

• • •

They arrived at Kilchurn Castle as the sun was setting. The first thing Ian noticed after alighting from their carriage was a much more elaborate one standing near the stables, with gleaming brass spokes, mahogany door insets, and a ducal crest.

Rory came to stand beside him as Devon rode up and dismounted. "Looks like Argyll will be here, after all."

"I wonder why he's come up from Inveraray for a harvest ball," Devon said. "Seems like he'd be holding one of his own."

"I doona ken," Ian replied. "The dragoons took him a message—"

"Mayhap his brother requested he come," Carr said as he and Alasdair joined them.

Ian frowned. "Aye, but why?"

"'Tis the question, isn't it?" Alasdair asked rhetorically. "First, we get an invitation—"

"Ye doona think we were invited because Lady Woodhaven is at Strae Castle? English protocol?"

Alasdair shrugged. "It could be, but Henry may have seen it as an opportunity to use her as well."

Rory snorted. "Campbells have always been ones to take advantage."

"I'll nae argue with that," Carr said.

"Use Em…Lady Woodhaven in what way?" Ian watched as the ladies were met at the entrance to the castle and they disappeared inside. He didn't want to think of Emily being a pawn in some devious game of political chess.

"She is English. Argyll spends more time in London than he does in Scotland." Alasdair looked speculative. "If he's been privy to inside information about our lands possibly being restored—some of which were given to the Campbells—"

"*Taken* by them, ye mean," Rory said.

"Aye, we can thank Mary, Queen of Scots for that," Devon added.

Alasdair nodded his assent to both of them. "Either way, Argyll might want to convince the countess to stand with them..."

Carr looked at Ian as Alasdair's voice trailed off. "Especially since some of the land from Lady Woodhaven's deed might be included," he finished.

Ian was silent. Emily wanted the MacGregors to have their name and honor restored. He knew that. But did she know that she could possibly lose the land given to her? King George had awarded her the castle *and its holdings,* but if Parliament decreed the *lands* be restored, Emily would have no source of income to maintain the castle, even if she kept it. And, after what she'd told him, he knew how important it was that she provide for her sisters.

Would she stand with the Campbells if it came to that? Ian grimaced. The worst part was he couldn't fault her if she did. He understood family. Wasn't he trying to do the same thing, not only for his brothers and sister, but also for his clan? The matter of having to make a choice between her needs and his clan's seemed to be looming closer, even without Devon's clamoring.

"'Tis only speculation on our part," he said. "Nae use inviting trouble where none may be."

"Think again." Rory pointed toward another carriage with a crest, turning into the drive. "That is the Earl of Bute arriving, nae?"

"*Hmmm*," Carr said, "it seems the clouds are gathering."

"But are we in for a storm?" Ian asked. "Lord Mount Stuart said his father supports the bill. Mayhap he will speak in our favor to Argyll."

Devon gave him a look as if he were daft. "Have ye been reading faerie tales lately? Ye ken things never turn out right for MacGregors."

Not wanting to upset his brother, Ian just shrugged. Besides, it was hard to argue the point, given their clan had been outcast or labeled outlaws by no less than eight monarchs for the past two centuries.

"Well, then, as our Irish relatives would say, 'tis time for our luck to change," Carr said with a smile.

Alasdair nodded. "Aye, and I'll be leaving soon to gather our clansmen in Ireland, as we discussed."

Devon pointed to the carriage. "I doona see Mount Stuart with the earl."

They fell silent as they watched the man descend and be greeted by Argyll himself. No one else alighted from the carriage and the footman closed the door, motioning for it to be taken away.

"Do ye still think it bodes well for us?" Devon asked. "The former Prime Minister and the Duke of Argyll meeting in secret?"

"Hardly in secret, brother," Carr said. "Neither of them is attempting nae to be seen."

His brother glowered at him. "Ye ken what I mean. Meeting in the Highlands instead of in London, or even Inveraray, can only bode ill."

"Mayhap they want only to take each other's measure before Parliament begins," Carr answered.

"Ye've been sitting in faerie dust, too," Devon muttered. "Or mayhap the Sassenach has bewitched both of ye."

Ian drew his brows down. The last thing Emily needed was for a damn rumor to start about witchcraft, for God's sake. "Ye doona like being suspected of foul play, Devon, so watch what accusation ye make."

His brother had the decency to look somewhat embarrassed, although he didn't apologize. "Think of it this way then. She knows the Earl of Bute. She admitted as much. How do we ken she didna send word to him?"

"Now ye are the one bespelled by the Fae," Ian barely managed to keep his voice level. "How would she have been able to do that?"

"She sent for Everard from White's Club," Devon retorted. "'Tis nae that hard to send a missive."

His other three brothers looked at him. Carr's and Alasdair's expressions were impassive, so he couldn't tell what they were thinking. Rory looked skeptical.

"Lady Woodhaven would have nae cause to do so," Ian said.

"Nae?" Devon asked. "Mayhap she wants to ken what the bill is going to say so she can decide who to support. Us or the Campbells."

"Lucifer's horns!" Ian considered pounding his eejit brothers' heads together. "Ye make her sound like some conniving mercenary. All Em—Lady Woodhaven wants is a home for herself and her sisters. Can none of ye understand that?"

"'Tis a home she might nae have if the bill goes through Parliament," Rory said stubbornly.

Ian threw up his hands. "Ye are eejits! Nae more of this talk! We all have eyes and ears. We will see how this plays out. As I said before, 'tis nae use in inviting trouble—"

"Ye need to stop saying that," Alasdair said mildly, then pointed to the road. "I think the Camerons are coming."

Ian turned his head and groaned at the sight of a dozen

or more men thundering toward them. They might not be wearing their tartans or carrying their standard, but there was no denying their fierce leader or their war cry.

And, from the way some of them swayed in their saddles, they'd been making good use of the whisky in the flasks. Sober, they were barely congenial to MacGregors. Drunk… Well, anything could happen.

Chapter Twenty-One

Emily gazed around the private dining room at Kilchurn Castle. It was nothing like the one at the MacGregors'. Unlike their round table that seated only a dozen or so, this long, polished mahogany table could seat nearly two score, and it was near full this evening.

The Duke of Argyll sat at the head, with the Earl of Bute to his right and his brother Henry to his left. Since they had obviously followed English etiquette, as the dowager Countess of Woodhaven, she was seated above the salt, which put her next to Gavin Campbell. Directly across from her sat the head of Clan Cameron, a man with piercing eyes and steel-gray hair and, apparently, the only member of his regiment, apart from a daughter, who was sober. Thankfully, other than his somewhat-foxed son Neal, who was seated beside him, the others had been relegated to the Great Hall with other visiting clans for the evening meal. Ian's brothers and uncles had been sent there as well. Ian had been invited to the private chamber, albeit at the far end of the table. Even though the position was not one of prominence, she thought it boded well for the clan's recognition that he was included.

Hopefully, she would have an opportunity to talk with the earl later, since there had been only flurried greetings earlier.

"I am so glad that you were able to attend." Gavin leaned slightly toward her. "And I must apologize for not calling on you as I said I would."

"That is quite understandable," Emily answered. "I realize how important it is to get the harvest in."

"There is that," he agreed, "but I was called away to Inveraray and only just returned two days ago."

That caught her interest, since Rory had reported the dragoons going there. "It must have been important business to take you away at such a critical time."

He smiled. "I assure you that it was."

Drat. Was he going to play cat-and-mouse? Emily smiled back. "I hope it was not dangerous?"

He held her gaze. "Dare I hope you would be concerned if it were?"

She returned his look. "Of course. Dragoons were spotted passing by Strae Castle, not very long ago, heading south."

Gavin looked disconcerted for a moment, then he shrugged. "The general at Fort William probably sent them on a mission."

Or maybe your uncle did, she thought, although she didn't voice the words. However, she'd spent five years in London Society observing how gossips gleaned their information. "But what kind of mission, do you suppose?"

"I… It could be any number of things. Highwaymen. A clan dispute. Cattle-reiving, even." He kept his smile in place. "These are the Highlands, you know."

Emily gave him a wide-eyed look that would have done Lorelei proud. "Forgive me for not understanding—I am still learning about Highland ways—but are those not trivial matters? I thought—and I may be wrong—but are the dragoons not here to ensure there are no more uprisings or rebellions?"

He nodded. "That is one of their duties."

"I have not heard any such rumors." She touched his arm briefly. "Surely, nothing nearby?"

Gavin looked at his sleeve where her fingers had been and then put his hand over hers for a moment. "I have not heard any rumors, either."

She withdrew her hand as casually as she could. Obviously, this conversation wasn't getting her any useful information, so perhaps it was best to change the subject. She knew the dragoons had stopped at Inveraray and that some of them had ridden south toward Bute, but had they gone there? That was the real information she wanted.

"Well, since the earl is here, I might ask him later if he has heard of any disturbances that we might be concerned about."

Something flashed in Gavin's eyes, but it was gone quickly and replaced with another smile. "I was not aware that you knew the earl."

"Oh, yes," Emily answered with her own smile. "We met on several occasions when my husband was still alive." She didn't add that on those occasions she was usually paying off markers. "It will be good to renew our acquaintance."

Gavin's smile wavered, but before he could respond, the younger Cameron spilled his wine. Unfortunately, most of it landed in Juliana's lap, since she'd been seated next to him.

"You bloody oaf!" She stood and started blotting the stain on her skirt with a napkin to no avail. "If you cannot—"

"What did ye call me?" He rose, too.

"*Juliana*." Emily gave her sister a warning look. Conversation had stopped and everyone was watching.

Her sister chose to ignore her. "I called you a bloody oaf."

He looked nonplussed, his face turning momentarily white before reddening. Out of the corner of her eye, Emily saw Ian disengage from a woman who had been holding on to his arm and push his chair back. She didn't have time to consider who that woman was other than she was very pretty. She just hoped Ian would reach Juliana before Neal turned violent.

"Ye called me a bloody *oaf*?" he repeated as if his ears had not heard correctly.

"I did and you are…umph!" She didn't finish as Ian pulled her out of harm's way.

"Ye'll nae strike this woman, Cameron," Ian threatened, "or ye'll answer to me."

Neal blinked, as if considering the fact that he might actually be harmed, and Emily sighed. Foxed as he was, it would take only a mere push to put him on the ground. She could probably do it herself, so she hoped Ian would restrain himself now that the immediate danger was past.

And then Neal Cameron did the strangest thing. He laughed. *Laughed.* As Ian raised a fist, he held both hands up. "Ye misunderstand, MacGregor. I've nae met a woman who dared to call me an oaf. Let alone a *bloody* one." He wobbled a little, then gestured toward Juliana. "I think she will make me a fine wife!"

Juliana stared at him, speechless for once. Then her eyes narrowed and she made a sound very much like a hissing cat before turning and running from the room.

His father yanked him into his chair. "Shut yer mouth."

His son just grinned. "Aye, a mighty fine wife."

• • •

Ian switched his focus to Emily, who'd gotten up and was hurrying out of the room after her sister. If the look of distress on her face hadn't been so dire, he would have laughed at the pure fury on Juliana's as she'd stormed from the room. He suspected it didn't have to do so much with her ruined gown as it did with Neal's announced intention. Of course, the man was well into his cups and probably wouldn't remember a word he said, but Juliana's indignant reaction was near priceless. Ian doubted even Rory could have goaded her into such a temper.

"I daresay our entertainment has begun." Gavin took a sip of wine. "And quite impromptu as well."

Ian turned his attention to him. What had Campbell been talking to Emily about that, judging from how often she'd smiled at him, had *entertained* her? He'd been sitting too far away at the other end of the table to be able to hear what was said. It hadn't helped that Breena Buchanan had managed to seat herself next to him and had not stopped talking. It had taken him less than five minutes to remember why he'd ended his very brief courtship of her a year ago. The lass chattered more than a cluster of squirrels amassing acorns.

Still, he didn't need to hear the exact words to know that Gavin Campbell had been flirting with Emily. He had actually put his hand over hers. Ian felt a muscle in his jaw flex as he tried to ignore the fact that she had actually touched Campbell first…and had she leaned in just a little bit? Breena had plucked his own sleeve about that time asking, with a pout, if he was paying attention. He was, but not to her.

The Cameron laird looked up at him. "Do ye have another point to make?"

Ian very much would have liked to make another point, only one directed at Campbell to leave Emily alone. But he was drawing attention to himself now that the wine episode had passed. Neither Argyll nor his brother had made any attempt to intervene, although they were watching from their end of the table, as was Lord Bute.

He sighed. If there was one person here tonight that he needed to curry favor from, it was the former prime minister. Getting into a verbal altercation with either the young Cameron or Gavin Campbell would only make the MacGregors seem more like outlaws. Certainly, it would not help his cause in any way.

"Nae." He looked at the blurry-eyed son. "Just a bit of advice, though." He doubted the man would remember, but he felt an obligation to Emily's sister. "Miss Caldwell tends to mean what she says. If I were ye, I'd let that fish swim away."

Neal winked at him. Or attempted to, anyway. Because of his inebriated state, it looked more like he'd gotten something caught in his eye. But his next words were clear, so he wasn't quite as drunk as Ian thought.

"I do like reeling in a fightin' fish." He grinned rather crookedly.

"How interesting," Gavin said.

• • •

"I cannot go back in there!" Juliana stopped stomping around the room that served as a ladies' retreat and looked at Emily, Lorelei, and Fiona, all of whom had followed her out. "Have a carriage brought around. I am going home."

Emily took a deep breath. "Remember that our host is the Duke of Argyll. He might consider it rude for you to leave."

Lorelei looked at her, horrified. "Surely not after her gown has been ruined!"

Fiona tilted her head. "The stain could be removed if we could get some cold water and soap."

"Then she'd have to walk around in a *wet* gown," Lorelei said.

"'Tis better than to have it ruined."

Juliana rolled her eyes. "The dress does not matter that much. I simply do not want to have anything more to do with that nasty man."

Fiona nodded. "Neal Cameron is right spoiled, he is. Likes to have his way, since in Scotland, he is still considered the laird's son."

"Well, he will not have his way with me," Juliana answered.

"Doona fash," Fiona said. "My brothers will protect ye."

Juliana gave her a skeptical look. "All your brothers?"

"Well, truth be told, I am nae sure about Devon."

"Or Rory," Juliana said drily. "He'd probably be more than happy to give me to that bloody oaf."

Fiona laughed. "Ye have that all wrong. Rory despises Neal."

Juliana shrugged. "All the more reason then, I would think."

"Why does Rory not like Neal?" Emily asked before her sister could start to rant on.

"'Twas a girl. Three years ago at a gathering of clans, Rory had his heart set—or at least his eye—on a neighboring MacFarlane lass. When Neal realized it, he decided to win her away." Fiona paused. "A proscribed MacGregor didna have much chance against a Cameron."

"If she was that shallow, then Rory should count his blessings," Emily said.

"Och, aye. He didna pine for long." Fiona paused once more. "But the lass came to Rory the next day with bruises on her arms and told him Neal had raped her."

Emily could practically hear the silence around her. "What happened?"

"Nothing. When Rory went to confront him, he denied it and said the girl was lying. His father vouched for him."

"So nothing came of it?"

"She didna get with child and the laird of Clan MacFarlane let it go." Fiona sighed. "Right pretty she was, too."

Which reminded Emily of the woman who'd been sitting next to Ian. She was pretty, too. Could it be the same woman? "Is the girl here tonight?"

Fiona shook her head. "Her father married her off to a Hamilton widower of some years who needed a young wife to look after his eight children. They moved to Glasgow."

Emily felt empathy for the girl. She hadn't had to take care of a nest of children and her father would never have forced her into marriage, but the results had been similar.

"Are there no MacFarlanes here tonight then?"

"I doona think so."

"I noticed two or three other ladies seated at the table. Are they all Campbells?"

"Nae," Fiona answered. "one is Neal's sister, Margaret, and the one sitting next to her is her cousin."

"And the other?" Emily finally asked when it seemed Fiona was not going to volunteer any information on the woman seated next to Ian. His sister looked uncomfortable, and Emily felt a sudden chill.

"That would be Breena Buchanan."

"And who is she?" Lorelei asked.

Emily silently blessed her sister at that moment. Lorelei no doubt was just curious, but it saved her from having to ask the dreaded question.

Fiona fidgeted with her sleeve. "Last year, Ian paid her some attention."

Juliana glanced at Emily, then at Fiona. "It seems he still does."

Emily felt her face heat and quickly looked down to smooth her skirts. Trust Juliana to be so blunt. And yet…she wanted to know if it was true.

"Nae, Ian is only being polite tonight," Fiona answered.

"He decided she was nae the one for him shortly after that."

Emily fussed with an invisible wrinkle and wondered if he'd told Breena. She certainly didn't act as though she'd accepted it.

Quite the opposite.

• • •

By the time the trestle tables had been put up and the benches set aside to make room in the Great Hall for the actual ball, Emily's nerves were frazzled. A carriage had been brought around for Juliana, since she was adamant she did not want to see or speak to Neal Cameron again. Fiona's revelation about Breena hadn't helped, either, especially since the woman was clinging to Ian when Emily finally reentered the hall.

"Is all well?" Gavin asked as he joined her.

No, she wanted to say. While she'd made Juliana's apologies to the duke, Neal Cameron had overheard and said it was a ridiculous excuse. Before Emily could stop her, Lorelei had then picked up a glass of wine to toss on him. His reflexes were quick for a drunk and he blocked her hand, which unfortunately resulted in the contents spilling onto Lorelei instead. She was now accompanying Juliana home in quite a high temper. Alasdair had gallantly offered to escort them. Emily only hoped he'd still be on speaking terms with her sisters when that journey ended. But Gavin was obviously waiting for an answer.

"As well as can be expected given the unusual circumstances."

"Most unfortunate for your sisters," Gavin replied. "Cameron can be quite the oaf, indeed."

That was the mildest word Juliana had used. While they were waiting on the carriage, she'd added others…lout, cad, swine, buffoon, and cur to name just a few. Perhaps it was just as well she had gone home, since Emily was quite sure the Duke of Argyll would not appreciate her inciting a brawl.

"The music has started." Gavin broke through her reverie. "May I have the first dance?"

She could hardly refuse, since this was his home. As she laid her hand atop his offered arm, she saw Breena tugging Ian along, and an unfamiliar sharp pain shot through her. Regardless of what Fiona had said, it didn't look like Ian was making that much of an effort to decline. At least it was a country reel, which would keep them separated much of the dance.

The dance was livelier than those in London, but she picked up the steps quickly enough. She passed Ian several times throughout the turns and twirls and each time their hands touched, however briefly, a tingle ran up her arm. It was not a reaction she had with any other. She wondered if Ian felt it, too. His whisky-colored eyes seemed to darken each time they met.

A good half hour passed before the music finally stopped. Emily was hot and out of breath, although none of the Scots women seemed to be affected. Obviously, they were used to dances lasting four times longer than what she was accustomed to, but it also made her aware that life in the Highlands required a certain amount of fortitude.

"Would you care for some refreshment?" Gavin asked. "There are several beverages to choose from, if you care to walk over."

Emily glanced toward the far end of the hall where a table had been set up. Ian and Breena were standing near it, and the last place she wanted to be was near them. Before she could politely decline, a servant hurried over and whispered something to Gavin. He scowled slightly, then turned to her.

"You must forgive me. I have a matter to attend to."

"Of course." At the moment she was so relieved, she

didn't even care what that matter might be. "I will just take some air."

He moved away, talking in low tones to the servant. Turning, Emily left the Great Hall and went down the steps to the courtyard. The evening breeze was cool, which felt wonderful on her overly heated skin. Rounding the side of the castle, she entered the gardens through a stone archway and stood for a minute, inhaling the scent of heather lining the walkway.

Several oil lamps suspended on metal poles cast dim light into the shadows. It did not appear to be a manicured garden like the ones on English country estates. Various shrubs and bushes were scattered about, but in the center two chestnut trees towered over a folly similar to the one at Glen Strae. Hearing the strains of music begin again, she decided it would make a good refuge so as not to endure another rigorous dance. And she had no desire to watch Ian with Breena.

She was near the entrance to the folly when she heard a low moan coming from inside. It was followed by another, slightly louder. A whimper. Good heavens! Was an animal hurt? Emily rushed up the three steps and stopped so abruptly she nearly toppled over.

No animal, save for human ones and certainly not hurt at all. In her foolish quest for privacy, she hadn't considered lovers might be trysting. And not just any lovers.

Devon glared up at her, a half-naked Margaret Cameron in his arms.

Chapter Twenty-Two

"Emily! Lady Woodhaven!"

Ian was calling her name. She gave Devon a cursory look, then turned and practically ran down the path she'd just taken. It would not do to have Ian finding his brother in a compromising position. Especially not with Neal Cameron's sister. Emily didn't even want to think about the consequences of that.

"Lady Woodhaven! Are ye out here?"

His voice sounded louder, which meant he must be heading toward the garden. She slipped through the archway and took a deep breath as she smoothed her skirts. "Yes, Mr. MacGregor, I am here..." She hurried toward the front of the castle, colliding with Ian as he rounded the corner. His large hands went around her waist, steadying her.

For a moment, she reveled in their strength. "I...came out to get a bit of fresh air."

Ian dropped his hands. "I saw ye leave and thought something might be amiss after Campbell walked away so abruptly."

Had he been watching her? From across the hall? She had thought him engrossed with Breena... The thought that he was not all that enthralled sent a pleasant little shiver through her.

"Are ye cold?"

Without waiting for an answer, Ian removed his frock coat and settled it over her shoulders like a cape. The warmth was comforting, as was the faint, male scent of him. She pulled it closer. "Thank you."

For a moment, he held her gaze, then let it drift to her lips. Instinctively, she moistened them, tilting her head as he lowered his, brushing softly across her mouth.

"Would ye like to stroll in the garden?"

Reality returned with a jolt. *The garden.* Drat it all. Devon was in there. As much as she wanted to have the privacy—and definitely more kissing—she couldn't take the chance of Ian finding his brother.

"I... It is a little chilly out here. Perhaps we should go in."

Ian narrowed his eyes slightly, then he straightened. "As ye wish, my lady."

Emily cringed at his formal address, all too aware that he'd taken her suggestion as a personal rejection. But what else could she do?

Ian was silent as they walked around to the front of the castle and mounted the steps to go in. He stopped once they were inside the Great Hall and bowed slightly. "If ye'll nae be needing my coat...?"

"Oh! Of course." Since he didn't attempt to remove it from her, she slipped it off, realizing as she did so that Glenda was glaring at them from not far away. Good heavens! The girl probably thought that they... Emily felt herself blush as she finished the thought herself. It would have been nice if it had happened. Very nice. But it hadn't. Reluctantly, she handed Ian his coat. He slipped it on just as the musicians started an allemande. On impulse, she laid her hand on his arm.

"Will you dance with me?"

He eyed her warily, probably wondering what kind of a game she was playing. And it was a game of sorts, but not one in which she made up the rules—she would much rather have been out in the garden folly at the moment—but she couldn't let Ian walk away thinking she had purposely turned him down. She smiled, wishing she were more of a natural flirt like Lorelei.

It still must have had an effect because, after a bit of hesitation, he smiled back. "Aye, if ye like."

"I do. They are playing an allemande."

They joined the others on the floor, forming two lines of couples, and extended their paired hands forward as they paraded the length of the Great Hall and back with a series of three steps and a pause. What Emily liked about this dance was that their hands were together throughout.

When the music finally stopped, Ian didn't release her hands immediately. Instead, he studied her. "Do ye ken what ye do to me, lass?"

Warmth flowed through her that had nothing to do with the exertion from the dance. This was when she should flirt or act coy, but she had never liked such silliness. "I think I do." When his eyes widened slightly, heat seeped into her face, but she went on. "You affect me, too." They were standing at the far end of the hall near a door and she glanced at it. "Where does that lead?"

"I suspect into a hallway to the kitchens."

She gave him a tentative smile. "Would it give us a moment of privacy?"

He grinned. "It might. Would ye—"

"Ah! There ye are!"

Emily turned, not particularly surprised to see Glenda

hurrying toward them. The girl had watched them rather sullenly from the sidelines as they danced. Hopefully, she hadn't heard what had just been said.

"What is it?" Ian asked, a trace of annoyance in his voice.

She didn't even spare Emily a look. "Ye must come quick. Neal has accused Devon of trifling with his sister and they are about to fight!"

Ian swore under his breath, then gave Emily an apologetic look as he turned away. "We will finish this conversation later."

Emily silently said a few choice words as he left. Of all the moments to be interrupted. And her trying to protect Devon had been for naught? She looked after Ian for a moment, then followed.

The altercation had moved into the bailey. By the time she got there, Neal and his father were standing beside Margaret who, somehow, looked miraculously well put-together, given the state of her undress when Emily had last glimpsed her. Even her hair was in place… Emily let her gaze slip to Devon. Where had he acquired the skills to be adept at serving as a lady's maid? Perhaps she didn't want to know.

At the moment, his fists were balled and he'd assumed a fighter's stance, even though Ian, Carr, and Rory were all trying to restrain him. He shook them all off and glared at Neal.

"Ye are calling your sister a liar?"

"I am calling ye one!" Neal growled. "I'll nae have a MacGregor sniffing around my sister's skirts."

Margaret frowned. "I told ye, Devon did nothing improper."

Emily looked down quickly to conceal her surprise. Nothing improper? A woman with her bodice down around her waist, stays undone, and a man with his shirt already out? *That* wasn't considered improper?

"I doona believe ye."

His sister punched his arm. "All we did was go for a wee walk."

Emily looked up at that, only to find Devon watching her. There was nothing apologetic in his look nor was it pleading. He simply stared, almost as if defying her to say something about what she had seen. Then he looked away.

Neal rubbed his arm. "Ye were in the garden with him nae an hour ago, weren't ye?"

His father stepped forward. "By God, if ye took liberties with my daughter, I'll see ye—"

"If I may?" Emily interjected. She looked around the group, pasting on what she hoped was a reassuring smile. Whatever had transpired between Devon and Margaret, the girl certainly wasn't crying foul which, in Emily's mind, put the matter to rest. "I happened to be taking the air in the garden earlier, about that time actually, and no one was up and about." It wasn't a *total* lie…the two hadn't been *standing*.

"There ye have it then," Ian said. "Surely ye will take the word of Lady Woodhaven?"

Neal made a disgruntled sound while his father sighed. "For now."

Carr nodded. "Then I suggest we go back inside before Argyll decides we are all still barbarians."

That seemed to break the tension. As they made their way toward the entrance, Devon swung his gaze back at her, eyes narrowing slightly, before he turned around to join his brothers.

…

Ian waited a good fifteen minutes until the Camerons showed no more inclination to escalate things, then he signaled to his brothers that they needed to talk. He left through the very door that he and Emily had been going to use to seek some "privacy," only *that* privacy was meant—he hoped—to have had a satisfying lustful ending. How ironic that the subject for *this* discussion was also lust.

Carr appeared a moment later, accompanied by Devon who wasn't looking quite as angry as Ian thought he should.

"Where's Rory?"

"He wanted to wait a minute to make sure nae one followed us."

"Good point." Although Ian didn't want to stand around in the hall where servants were sure to be coming through, he also wanted to make sure their temporary departure was not noticed. It felt like minutes passed before Rory finally entered the hallway.

"This way," Ian said. "If I remember, there is an office of sorts off the kitchen that the housekeeper uses." Luckily, the door was unlocked. He motioned them through, checking to make sure no servants had seen them. Then he closed the door, leaned against it, and looked at Devon.

"What?" his brother asked.

Ian was holding on to his temper by a thread. "Doona play me for a fool. What transpired between ye and the Cameron lass?"

"Ye heard Margaret. Nothing improper, she said."

"I ken what I heard *her* say. I also ken that *ye* said nothing."

"There was nae need." Devon shrugged. "If her kin willna believe her, why should they believe me?"

"*Her* kin is nae here," Carr pointed out. "*Your* kin is. Answer Ian's question."

A corner of his mouth quirked. "Why, brother, ye ken 'tis nae honorable to kiss and tell."

"'Tis nae the time for jest, *brother*," Carr replied. "Did ye take advantage of the lass?"

"Nae." He grew defiant. "I took only what Margaret freely offered."

"*Jesu*!" Rory exploded. "Are ye a complete eejit?"

Devon drew his brows together. "Only a fool would turn down what she asked me to do—"

"Lucifer's horns!" Somehow Ian managed to keep his voice down. "If ye got her with child, ye will have to—"

"We did nae go that far." Devon looked at each of his brothers. "Ye have my word on that."

"Still. If ye had been caught in a compromising position, ye would have had to marry the lass," Carr said.

"And we would have had *Camerons* for kin," Rory added. "Ye want that arse of her brother to be a part of us?"

"That is nae going to happen," Devon shot back. "I told ye, there will be nae bairn."

"Thank God for that," Ian replied. "And thank God nae one saw ye in the garden." "Aye." Carr nodded. "Had there been a witness, ye would be in deep trouble."

Devon was quiet for a moment. "I suppose I would."

It wasn't like his brother to acquiesce so easily, but they'd already been gone long enough. "We'd best get back to the festivities." He gave Devon a warning look. "I hope ye learned yer lesson."

To which his brother didn't reply.

• • •

Emily watched as Ian disappeared through the door at the far end of the hall, followed by two of his brothers. In another minute, Rory left as well. She suspected they were going to give Devon a stern dressing down, but at least he didn't need to admit to more than he wanted to. Guilt niggled at her for telling a lie, but the consequences of his behavior would have had far more serious repercussions if she had admitted the truth. Besides, if she hadn't been so naïve to think an animal had been hurt in the folly, she wouldn't have stumbled across the tryst in the first place. Neither Devon nor Margaret were innocents, obviously, but it truly was not her business.

"What has you so contemplative, my dear Lady Woodhaven?"

She turned abruptly to see Lord Bute standing a few feet away. She'd been so wrapped in thought that she hadn't heard or seen him approach. Not that she could tell him what she had been thinking about.

"I must apologize, Lord Bute. I fear I was simply woolgathering." She dipped a quick curtsy. "How good of you to attend the ball."

He made a small bow. "Well, one does not often refuse a duke's invitation."

Emily smiled at him. "I suspect, as a former prime minister, you would be allowed."

He smiled back. "I always enjoyed your quick repartee, my lady."

She gave him a droll look. "You may be the only one, my lord."

"Certainly not. I daresay many enjoyed your wit."

"Other than Albert, of course."

"Then he was more the buffoon than I thought him," Lord Bute said. "And forgive me for being blunt."

Emily shook her head. "I prefer that you be honest, even if it is blunt."

He gave her a thoughtful look, all trace of lightheartedness gone. "Actually, that is the reason I am here. I wanted to talk to you about the bill my son is going to propose."

"Do you mean about reinstating the MacGregor name?" Emily hoped her tone sounded casual. "I think that is long overdue."

He studied her. "Do you?"

"Of course. It is rather ridiculous for an entire clan to be proscribed for events that began during Mary, Queen of Scots' reign."

"Well, there have been other incidents over time," he answered. "For example, Rob Roy did not exactly add accolades to the family name."

"I suppose not," she acknowledged, "but I am learning that cattle-reiving is somewhat of a Highland tradition."

"It is, at that." He smiled and then he sobered. "But more importantly, you need to know how reinstating the MacGregors to their full status may affect you. Specifically, the deed to your holdings."

Emily frowned. "King George issued the decree for that deed himself."

"And I am sure he meant for you to keep it." He hesitated. "But there is the chance that once the MacGregors are restored, they will ask for the deed to be revoked."

She frowned. "Do you mean…all of it? The castle and the lands?"

"I do not know that for certain, but it is a possibility that you should be aware of." He reached over to pat her hand. "I wanted you to know."

She stared after the earl in stunned silence as he left her side. She would lose everything. Her sisters would not have a Season next spring. They wouldn't even have a home if she lost Strae Castle. Surely, Ian wouldn't do that. Then the reality of the situation struck with the force of a tidal wave.

It might not be Ian's decision. He would be the official head of the clan once more and he would have to do what was best for the clan. She understood that.

But what was best for Clan MacGregor probably didn't include three Sassenachs.

Chapter Twenty-Three

Dawn was breaking by the time they returned home from the ball. Emily burrowed her head into comforting warmth that seemed to surround her, only to be disturbed from a wonderful dream of Ian, when the carriage finally rolled into the bailey of Strae Castle and came to a stop. Slowly, she opened her eyes. Then she bolted upright, jarred into full awaking.

She hadn't been dreaming. Lulled by the steady clopping of horses' hooves and the rhythmical sway of the carriage, she remembered starting to fall asleep. Somehow, she'd ended up in Ian's arms, her head on his shoulder, snuggled against him. Fiona and Glenda sat across from them.

Unlike a ball in London where the revelers *danced* until dawn, their late—or early—arrival home was because they'd had to travel miles that night. Some of the more distant clans, like the Camerons, had brought tents, but Ian said they had enough clansmen with them to not worry about villains attacking.

"Did ye sleep well?" he asked as though it were the most

natural thing in the world for her to have fallen asleep with him.

Emily swiped at her hair, feeling flustered. Fiona looked amused, but the sour look on Glenda's face told a different story.

"I apologize—"

"Doona." Ian grinned at her. "I am nae complaining."

That drew a deep frown from Glenda, and Emily didn't know what to say. The girl was obviously infatuated with Ian, although trying to explain that to someone but four and ten wasn't going to have any effect. The Lord knew she'd tried often enough with Lorelei. So instead, she changed the subject.

"I hope Alasdair made it back without having his ears blistered by my sisters."

"Well," Ian said, "he had the option of riding atop with the coachman, although I suspect he dinna take it."

Emily gave him a quizzical glance. "Why not? The air was not chilly outside and the company probably much better. I suspect Juliana's temper hadn't cooled off much nor Lorelei's wailing over having to miss the ball."

"Knowing Alasdair, he agreed with Juliana—Neal Cameron is an arse—and he more than likely promised Lorelei he would dance with her when they got home."

"That would be a thoughtful gesture, but not *quite* the same as actually attending the ball," Emily said.

"My brother can be quite persuasive when he puts his mind to it." Ian grinned again. "And I suspect he wouldna complain about having the lass to himself. He fancies her."

"Then he's a fool," Fiona said. "Lorelei canna wait to get to London next spring for her Season."

"Besides, he should marry a Scottish lass," Glenda said, looking at Emily with narrowed eyes, before smiling brightly at Ian. "All the MacGregors should."

He frowned, but before he could speak, Fiona intervened. "'Tis a good thing Alasdair is leaving for Ireland soon."

"Oh?" Emily thought it best to steer away from both Glenda's sly remark and the topic of marriage. "How long will he be gone?"

"It could be months," Ian replied. "Many of our clan moved to Ireland when the proscriptions were nae lifted after Culloden, so MacGregors are scattered throughout the land."

"He is going to contact all of them?"

"He will try." Ian hesitated. "With Lord Mount Stuart proposing the bill in Parliament next month, Alasdair needs to let them know they will be free to return."

"As *MacGregors*," Glenda said.

"I see." And Emily also heard what hadn't been said. Once they returned, they would want their lands back. *Her* lands.

Or maybe not hers for long.

• • •

Ian was hoping to catch a few winks before tackling the day, but as soon as he entered the castle, he saw his uncles waiting for him, along with his brothers. They'd all gotten home hours ago, since they'd brought their horses and weren't slowed down with a carriage. They'd probably had some *sleep.*

From the serious expressions on all their faces, any thought of sleep vanished, along with his musings of holding Emily again. The scent from her hair lingered on his clothing and he had a very vivid recollection of how perfectly she had fit against him while she slept…although *sleeping* wasn't what his cock wanted to do at all. With a sigh, he pushed those lusty thoughts aside.

"What is wrong now?"

"The library," Donovan said as he turned down the hall.

"We need privacy."

Ian doubted this matter was about Devon. First of all, his brother didn't look angry or even irritated. Secondly, he doubted either of his uncles cared that much if Devon had taken advantage of the lass, as long as he hadn't gotten caught.

He closed the door behind him. "Well?"

"Ye should ken that while ye were having your talk with Devon, the Sassenach was in deep conversation with Lord Bute," Donovan said.

So his uncles did know about Devon. Not that it mattered now. "What do ye mean?"

"They were all English-like," Broderick said. "She curtsied and he bowed. Then they laughed and talked as though they were friends—"

"Lady Woodhaven said they'd met before," Ian interrupted.

"—good friends. *Verra* good," Broderick continued.

"And when they finished talking, the earl took her hand and nodded," Donovan added.

"Like they had come to some kind of agreement," Broderick said.

Ian frowned. "Agreement? Did ye hear it?"

"Nae, I was too far away and it was too noisy."

"Then how do ye ken it wasna simply a conversation?"

Rory snorted. "About the weather mayhap?"

Ian ignored his sarcasm. "I doona ken that, but Lady Woodhaven was married to an earl and Lord Bute is also an earl. Aristocrats travel in the same circles so 'tis nae unusual for them to talk."

"Aye, but about *what*?"

"Rory does have a point," Carr said. "The fact that both the Duke of Argyll and the former Prime Minister came to Kilchurn Castle for a harvest ball seems odd."

"Unless they wanted to conspire with Henry about

keeping us proscribed and nae getting our lands back," Rory answered. "Ye remember Devon and I followed the dragoons. They were delivering a message from Henry to Inveraray and then some of them rode south, mayhap to Bute."

"We doona ken for sure."

"It does make sense, though," Alasdair said. "Gavin Campbell invites Lady Woodhaven and her sisters to the ball and we are included only because it would look strange if we were nae. She accepts. Henry sends word to his brother and Lord Bute that she will be attending. What better way to meet and mayhap get her opinion of us?"

"Aye, her opinion could go a long way in helping Bute decide whether to support the bill or nae," Carr replied. "Unfortunately, it stands to reason that she will want to be assured of her deed remaining valid, so her opinion might be negative."

Ian frowned. "Em…Lady Woodhaven has told all of us she hopes we get our name restored."

"Our name, aye, but the land deed is a different thing."

He couldn't argue with that, knowing why it was so important to her. It was equally important to them. Ian grimaced, feeling like he was about to be drawn and quartered. He was the chosen leader of the MacGregors, even if it wasn't lawfully recognized, and he was honor bound to do the right thing for his people. If he defended Emily, he would be betraying his clan, but if she lost everything, *she* would feel betrayed and he would lose her. Like a lightning bolt, the thought struck him that he had begun to care for her.

"Are ye listening?" Alasdair asked.

Somehow he managed to pull himself together. "Aye. Ye were speaking about…about…"

"What Lady Woodhaven's real opinion of us might be."

There was resignation in his brother's tone, although he wasn't sure whether that was from his lack of attention or that there might be real cause for concern. Ian looked at each of his brothers and uncles. "Ye have never heard her say a bad word about any of us MacGregors."

"Nae to our faces, but that doesna mean she willna try to sway Bute," Rory said.

"I think ye all do her a disservice. Em…Lady Woodhaven wants to be accepted by us." Ian fully expected Devon to explode at that, but his brother remained strangely silent. It was Broderick who scoffed.

"She is a Sassenach."

"She canna help where she was born."

"When have the English ever regarded Scots as equals?" he asked. "Have ye forgotten Culloden already?"

"I have nae forgotten. But remember, we were allowed to remain here because we dinna take up arms against the Crown."

"Only because Bonnie Prince Charlie's strategy to restore the throne to a Stuart was nae well-planned and the young buck wouldna listen to his elders' reason," Donovan said.

Rory nodded. "Aye. The MacGregors were nae so easily convinced to run off half-cocked."

"Likely because our survival depended on our wits," his uncle said.

"Be that as it may," Ian interjected, "the English have nae cause to distrust us now or to uphold the ban."

"The question is, can we trust *them*?" Carr looked thoughtful. "Both our uncles have a point. The Campbells could have as much to lose as Lady Woodhaven if Parliament sees fit to restore the lands awarded to them during Queen Mary's reign."

"That is nae likely to happen, given the amount of time gone by."

"Still, it might well be the reason Gavin heads to Cawdor,"

Alasdair answered.

Ian gave him a puzzled look. "What do ye mean?"

"I overheard Gavin complaining that he was being sent to Cawdor to rally the Campbells there. Mayhap Argyll is going to fight the bill, even if Bute doesna."

In spite of that dire possibility, Ian felt a sense of relief that Gavin would not be around for a while. He hadn't much liked seeing the man fawn over Emily and dance with her. He'd had no doubt the cur would come calling. At least, that would be postponed for now. The man's absence would give Ian much-needed time to sort things out in his own mind to decide what to do about his newfound feelings.

And, more importantly, how to approach Emily about them.

"All we can do is wait," he said, but he wasn't sure he was referring to the Campbells or to himself.

• • •

Everyone seated at the round table for dinner seemed tired, if not exhausted, much of which could be attributed to the wee hours of the morning when they'd returned from Kilchurn. While Fiona and Glenda had trundled off to bed shortly after coming home, Emily had had to deal with her sisters.

Juliana had still been furious, not at having wine spilled, but by Neal Cameron's boorish behavior and assumption that she would *want* to marry him. She would rather take vows and the veil, she had informed Emily with enough ice in her tone to freeze the River Clyde, before that happened.

Emily feared that Lorelei, on the other hand, might set fire to the solar with her temper running hot. Not only had her gown been ruined—by her own hand, although Emily didn't point that out—but she had missed the ball. Missed the first social event to take place since their arrival *and* missed the opportunity to practice her flirting skills with a number of young men that she'd noticed. How was she ever going to attract a worthy husband during London's Season if she didn't practice?

Emily thought it prudent not to bring up the conversation she'd had with Lord Bute… That if they lost their deed, there might not *be* a Season for Lorelei, and the possibility of taking the veil might actually become an option. There was no use in upsetting her sisters even more.

Still, she pitied Alasdair having to endure the carriage ride home. She glanced at him now. He seemed unaffected and was actually smiling at Lorelei. Perhaps he had joined the coachman on the bench for the ride home, after all.

She turned her attention to the conversation Ian was having with his uncles.

"We are going to have to begin cutting the peat before the rains start," he was saying. "We have little of last year's supply left."

"Aye," Donovan answered. "The near side by Gwendolyn's cottage should be dry enough."

"Do the barley sheaves not have to be brought in before the rains start as well?" Emily asked.

Ian nodded. "We will check on them tomorrow and then send most of the men out to start bringing them in."

"It seems to be a bigger crop this year than what was reported last year." The uncles gave her sharp looks while Ian busied himself cutting his meat. "At least, that is what I have been able to determine by looking at the records you have kept." She looked at the men who were all suddenly silent. "But I may be wrong."

Ian finally spoke. "Ye are nae wrong. This year has been verra good."

"Excellent!" Emily replied. "Especially since we have a contract with White's for the whisky." She turned to the uncles. "And there is enough storage at the distillery for this year's crop?"

"Aye," Donovan said. "We keep the grain in dry storage bins and take out only enough that will fill the floor to begin malting."

"I do not think I saw the storage bins when I toured the facility."

"That is because they are midway between the fields and the distillery." Broderick paused. "Mayhap ye would like to tour those, too?"

She looked at him, surprised at the suggestion. He didn't look like he was being sarcastic. And his tone was even. He lifted an eyebrow questioningly and she nodded. Perhaps he and his brother were finally beginning to accept that she had a true interest in learning the whisky business. "I would like that."

"Ye can come over tomorrow then."

Ian frowned. "We have got to check out the peat bog tomorrow."

"And Donovan and I have to check the barley," Broderick answered. "I am sure Lady Woodhaven will be safe riding over by herself in broad daylight."

"Of course I will," Emily responded. "It is only a mile or two. Besides, Muirne could use a run. I have not had a chance to ride her in several days."

"Then that is settled," Broderick answered. "We will expect ye in the morning."

Devon glanced at his uncle and then looked at her. For just a brief moment, she thought he was going to say something, but then he turned away. She'd not had a chance to speak to him since the incident at Kilchurn, so she had no way of knowing whether he'd be a bit more receptive to her now. She sighed inwardly. At least, he no longer looked hostile or angry.

"I still doona like ye being on the road alone," Ian said. "There will be other clans traveling home."

Juliana narrowed her eyes. "Do you think Camerons may be about?"

"Nae," Ian replied. "They live to the north of here."

"Doona fash," Rory said. "Once Neal sobers up, he'll nae even consider taking a Sassenach to wife."

Juliana turned her fury on him. "Not that it is your business, but who told you?"

He grinned. "Word spread like floodwater from the Clyde. *Everyone* kens."

Emily was pretty sure he said the last simply to goad Juliana, which wasn't very wise, given her frame of mind. And he might just deserve the tongue-lashing he would get, but unfortunately, Glenda chose that moment to lend her support to him.

"'Tis just what I said last night." She slanted a glance at Ian before looking quickly away. "Nae self-respecting Scot would marry a Sassenach."

"I think you have that backward," Juliana retorted.

"*Juliana.*" Emily used the tone she reserved for the direst of times. This certainly was one of them. Thankfully, her sister recognized it. She stabbed a potato with her fork with enough force that her simmering wrath was clear.

Ian gave his ward a severe look. "Ye are excused, Glenda."

The girl looked mulish, started to open her mouth, then shut it. She shoved her chair back, glared at Emily, and stomped from the room.

Ian frowned. "I am sorry—"

"It is all right," Emily said. "I think everyone is tired. Shall we just eat?"

He looked like he wanted to argue the point but finally nodded. Emily breathed a sigh of relief. A crisis had been averted. At least for now.

• • •

Emily deliberately lolled in bed the next morning, not that it was hard to do after not getting much sleep the night before, but more importantly, she wanted to wait until Ian and his brothers had left for the peat bog before she went downstairs. She had a feeling he'd find a way to keep her from going to the distillery if he saw her.

The breakfast room was empty when she got there. Her sisters were probably still in bed recuperating, which was just as well, since she didn't feel like listening to any more complaints. She had hoped Fiona would be about and might want to ride over to the distillery with her—her company would at least please Ian—but she was nowhere around. Not surprising, since it was the middle of the morning. Fiona often helped Old Gwendolyn deliver her potions and tinctures to those who were ill.

Emily helped herself to some cheese and bread that were still on the sideboard, took an apple to give to Muirne, and headed to the stables. The only person she saw was a young lad about twelve who was mucking out a stall.

"Where is Jamie?" she asked him.

"Some of our mares got out of the far pasture. Master and the other grooms went to catch them," he answered. "Can I do something for ye?"

"Yes, please. Would you saddle Muirne for me?"

"Right away." The boy grinned and scampered off. A few minutes later he led the filly out. "Here she is."

Emily fed her the apple, which she happily crunched, then led her to the mounting block. As she swung her leg over the saddle to ride astride, she wondered if she'd ever prefer a sidesaddle again. The breeches Fiona had lent her when she first arrived were so practical. She laughed aloud, imagining what the ladies of the *ton* would say if they saw her riding astride in Hyde Park. No doubt there would be a number of cases of the vapors for sure. But she wasn't in London and this wasn't England.

And Scots, she had learned, were much more pragmatic and practical.

She pondered that as she turned Muirne toward the distillery. Although the ball at Kilchurn had overtones of English Society, since the Duke of Argyll and Lord Bute both spent much of their time in London, the stalwart nature of Scots had also been evident. The women didn't care if their hair came down or their ankles showed while dancing. They simply enjoyed the country reels to a degree that no English lady would allow herself to engage in. The men were robust, hearty, and forthright. Emily winced a little. Perhaps a bit too forthright, given the Cameron debacle. No one minced words. Emily found that rather refreshing, even if it made her more aware that she was still looked on as an outsider. But the attacks seemed to have stopped, so perhaps Ian had made clear that as laird, albeit an outlawed one, she was under his protection.

His *protection*. Where once she would have scoffed—after all, her husband's protection had been anything but—except now the idea gave her a warm feeling inside. It made her feel cherished. She knew that was probably a silly notion, since Ian had a responsibility to protect all under his roof and had said as much. Still, she wondered if maybe he did care for her. At least, a little. They'd shared a wonderful kiss in the folly and had almost had another opportunity to do it again. She wasn't so naïve as to expect a man to declare undying love because of a kiss, but if it had affected him even half as much as it had her, that said something. She just wasn't sure what.

Emily shook her head to clear it. She was not some giddy, wide-eyed debutante. There was no sense letting herself imagine all sorts of scenarios that probably wouldn't come to pass. She turned her attention back to the road.

Passing by Gwendolyn's cottage, she noted the door closed and there was no sign of the wolfhound, so she had probably been right that Fiona was making rounds with the healer.

She reined in the filly, pausing to look over the landscape. The peat bog was not far away. She could see men in the distance, bending to their work, and wondered how far they would be able to go before they confronted an oozing mess. For a moment, she considered riding over to watch Ian work, but her presence would only remind him she was riding alone. Reluctantly, she turned Muirne in the other direction.

The road stretched out ahead of her, flat and smooth. Beneath her, she could feel the filly's anticipation of a good run. Emily laughed and leaned over the horse's neck, whispering in her ear.

"Let's go!"

Without breaking stride, the filly launched into a rocking-chair canter and then faster as Emily urged her on. The wind whipped the mane in her face and her hairpins fell out, letting her hair fly freely behind her. Powerful muscles bunched under her, the steady rat-tat-tat of hooves filling the air as the horse snorted and tossed her head. Emily had never felt so free.

And then she felt the saddle slip. Emily grabbed for the mane, which loosened her hold on the reins, allowing Muirne to stretch into a full-out gallop. As she did, Emily felt herself go airborne.

For a moment she floated in the air before she landed hard and the world went black.

Chapter Twenty-Four

Ian hated working in the bog. It was messy, stinking, backbreaking work, but he never asked his men to do something he wouldn't do himself. Today had been especially bad because the muck wasn't quite dry enough and had sucked at his boots with every shovelful unturned.

Now he perched on the edge of the horse trough in the bailey and pulled off his mud-laden boots. Maggie would skin him alive if he even attempted to track through the kitchen in them. He was tempted to roll back and drop himself into the trough to wash the dirt off, too, but the horses wouldn't appreciate it. Besides, the temptation of a *hot* bath was more than enough incentive to pick himself up.

He took the servants' stairs up to his chamber, knowing Hamish would have seen him in the yard and sent some lads up with hot water. Since it was only the middle of the afternoon—he'd finally yielded to the bog—he allowed himself to linger in the copper tub until the water turned cool. Besides being practically a sinful luxury, it gave him some quiet time to reflect on Emily.

He could still feel how perfectly she fit against his side as she'd fallen asleep in the carriage. How warm and soft she'd been and the delicate scent from her hair. How she'd burrowed her head into his shoulder with a satisfied moan… A moan he'd like very, very much to make her do while she was awake and lying beneath him in the throes of passion.

And he had no doubt Emily Woodhaven was a passionate woman. She might appear quiet and calm and quite sensible, but the kiss they'd shared—the one that she'd asked to prolong after Devon had interrupted them, said otherwise. So did her bold invitation to go into the darkened hallway at Kilchurn. If only Devon had not been called out… Ian sighed. His brother did turn up at the most inconvenient times.

Stepping out of the now cold tub, he dried off quickly, donned some clean clothes, and went down to the Great Hall. While it was still too early for the evening meal, the workers were enjoying well-earned kegs of ale. Many were already refilling empty tankards as he entered. None of the women were in sight, but he saw Carr near the dais and walked over to him.

"Did Alasdair get off all right?"

His brother nodded. "Hamish said he left for Glasgow shortly after we went to the bog."

"If he catches the tide right, he'll be in Ireland tomorrow then." Ian looked around the room. "'Twill be a pity he willna be here when Lord Mount Stuart presents the bill."

"Ye are that sure it will pass?"

"It has to."

Carr raised a brow. "Have MacGregors nae been saying that for the past two hundred years?"

"Aye," Ian said, "but this time we have a former prime minister to lend his support to it."

"Ye have that much faith in him?" Carr asked. "Did he tell ye so?"

"He seemed to be most favorable when I spoke to him," Ian replied.

"Favorable is nae a definite."

"True, but Argyll was with him when we spoke." Ian grinned. "But 'twas Emily who told me about their conversation. He will support us."

"So the countess is on our side then?"

"Aye." Ian paused. When Emily had told him that Lord Bute would back the restoration, she had sounded a bit constrained, but then she'd smiled and said he had nothing to worry about. "I trust her."

"I do, too, although I canna speak for our brothers," Carr replied.

Ian looked around the hall again. "Where are they, by the way?"

"Rory heard that some of the mares had gotten out of the pasture this morning so he went to check with Jamie." Carr shrugged. "I doona ken where Devon went."

"*Hmmm.* I wonder where the women are?" He'd no more than finished the sentence when he saw Fiona enter with Lorelei and Juliana. He frowned when he didn't see Emily and then the hair on his nape began to rise as all three of them hurried over to him.

"Where is Emily?" he asked as soon as they reached him.

"We doona ken," Fiona said, a little breathless like she'd been running. "I thought she was still at the distillery—"

"But her horse just came back," Juliana cut in. "Without her."

"*What*?" Ian didn't wait for an answer and raced down the length of the hall, leaving his men to stare at him, some of them with tankards half raised. He paid no heed to their calls. Carr could handle it.

He nearly collided with Devon coming up the stairs to the front door. In his arms, Emily hung limply.

"I found her on the road to the distillery," he said, handing her over.

Ian cradled her, making sure her head didn't loll. Thank God she was breathing. He had a horrible feeling of déjà vu. "Fetch the physician and Gwendolyn," he ordered as he strode swiftly to her chamber, her sisters and Fiona on his heels.

He kicked open the door and went to lay Emily on her bed—just like last time. Maggie bustled in behind him and he found himself shoved out the door—*just like the last time*—while the women took over.

Only this time, as he waited, something was different. This time he realized that Emily was the most important thing in his life. More important than reclaiming Strae Castle—or even their land—if she weren't here to share it. Without her, what else mattered?

He needed to find out who was trying to kill her before they succeeded.

He stared at the door, then at the empty hallway, cursing the time it took to wait before he could see her. When Devon returned, he'd find out what had happened. It seemed for once Devon had turned up at a convenient time.

Ian paused. Or had he? Why had he been on that road?

Ian closed the door to the library several hours later and sighed. It seemed he was spending more time in this room than in his own bedchamber lately. Which might be just as well—if it weren't for the *reason* he was in here—because he was harboring more and more lustful thoughts about Emily joining him in his bed, along with all the things they could do besides sleep.

He looked at his assembled brothers, sister, and uncles.

Their expressions, with the exception of Fiona, were resigned. They all knew why they had been summoned to this room. Again.

"The physician did say she was going to be all right," Carr said.

"And Old Gwendolyn is staying with her this time," Fiona added.

"I ken that." He studied each of the men. "But these attacks need to stop."

"We doona ken this…accident…was an attack," Broderick said. "Jamie said the girth strap was frayed and caused the saddle to slip."

Ian grimaced. Once Emily regained consciousness, she'd told them she felt it loosen before she fell. He'd gone straight to the stables to look at the saddle himself. The leather strap that pulled the cinch tight was intact, but the cloth part that went under the filly's belly had torn apart. It didn't look like it had been cut because, as his uncle said, the threads were frayed and the girth looked like it had worn through. He asked Jamie why he hadn't inspected Muirne's saddle first and found out he'd been out rounding up the mares that had gotten loose. A stable lad had actually saddled the horse. When he'd turned his questions on him, the lad trembled so much Ian feared he'd soak his breeches.

"I've nae proof, but it seems too much of a coincidence." He held up his hand and began ticking each finger. "First, there was a loose board on the steps that caused her to fall and could have killed her—"

"Didna ye say she got the sheets tangled?" Donovan asked. "The board could have come loose when she pulled at the sheets."

"I didna find any nails on the floor."

"They could have gotten caught in the sheets."

"They were nae found." He continued. "Second, alcohol

was put in the tea and made her fall asleep when she should have been kept awake—"

"Which is why Gwendolyn is with her now," Carr said.

"Aye." Ian was taking no chances this time.

"And whoever put it in there might have meant well." Rory glanced around. "Have we nae all added a dram to tea now and then?"

"Mayhap, but what about the wine? Someone put hemlock in it."

There was silence after that remark.

"Poison is a woman's weapon. Glenda might have done it." Broderick shrugged when everyone looked at him. "We all ken she has taken a liking to Ian."

"Something I have tried to discourage," Ian replied.

Broderick studied him for a moment. "Women doona always ken what's best for them, do they? They doona listen—"

"Glenda might be willful, but to attempt murder?" Ian frowned. "I canna believe she would do such a thing."

"I canna, either," Fiona said.

"Even if Glenda did such a foolish thing, she willna have the chance to do it again," Carr said. "She kens we all eat off the same platters and drink from the same flagons as she does."

"So she tries something else then."

"Ye think she had something to do with what just happened?" Carr asked. "I doona think Glenda even kens how to saddle a horse. She doesna like them."

"I agree," Fiona said. "We should just be thankful Devon found Emily when he did."

"Aye. 'Tis." Ian turned his attention to his brother and took care to keep his tone casual. "How did ye happen to be on that road?"

Devon stared at him, his eyes growing dark. "Are ye

accusing me of something?"

"Nae." Ian closed his eyes briefly, wishing his brother wasn't so quick to anger. "I am just asking a question."

A muscle twitched in Devon's jaw. "Since we couldna work in the bog any longer, I decided to ride over to the distillery."

"Why?" Broderick asked.

"To check with ye on the barley." He lifted one shoulder in a half shrug. "Mayhap I thought to make amends with Lady Woodhaven and escort her home if she were still there."

Complete silence met that remark. Devon looked around, his eyes narrowing as he shoved back his chair so hard it fell over. "But why should any of ye believe me? Ye probably think I did something to the saddle and wanted to make sure my plan had worked."

"Devon…" Fiona started to say, but it was no use.

Their brother had already left, slamming the door behind him.

• • •

Emily looked up at the sound of a rap on her door, but before she could call to enter, it opened and Ian poked his head around.

"Are ye feeling well enough for a visit?"

"Of course!" Emily pushed herself a little higher against the headboard. "It seems I find myself near helpless once again."

"Not helpless. More like a victim."

"Again," she said softly.

"Aye." He turned to Gwendolyn. "Ye may go. I will make sure the lady stays awake."

Emily wasn't sure, but she thought there might be a glint of mirth in the healer's eyes.

She nodded as she gathered her basket and shawl. "'Tis nae else to be done other than she needs rest."

The last was said in a more authoritative tone, as if she were warning him. He grinned at her. "Ye have my word."

Emily didn't know exactly what he meant by that, either, but in another moment the door closed and they were alone in her bedchamber. It suddenly seemed much smaller with his presence. He sat down on the edge of the bed, not touching her, but the room also became instantly warmer. Much warmer.

"Did someone sabotage the saddle?" she asked bluntly. It was something she had to know.

"I canna say. The girth was frayed, nae cut."

"It could have been worn then?"

"'Tis possible."

She studied him. "But you do not think it was an accident."

"If it had been worn so thin that it was a danger, Jamie would have replaced it." He was quiet for a moment. "The only people who were aware ye would be riding this morning were my…my kin."

His eyes were sorrowful and his mouth drawn as he uttered the words. Emily reached out to touch his cheek. "Do ye really think someone in your family capable of murdering me?"

Ian caught her hand and pressed a kiss to her fingertips. "I doona want to think that. Devon—"

"No." Emily shook her head. "I know your brother hates the English. He has good reason after what he went through. And I have been told that I look like Isobel—"

"Ye are nothing like her!"

"That is my point. Although Devon stays angry much of the time, I do not think him mad. He knows I am not like his stepmother. And," she added, "I do not think him capable of killing a woman."

"I hope ye are right."

"I think I am. Remember, there were servants in our dining room last night. Any one of them might have mentioned my intent to ride this morning." She smiled. "Servants, regardless if they are part of the clan, love to gossip. Sharing private information about what the *laird* and his family are up to moves them up a notch in the hierarchy, so to speak. Besides," she added, "everyone here knows I like to ride. If the girth strap was truly compromised, someone could have done it earlier and just waited for the next time I rode out."

"Ye seem to be taking this new *accident* verra well. Are ye nae afraid?"

"I have been thinking," Emily replied. "Lord Bute explained to me that when your name is restored—"

"It could be *if*."

"*When*," she said, "your name is restored, there is a real possibility that you will be able to reclaim your land, or some of it anyhow."

"If that happens, I will nae toss ye out." Ian's brow furrowed and then cleared. "Aye! I should have thought of it myself! If we marry, the problem is solved!"

"*What?*" Emily stared at him, not sure she'd heard correctly. "That is not a solution."

"Nae?" He looked puzzled. "Ye will be totally under my protection if ye are my wife. 'Tis settled."

"No."

He tilted his head to look at her as though she were some strange creature he'd never encountered and she supposed, maybe she was. There were probably a dozen women—certainly Breena—who would leap at the chance to marry Ian, for whatever reason, but she wasn't one of them.

He'd never understand how much she valued her freedom. She held the title to Castle Strae. How many women could own land in their own right? She would have enough *discretionary* income—her *own* income from additional profits at the distillery—that no man could tell her how to spend. She could give Lorelei her Season in London and Juliana, too, if she wanted it.

"No one would *dare* harm ye, if ye were my *wife*."

Emily chewed her lip. "I thank you for the offer, but I cannot accept." She'd married out of necessity once and she was not going to travel that road again. Certainly, Ian was nothing like her late husband. Ian would never hurt her, she instinctively knew that. And he would protect her. She knew that, too. But it wasn't enough. Her parents had loved each other and if she couldn't have that, she would not marry again. And he had said nothing about love. His proposal was simply a solution to a problem. She laid her hand on his arm. "Please understand. It is not that I do not desire you—"

"Ye desire me?"

"Yes..." She didn't get to finish the sentence because his lips were on hers.

Ian edged closer and gathered her to him. She sighed and relaxed in his embrace, her arms going around his neck as she parted her lips to allow him entrance. His tongue swept in, hot and firm, claiming her mouth, demanding she yield to him. His arms wrapped tight around her, crushing her breasts against him as he angled his head to better capture the kiss.

And then he pulled back, his hands sliding up her arms to push her back gently. "What am I thinking? Ye just had a hard knock on your head—"

"Which has not altered my thinking." She slid her fingers down his chest. "I do not want to stop."

He took a shuddering breath and laid his forehead against her. "Neither do I, lass, neither do I. But this is nae the time nor the place."

"But..." A knock at the door interrupted her argument.

Ian stood quickly as it opened and Maggie stuck her head around.

"Jamie is asking to talk to ye," she said to Ian.

"I will be right there." He turned to Emily and winked. "We will continue this…discussion…later."

She smiled as he left. "I look forward to it."

Chapter Twenty-Five

He'd just proposed marriage—for the first time in his life—and he'd been turned down. Ian was still smarting a bit over that when he joined his brothers, uncles, and the ladies the next morning to break their fasts. If *any* of his brothers found out, he'd be the butt of their jokes for months.

Emily was already seated at the round table, looking fully recovered from her fall. She glanced at him and he thought he saw a faint blush steal across her cheeks before she turned to speak to one of her sisters. Since none of the women were gawking at him, he assumed she hadn't told them about his proposal.

Not that he had given up on the idea. MacGregors hadn't survived as outlaws for nearly two centuries to simply accept rejections of any sort. And, damn it, Emily needed protection, whether she thought so or not. What Jamie had wanted to talk to him about yesterday was that the cinch on Muirne's saddle had been replaced with an old one from a pile of discards. Which meant someone had deliberately changed it. And someone may have opened the gate that let the mares out so Jamie and the experienced grooms would not be around to saddle the horse.

He tried not to let those worrisome thoughts show as he helped himself to eggs, ham, and potatoes from the sideboard and took a seat, then turned to Emily. "How are ye feeling this morning?"

"A bit sore from the fall," she answered, "but otherwise, I'm fine."

He wanted to say more but held his peace. All of the incidents could have been committed to scare Emily away rather than actually murder her, but he hated thinking one of his kin, or even another clan member, was responsible.

But that was wishful thinking. He looked around the group.

"What are the plans for today?"

"Donovan and I are bringing the last of the barley sheaves in," Broderick replied.

"We'll be cutting peat," Rory said, "if the bog's dry enough."

"It ought to be," Devon added, "since the sun was out most of yesterday."

"What about ye?" Carr asked.

"I'll be taking the wagon over to Taynuilt to get some supplies." Ian glanced at Fiona. "What will ye ladies be doing?"

His sister tucked her chin subtly in a semblance of a nod to acknowledge she understood his concern to stay near Emily. "We—all four of us—are going to Gwendolyn's cottage to help pack herbs. She's getting ready to take them around to the crofters, since cold weather will soon settle in."

"And Glenda?"

"I have nae seen her this morning, but I will ask."

Ian nodded. "'Twould be good if she went along."

Fiona's eyes widened fractionally, an indication that she

realized the girl might be a suspect. “Aye. It would.”

He finished his food while covertly watching the others. Nobody seemed to be upset that Emily had recovered from the “accident.” Devon didn’t even appear angry after yesterday’s outburst when he’d stomped from the room. But then, Emily seemed to be convinced Devon was not the culprit. With all his heart, Ian hoped she was right. That his volatile brother was not involved in any of this. But if not him, who?

He sighed as he stood to leave. When he returned home this evening, he would have a long talk with Carr and decide on how to proceed. At least everyone’s whereabouts were accounted for today, and Emily would be safe with Fiona at the cottage.

For now, it was all he could do.

• • •

It was late afternoon when Emily and her sisters returned with Fiona from the healer’s cottage. She’d spent an enjoyable day helping pack the herbs into little packages that would be used for various ailments and winter fevers for the folks who lived around the area.

Glenda had arrived shortly after they did, and Emily had been impressed by how much the girl knew about the various plants and concoctions. She briefly wondered if Glenda had actually put the hemlock into the wine, but the more Emily listened to the interaction of Old Gwendolyn with the younger girl, the more she realized that the healer was training her to perhaps take her place.

That assumption was validated when Gwendolyn announced Glenda would be accompanying her on her trip this time, stopping overnight at one crofter’s hut or another. They’d both set off on the healer’s horse with Cedric, the wolfhound, bounding beside them.

Ian's brothers and uncles had also returned to the castle, although there was at least two hours until sunset. Most of them were in the Great Hall, drinking ale. She met Broderick on the stairs as she made her way to the solar. He smiled quite genially as they passed and she smiled back, wondering if, perhaps, Ian had said something to his kin about their conversation after all.

When Emily entered the room, Lorelei was twirling a sprig of heather. She held it up to her nose.

"This would make a nice perfume."

"We use it in some of our soap-making, but I doona think anyone has ever thought to press the flowers into perfume." Fiona shrugged. "We are nae London Society here."

"Still." Lorelei looked at Emily. "Do you not think one of the shops on Bond Street would be interested in a new scent?"

"It would be a welcome relief," Juliana said. "Some of those French perfumes are terribly *flowery*."

Emily took the sprig from Lorelei and held it to her nose. The scent was light and not too sweet. "It might be worth looking into."

"You sold whisky to White's," Juliana said.

"Yes, but the whisky is already distilled and more is being made. We would have to set up a perfumery and start from scratch."

"At least the process would not take as long."

"That is true." Emily turned to Fiona. "Do you think Glenda might be interested in helping with this?"

"I doona ken, but we can ask when she returns."

Emily nodded. Perhaps this would be a way to involve Glenda and get to know her better. Sitting down, she picked up a gown she'd left in the solar that had a small tear in the skirt. She hated asking the servants to do mending for her, since they already had their own families to take care of, and the last thing she wanted anyone in the clan thinking was that she thought herself superior. Besides, there was enough light left to fix the small rend.

Thirty minutes later, she bit off the thread and smoothed the stitches she'd made. Although she was not an accomplished seamstress, she thought her work was quite acceptable. Standing, she stretched and yawned.

"I think I will take a short nap before the evening meal."

"Aye," Fiona answered absently, engrossed in a game of checkers with Lorelei. Juliana just waved a hand and didn't look up from the book she was reading.

Emily walked the short distance to her bedchamber and opened the door. The coals in the brazier had not yet been lit, leaving the room cool now that dusk was approaching. With a sigh, she took the oil lamp hanging from a sconce and turned the wick up to illuminate the room. Making her way to the tinderbox, she noticed a folded piece of paper propped up against it. She set the lamp down and picked it up.

I will secure a room at the inn in Taynuilt tonight. Will ye come? We will have the privacy we need. Ian

'Tis better if ye do not bring a horse, since it will raise questions. The bog was dry enough yesterday for ye to cut through and will save ye time.

Emily folded the note and laid it down, her hand trembling with excitement. They'd been interrupted last night. He had said this room was neither the time nor the place so he must have planned this and left the note this morning before he left. Her hand flew to her mouth. When had he expected her to find this? They'd spent most of the day at the cottage and she hadn't come to her room before going to the solar. Had he been expecting her earlier? Was he waiting for her now?

Thinking maybe she wouldn't come, since it was already near dark?

She hastily scribbled a note to Maggie that she wasn't feeling well and was taking to her bed and didn't wish to be disturbed. Then she hurried to the wardrobe and took out her sturdy walking boots. Ian was right that taking Muirne out this time of day would only create questions or, worse, one of the grooms would insist on coming along. He had said the bog was dry and his brothers had been working it most of the day. Grabbing her woolen cloak from a peg near the door, she swung it over her shoulders and stepped out into the hall.

All was quiet. Her sisters and Fiona were still in the solar, the men were gathered in the Great Hall, and the maids would be preparing the evening meal. Emily used the servants' stairs and left the note on the housekeeper's desk near the back door and let herself out.

The gloaming had settled as she made her way around the corner of the castle and to the postern gate. Once outside the walls, she took a deep breath of cool, crisp air and started walking.

She passed the healer's cottage, silent and still now that Gwendolyn was making her autumn rounds. By the time she reached the bog, darkness had fallen, lit only by a sliver of new moon.

Emily took a moment for her eyes to adjust to the lack of light. She remembered what Ian had told her about the boards sinking below the surface where the bog was treacherous. In the distance, she could see moonlight reflecting off them. If they were visible, the ground should be safe to that point.

She started to cross the upturned rows of peat, stumbling a bit at the unevenness of the earth. The soil felt damp but not wet. Still, it was just a matter of minutes before the leather soles of her boots were soaked through. The ground seemed to be more uneven as she walked and she nearly turned her ankle several times as she navigated the heavy clumps, her legs beginning to ache with the effort. At least she could see a cluster of rocks not too far away on her right, so she must be nearing the other edge of the bog.

Perhaps she would rest a minute when she got there. She turned and headed for the boulders. Her foot slipped and she stumbled slightly, balancing by pushing her other foot down.

When she tried to lift it, it stuck. So did the first foot. And then she heard a sickening, sucking sound as mud and water oozed over her boots.

Chapter Twenty-Six

Darkness had fallen by the time Ian turned the team through the raised portcullis and drove across the bailey. He had meant to be home hours ago, but the cooper had learned of some used oak barrels available that were necessary to allow the whisky to mature. Since they would now be producing more casks, they'd need all they could get. Unfortunately, the barrels had been in a warehouse ten miles away.

He turned the weary horses over to Jamie and made his way to the castle. The evening meal had already passed, but folks were lingering over tankards in the Great Hall. Some of his kin were still seated on the dais, having obviously taken their meal there tonight. Just as well, he thought. Emily, in light of what she'd offered to do, should be seen more often joining the clan. Her seat was empty, although her sisters were still there. He glanced toward Carr, engaged in conversation with Rory. He definitely wanted to talk to him, but it could wait a few minutes.

"Where is Emily?" he asked as he approached the dais.

"She was not feeling well," Lorelei replied.

The hairs at his nape prickled. Had someone tried to poison her again? "Did ye check on her?"

"She left a note for Maggie not to be disturbed."

"But ye didna check?"

"My sister may seem a docile kitten most days," Juliana said, "but when she is not feeling well, she is more like a lion with a thorn in its paw. Better to leave her alone."

He'd never thought of Emily as *docile* nor a kitten for that matter. More like a she-wolf, protective of her sisters.

"Juliana is right. Emily does not get ill very often, but when she does, she just wants to be left alone." Lorelei lifted one shoulder in a half shrug. "Besides, she did say she wanted to take a nap."

Something didn't seem right. "When was this?"

"Earlier."

Ian took a deep breath, willing himself not to raise his voice. "*When*, precisely?"

Juliana frowned at him. "It was just before Devon came to the solar to fetch Fiona."

"For what?"

"He didn't say."

Ian glanced around for his brother. He wasn't with Carr and Rory, and Ian didn't see him anywhere. The hair at his nape prickled again. "Where is Fiona?"

"We have not seen her since she left the solar."

Ian stared at both of them, then he turned and ran out of the hall toward the back of the castle where Emily's chamber was. Not bothering to knock, he pushed open the door.

Her bed was empty.

It had not been slept in.

He looked around. Nothing seemed to be out of order. No signs of a struggle. Emily's slippers lay on the floor by the wardrobe so she must have changed shoes. Then he noticed that her cloak was gone. He suddenly felt like Paden had kicked him with a well-placed hoof in his stomach. Had Devon—he didn't want to think it—lured her out? And Fiona—Lucifer's horns!—his sister could not be involved with any plot of Devon's. Had she gone after them?

He ran a hand through his hair in frustration, not knowing what to do. Then he spotted the note lying on the dresser. He reached it in three strides and picked it up. A moment later he howled at the walls and went racing out.

• • •

Emily shivered. The night air had turned cold and she'd dropped her cloak when she first began to struggle. She didn't dare try to reach for it now, since she was already near knee-deep in the sucking goop. Each time she moved, the mess shifted, pulling her down. The rocks couldn't be more than ten or fifteen feet away, a safe haven. But it might as well have been miles.

A hysterical bubble rose in her throat and she fought the panic that was rising. How could she have miscalculated so badly? The boards—she looked again, trying to locate them but from her location now she couldn't see them. Or…maybe they had sunk. She had no idea when they had been put into place or how long it took, although, where she had walked should have been dry. The note had said it was. Would Ian still be waiting for her? Or would he think she had decided not to come? He wouldn't get home until morning. Would anyone think to look for her? She'd left the note for Maggie and her sisters knew to leave her alone… Oh, dear God. She had been such a fool to walk through a bog at night.

She froze suddenly and stopped breathing as the sound of water seeping from the overturned peat began to rise around her boots. For a moment, she stared at it, feeling the hysterical bubble rise in her throat once more.

And then she screamed.

• • •

Ian was nearly out of breath from running out of the castle to reach the bog when he heard the scream. Damnation! It was faint. He swiveled his head to attune his ears from the direction it had come. He could see nothing at this edge of the bog, but if Emily had wandered in past the boards…

He squinted in the dim light from the moon. The boards had been placed fairly close to the newly turned rows yesterday, since the mud had been like thick soup and it hadn't been safe to go farther in. They were gone now, and he frowned. They'd been placed near the upturned peat and couldn't have sunk under the turf. He peered out over the bog and felt his eyes widen as he saw the boards floating a good hundred feet away. How they had gotten that far out he didn't know, but if Emily had taken them for a guideline and walked into the sodden mess…

Another scream rent the air. It sounded like it came from the far end and he sprinted toward the sound. Several times he slipped and nearly fell as he skirted along the edge. It would have been quicker to dart through, but not safe. The cry came again, ceasing suddenly. *Dear God! Don't let the muck have sucked her under!*

He ran faster, charging through gorse scrubs that tore at his breeches and over rocky terrain until, as he rounded a set of boulders, he saw her, standing thigh deep in muck.

"Doona move! Doona thrash!"

She turned her head. "Ian! You came!"

"Aye. I'll get ye out. Just doona move."

"I…I won't…"

Ian pondered for a moment. Luckily, Emily was close to solid land, but seeing how far she'd already been pulled down, he couldn't wade out and get her or they'd both be stuck.

He calculated the distance and then began stripping. Pulling off his boots, he unlaced his breeches, then pulled his shirt over his head. Tying one of the sleeves to one leg of the pants, he formed a makeshift rope that was near eight feet in length, but would it reach?

Holding on to the free sleeve he swung the heavier end over the surface. Emily tried reaching for it, but it fell short and she whimpered as the oozy mess sucked at her.

"Doona move! I'll come to ye."

"You will get mired, too."

"Nae if I am careful." Ian edged his way down from the rocks and stepped onto the soaking ground. It moved but didn't give way. He ventured another step, feeling how soft it might be before putting his weight down. Another step and he felt the pull at his foot. He stopped and considered the distance between him and Emily. His clothing rope might just reach her.

"Try nae to move yer legs, bend forward from yer waist," he instructed as he did the same. "And grab hold." He swung the rope out again. It landed with a muddy splash just in front of her and, as Emily tried reaching for it, she fell forward.

"Damnation!" Ian pulled his foot free, about to take another step, when he felt the cloth tighten. Emily had managed to grab onto it. "Hold on with both hands, *mo cridhe*."

"I am."

Her voice sounded weak and even in the moonlight, he could see her face was white. Carefully, he took one step back, then another, keeping the clothing line tight. When his foot struck solid ground, he dug in his heels and reeled Emily out of the mud with a steady pull. The goop made a loud, sucking pop as it released her from its grip. She stumbled and the sudden give on the rope tumbled him backward, pulling her down on top of him.

For a moment, they both lay there, panting and covered in mud.

"You saved my life," Emily finally said, one small hand splayed against his bare chest. "I hoped you would come."

He tightened his arms around her. "I dinna write the note, *mo cridhe*."

She stilled, then raised her head. "Then who did?"

"I doona ken, but I will find out when we get back to the castle." He sat up, raising her with him. For the first time, she seemed to realize he was naked, save for his small clothes. He thought he detected a blush. He untied his shirt. "I suppose I should get dressed."

Her hand lingered a bit before she sighed and dropped it. "I wish you had written that note."

He stopped halfway into his breeches, one leg lifted, and nearly fell over. He yanked them up. "Ye do?"

Emily nodded, watching as he fastened them. The awareness sent his cock to full attention. Her eyes grew big at the sudden bulge and he asked a tentative question, hardly daring to hope. "Why?"

"I... I wanted to make love with you."

The words were nearly whispered and she suddenly bent down to pick up his shirt, but he suspected it was more a gesture to hide her face. He placed his fingers under her chin when she rose and tipped her head up. "I would like that more than anything."

Emily smiled. "When we get back to the castle, I want to take you to my bed. After I get cleaned up, of course."

He laughed outright at that. Emily would always be practical. "I doona ken why we have to wait to get back."

Her eyes widened. "You want to make love...*here*?"

He shook his head. "I'll nae take ye lying on rocks out in the cold, lass. I was thinking that Old Gwendolyn's cottage will be empty."

"She would not mind if we used it?"

"In the Highlands, an empty cottage always has a welcome sign. We will leave it as we found it, but there is a bed and hot water to be had for a bath first." He tilted his head. "What say ye?"

"I say yes." Emily smiled at him. "I mean...*aye*."

...

The fright—and very real peril—of the danger that had just passed should have exhausted her, but Emily felt exhilarated. Perhaps it was one of those nonsensical reactions like laughing hysterically when you want to cry. Or, perhaps, it was anticipation of what was to come. Either way, the bog incident seemed a distant memory. At least, for now.

The cottage was dark when they arrived, but unlocked, and they removed their muddied boots and socks before entering. Gwendolyn had left several small logs in the hearth, kindling already stuck between them. Ian soon had a fire blazing and kettles hanging from an iron pole placed between yokes above it, heating water.

Emily pulled a large copper tub out from its corner niche and found two linen towels that she remembered the healer spreading over some bushes to dry that morning. They still smelled of fresh air. A cake of heather soap lay in a pewter dish near a wash basin. Within minutes, steam was rising as Ian poured the water into the tub.

He turned toward the door. "I will leave ye to your bath."

"You will need one, too," Emily said, "since I spattered mud all over you."

"I'll use the water when ye are through."

Emily wrinkled her nose. "It will be cold by then, not to mention dirty."

He paused with his hand on the doorknob and lifted an eyebrow. "What are ye suggesting?"

She swallowed hard and looked at the floor. She'd never been in the position of seducing a man before. She'd never *wanted* to. Goodness, she'd always waited to take her bath until her husband had been well in his opium haze and even then had locked her door to thwart his unwelcome intrusion.

And now, all she could think of was that she wanted Ian to stay. She swallowed again and looked up. "Since we're both filthy, we could share the bath."

His mouth quirked at that. "Is that the only reason? Because we're both dirty?"

She felt herself blush, hoping he'd mistake it for the heat in the room. Her reasoning sounded inane, even to her. More like suggesting two children get cleaned up rather than being seductive. "I…do not know…"

"I ken." In three strides he was at her side, cradling her face in his hands. "Do ye trust me?"

She looked into his eyes. "Yes."

"Then let me show ye what else a bath can be used for."

With those words, he tugged at the bedraggled ribbons lacing up the front of her gown. It was a simple garment meant for working in and didn't require petticoats or stays. It took only a moment or two for his deft fingers to undo the ties, and he slid the gown off her shoulders, letting it fall to the ground. That left only her chemise, which, as water-soaked as it was, clung to her, leaving little to the imagination.

Ian's eyes widened as he looked down, and she felt her nipples harden under his gaze. He brushed his fingers lightly over one breast and a sound, suspiciously like a growl, came from him.

"I want to see ye naked."

He gave her a quick glance, then took both hands and ripped the chemise in half. Instinctively, she raised both arms to cover herself, but he stayed her. "Doona."

She dropped her hands, feeling a moment of mortification at standing completely nude in front of him, but the feeling turned to something else when she noticed the large bulge in his breeches that strained for release even as it grew. An odd tingling sensation began in her belly.

"Ye are beautiful," he said and quickly stripped off his own clothing.

She barely had time to register how very large his member was—Good heavens! He was at least twice the size of Albert!—before Ian was lifting her and placing her in the tub. Water lapped over the side as he climbed in beside her. His broad shoulders nearly touched the edges of the tub, and she saw a dusting of dark hair across his hard chest, a thin line of which ran down his belly and below the surface of the water.

Ian pushed his legs under hers, and his biceps flexed as he lifted her thighs to spread them around his hips. It was an intimate position, and she wondered if he'd simply impale her. He certainly looked ready. Instead, he traced her cheek with his thumb.

"Lie back and let me wash ye."

She gave him a startled look, but he was already pressing her down gently. As small as the tub was—at least with both of them in it—she could lean her head against the rim quite easily. She was quite comfortably inclined as well, although her position had her breasts poking up from the surface. Ian's golden eyes darkened at the sight, and she suddenly felt quite wanton.

"I like when you look at me like that."

He grinned. "I am planning to do more than look, lass."

Her whole body tingled, although she didn't know what he actually planned to do. Albert had not been one to linger at bed sport, for which she had always been grateful. Now, however, it seemed that every nerve ending awaited Ian's touch.

Ian lathered a washcloth and began stroking one of her arms with it. Slowly, as if he had all the time in the world. Although he wasn't doing anything more than getting rid of the grime, the sensation was amazing. He lifted her arm, bringing the cloth down along her ribs, just grazing the side of her breast. Her breathing shallowed and her breast suddenly felt heavy and achy with need. He smiled—did he know what she was feeling?—and did the same with the other arm, this time his knuckles brushing alongside the other breast.

Emily's breathing hitched. She wanted him to touch her. Really touch her. Instead, he dipped the cloth and squeezed water over her collarbone and dribbled it across her nipples, which peaked immediately.

"Please..." She broke off.

"Please what?" He dragged the washcloth lightly over her again. "What do ye want me to do?"

"I...want...you...to touch me," she whispered.

"Like this?" He lightly traced around one breast with a finger.

A moan escaped her. "M...more."

He dropped the cloth and cupped both breasts, kneading them. "Like this?"

"Y-yes."

He grinned again and rubbed a nipple between his forefinger and thumb. "Or like this?"

"Ahhh!"

"Or maybe this." Ian leaned forward and laved the other nipple with his tongue, circling the areola.

A squeak emerged from her as she closed her eyes in bliss. How could this feel so wonderful? She was lost in heady sensation as he covered her nipple with his mouth and began to suck while pinching and pulling the other one.

And then she felt his free hand slide down her belly to the apex of her thighs, which were brazenly splayed open under the water. His fingers separated her folds, stroking them in rhythm to the suckling of her breast. A strange pulsing began between her legs as her body responded. She felt herself rising as though riding a wave, then plunging into a trough, only to rise higher with each of his strokes. Something was building inside her like a sea building in a storm. Some aching need she'd never felt before. Something… She wanted…whatever was gathering inside her…

And then his thumb pressed against that little nub that had been throbbing, and for a second the world went black as a rogue wave crested, washing over her.

She opened her eyes to find Ian watching her, his whisky-colored eyes darkened with his own desire. Almost before she had time to recover her breath, he lifted her against him, pulled her legs tight around his waist, and took her mouth with his, tongue delving deep inside while his manhood penetrated her.

The initial shock of his filling her, stretching her wide, quickly changed to more want and more *need*. She whimpered as the odd tension built again, the waves rising higher this time, the troughs plunging deeper as his hips undulated against her, his thrusts deep and hard. She met those thrusts with her own, not caring at the moment whether she was being rent in two, knowing only that she wanted him deeper, harder… Their tongues did battle as their bodies strove to become one.

And then his hands were around her waist, lifting her, his shaft nearly leaving her. She cried out her displeasure and he slammed her down on him, his manhood pounding into her before the wave crested once more.

For long minutes, she lay against him, her body weightless as she floated in her own sea of pleasure and contentment. The metaphors were all true. The sea just crashed, the earth had moved, the volcano erupted… All the times she'd listened to other women speaking of bed sport as though it were actually enjoyable and laughed at them. Ha. The joke was definitely on her, because bed sport was all of that and more. Much, much more.

Finally, she roused herself enough to lift her head and gaze at him.

A corner of his mouth lifted in a half smile. "I told ye I was going to do more than look…"

Chapter Twenty-Seven

Emily woke the next morning to something very warm and solid in her bed. Slowly she opened her eyes and then realized it wasn't her bed she was sleeping in. It was Ian's and he was lying beside her. When she looked at his face, his golden eyes were watching her.

"How long have you been awake?"

"Not long enough. I like watching ye sleep. Ye are like a soft kitten, curling yerself against me."

"I did not…" She stopped, since she couldn't argue the point that she had her arm over his chest and one leg intertwined with his. "I remember *you* holding *me* when I fell asleep."

"Aye. And ye snore."

"I do *not*!"

He laughed. "Well, a snuffling sound."

She tried to look indignant, but it was hard with his already hard cock pressing against her belly. She was a little sore from the three additional times they'd made love after they got back, but that didn't mean her body didn't want *him*.

Again.

With a sigh, she sat up. “We had better not keep your family waiting any longer.”

He made a disgruntled sound, but he sat up, too. They’d returned to the castle shortly before midnight and found everyone gathered in the Great Hall, but she had been near exhaustion and Ian had told everyone to go to bed and he’d explain in the morning. At the time, she hadn’t given any thought that it might seem odd that Ian had taken her to his bedchamber. Now that would be one more thing to explain. At least, to her sisters.

She looked at the sun streaming in his window. “It must be midmorning already.”

“Aye, ’tis.”

He went to his wardrobe for clean clothes and she realized the only gown she had was the dirty, torn one from last night. “I hope I do not run into a servant on the way to my room.”

He arched a look at her. “It willna matter if someone sees ye. We are going to get married.”

“I…do not think…”

He stilled. “After last night, ye still doona want to marry me?”

She hesitated. The idea of having Ian beside her every night—experiencing what she never thought she would—was tempting. She knew her feelings for him had deepened, but he had not said he loved her. She was old enough to know that, to men, lust and love were not the same. If she were even to *consider* giving up her freedom—Lord, why was she even thinking that she would?—it would have to be for love on both their parts. She shook her head.

“Why nae?” He looked almost wounded. “Whoever is attempting to harm ye—”

“Kill me, you mean. It is no use denying it.”

Ian grimaced, a muscle ticking in his jaw. “That will stop

when I take ye to wife."

"That will not solve the problem," she said. "If this person stops, then we will never know who it is and I will always live in fear."

He frowned. "What are ye proposing then?"

"I am not sure. I think we need to find out who is behind this."

"I doona want…" He was interrupted by a knock on the door. "Who is there?"

"Carr."

Ian went to the door to open it. "What do ye want?" he growled.

His brother raised a brow. "A messenger just arrived from Lord Mount Stuart. Parliament is going to un-proscribe us. The MacGregors will be a proud and lawful clan again."

• • •

Less than thirty minutes later, Ian, his siblings and uncles, as well as Emily and her sisters, were all gathered in the library. The envoy that Lord Mount Stuart had sent was looking a little discombobulated, but that was probably because everyone was trying to talk to him at once—at least, everyone on Ian's side of the room. Emily and her sisters were sitting still as garden statues close to the hearth.

"Ye are certain his lordship has the votes?" Carr asked

The envoy—Mr. Smythe—nodded. "King George himself mentioned to Lord North that allowing MacGregors to claim their name again might be justified."

Ian hid a smile. The current prime minister would not go against the king's request. More than likely it had been suggested by Lord Bute, who had been tutor to the king and still maintained a favorite position with him. Ian glanced at Emily, wondering how much of an influence she might have had. She had been seen in conversation with Lord Bute at the Campbell's feast. And just recently—*very* recently he thought with an inward grin—she'd said "when" their name was restored. Not "if."

"When is this going to happen?" Donovan asked.

"Sometime in December, according to the roster," Mr. Smythe replied.

"Does that mean our lands will be restored?" Rory asked.

"And the castle?" Broderick added.

"You will be able to petition for your lands to be restored, although it will be a somewhat lengthy process," the envoy answered, "but the deed to the castle will be the king's decision to make."

Ian's rather lustful thoughts disappeared. Emily was clenching her hands so tightly he could see they were white, even from where he stood. He wanted to remind her that he'd told her he wouldn't throw her out. He started to say as much when Donovan spoke.

"'Tis time we take back what is ours."

"Aye. MacGregor holdings should nae be in the hands of the English." Broderick looked at him. "Ye are our laird, by Scottish law. Do ye nae agree?"

Ian opened his mouth, then closed it. The Crown didn't recognize lairds but the Scots still did. His duty was to protect his lands. Not only did his clan expect it, he would no doubt be exiled from them—and truly wander in the mists—if he did not claim what had been rightfully theirs. He glanced at Emily, but she wasn't looking at him. Well, this would simply be one more reason why she should marry him. Surely she would see the reasonableness of that now. He took a deep breath.

"Aye, Clan MacGregor must have our lands back."

• • •

Emily wasn't sure how she managed to hold herself together until she reached her bedchamber, but somehow she'd found the strength to hold her head up and walk out while the men were talking about celebrating. She'd refused to look at Ian.

He had betrayed her.

She shut the door practically in her sisters' faces. They'd both wanted to come in, but she told them she had some thinking to do. Juliana had been furious about the news and Lorelei had a dozen questions and, until she could sort things out, she just wasn't ready to deal with either of them.

Clan MacGregor must have our lands back. Those were Ian's words. He hadn't said "theirs" and he hadn't corrected his uncles when they both said the English should not have a claim. They'd meant her. *She* should not have a claim.

Emily sank into the chair by the hearth and stared at the cold ashes. Her heart felt like those cold ashes looked. Spent. Where hope had leaped like fire only this morning, now she felt her heart, like the ashes, could be swept up and discarded.

It wasn't that she didn't understand. She'd been in Scotland long enough to realize how important a clan's holdings were. She had even given thought to offering Ian a proposal—not for marriage—but one where they would share equal profits. That was no longer applicable. Once Parliament restored the MacGregors' status, they could—and would—pursue getting their lands back. No doubt they'd also petition the Crown for the title to the castle as well. If King George acquiesced, she would be back where she started.

She desperately needed a plan. Slowly, as she continued to stare into an empty hearth, one began to form. It wasn't what she wanted, but she thought Ian might agree to it, since it would make things easier for his clan. As she stood to go find him, a knock sounded on her door. A moment later, it opened and Ian poked his head around as though she'd conjured him.

"May I come in?"

"Yes. I…was just coming to look for you."

Ian closed the door. "Ye were?"

"Yes. I have a proposal."

He grinned. "I kenned ye'd see the way of it."

"The way of it?"

"Aye. Marriage to me solves all the problems, does it nae?"

Her silly heart skittered. If only it were so easy. But she knew he was offering a business proposal, however much they'd enjoyed their bedding. Lust was not love and he had yet to even hint at that. Love was not something that could be forced, either. She might love him— Dear God, she had come to that realization while she was doing her thinking—but she didn't want to go through life with a husband who didn't love her back.

Slowly, she shook her head. "It does not. Your uncles made it quite clear earlier that I am not welcome here—"

"They can move elsewhere."

"No." She felt tears sting her eyes and willed herself not to cry. "Can you not see that I would just be breaking up your family? You finally have the chance to be their true laird. I do not want to be an obstacle."

"An obstacle?"

"Yes. Now—after centuries—you finally have the opportunity to be a proud clan again."

He was silent and she knew that his silence was the answer. It wasn't the one she wanted, but it proved she'd made the right decision. "Here is what I propose. I will turn over the deed to the castle and the lands willingly. In return, I want enough money to purchase a small house. I also want ten percent of the profit from the sales of the whisky going to White's annually. That will allow me to have financial independence."

He furrowed his brow. "I told ye I would nae throw ye and yer sisters out. Why would ye need financial independence?"

Here was the crux. If she stayed, her heart would be broken, not that she was going to confess that. She didn't want his pity, for God's sake. "Because I cannot continue like this. I *will* not continue like this." Emily took a deep breath and lifted her chin. "My sisters and I will be returning to London."

Chapter Twenty-Eight

Ian stared at Emily, not sure he'd heard her correctly. "Ye want to go back to London?"

"I… Yes. That would be best for both of us."

He felt like his horse had kicked his gut with a well-shod hoof. He had come up here to convince Emily that, now more than ever, they should marry. "I doona understand, lass. If we marry, we both benefit. The MacGregors get their land back and ye become a MacGregor."

She stared at him for so long that he began to wonder if she'd taken leave of her senses. "Do ye nae see 'tis practical?"

The question seemed to revive her. "Yes, it is practical. Yes, it would benefit both of us. You would be spared the expense of time and money to reclaim your lands. I would have a place to live—"

"So there ye are." Ian spread his hands. "I will see to a special license then."

"*No.*"

He frowned. "Why nae? We suit. Ye canna deny we do well under the sheets—"

"Lust is not love!" Her hand clamped over her mouth and she looked horror-stricken. "Never mind I said that. I meant–"

"Ye meant..." Understanding washed over him like a breaking wave that he hadn't seen coming. "Ye doona think I care for ye?"

She hesitated. "I suppose you do care. You did save my life."

He blinked, not sure what she meant. "Of course, I saved yer life—"

"Just like you would anyone's."

"Not just anyone's. Do ye have any idea of how I felt when I came home and found the note ye thought was from me? Do ye ken what came over me when I thought ye were in danger? And worse, when I found ye in the bog, half sucked under? I...I...doona ken what I would have done if ye had been...if I hadna gotten there in time..."

A second invisible wave crashed over him, making him wonder if he'd scattered some of his wits somewhere. If he had lost Emily that night... If whoever was trying to murder her had succeeded... Nothing else would matter. Becoming un-proscribed, having their name and even their lands restored...none of that would matter if Emily wasn't with him.

"I love ye, lass. I doona want ye to leave me."

She stared at him. "You...*love* me?"

"Aye. I guess I just now realized it." He held out his arms. "Will ye stay?"

For an answer, she leaped into his embrace and he covered her mouth with his, angling his head to deepen their kiss so she would know just how much. A soft moan came from her throat just as someone pounded on the door.

"Go away!" he nearly shouted.

The knock sounded again, louder this time.

"I do not think whoever is there is going to listen," Emily said as she leaned back.

Ian growled and stomped to the door, throwing it open to reveal Fiona.

"Sorry to interrupt," she said. "but Devon and I would like a word with ye and Emily. In my chamber, if ye please."

"Yer chamber? Now?"

"Aye, now." she replied. "What Devon has to say is for yer ears only."

Devon was standing by the window in Fiona's chamber, looking out over the back gardens. He turned as they entered and Ian hoped—*prayed*—that his brother wasn't going to offer a confession. He steeled himself for the possibility and felt Emily's warm hand on his arm. She shook her head slightly. He took a deep breath.

"What do ye have to say?"

Devon looked from him to Emily. "First, I want to apologize to ye. It seems I misjudged ye in my dislike for the English."

"*Dislike* is putting it mildly for ye." Ian looked at his brother quizzically. "What changed your mind?"

"Lady Woodhaven—"

"Please call me Emily."

Devon smiled at her. If Ian hadn't seen it, he never would have believed it.

"*Emily*," Devon continued, "caught me with Margaret Cameron in the Campbell's folly at the ball. She said naught when she could have gotten me in much trouble."

Ian looked at her and she shrugged. "I did not think it anyone's business."

Devon cleared his throat. "But 'tis nae what I need to tell

ye."

Ian felt dread flood through him. Was his brother about to confess? His face must have given his thoughts away because Devon tightened his mouth, the sullen look returning.

"I dinna do anything."

"Devon," Fiona said softly. "Remember what we talked about." She turned to Ian. "Devon sent for me yesterday, shortly after Emily left to take a nap. We went for a long ride because he didn't want anyone else to hear what he had to say."

That explained his absence, but it didn't necessarily excuse him. Ian nodded. "Go on then."

Devon took a deep breath. "I think Broderick is behind all the attempts to injure Lady…Emily."

Ian stared at him. "Why?"

"We all ken that Lady…Emily…looks like Isobel—"

"And is nothing like her!"

"Aye, but Emily is English and ye ken Broderick thinks Englishwomen are all whores."

Ian drew his brows together. "Just because our stepmother was wanton, doesna mean all Englishwomen are."

"Finish your thoughts," Fiona urged Devon. "Tell them why Broderick thinks so."

He took another deep breath. "The night Isobel was murdered, I was on my way to confront her about cheating on our father, but Broderick was at her door with a plate of marzipan—ye ken how Isobel loved it—so I hid. I saw him go in. I heard a laugh, then a stifled scream." He paused. "Broderick never came out."

Ian started, then his brow furrowed and his eyes narrowed. "The passageway. He escaped through the passageway. But why would he…" It took him another moment for the idea to register. "He was one of Isobel's lovers?"

"I suspect so," Devon answered. "I think he killed her

because he was jealous of the other men she saw."

"And ye never said anything?"

He shrugged. "I dinna like what Isobel was doing to our father."

"But—"

"I ken I should have, but I was four and ten. At the time, I thought it justice."

"And you think Broderick has tried to kill me because I remind him of Isobel?" Emily asked.

"I think it possible." Devon hesitated. "Jamie mentioned it was Broderick who told him he'd seen the mares in the far pasture. Jamie thought it odd because the distillery is in the opposite direction, but he was more concerned about fetching the horses back." Devon paused again. "Our uncle may be a bit mad."

Ian's mind raced. Now that he thought on it, Broderick had always been attentive to Isobel. The times his father had been called away to secretly take care of MacGregor business, Broderick had escorted Isobel where she'd wanted to go. He hadn't paid much attention at the time, since it had seemed natural that Broderick would take care of his brother's wife. But he'd also sat at Isobel's other side on the dais for their meals. A seat that Emily now sat in, beside Ian. Was his uncle's mind so twisted he thought Emily was Isobel?

Ian sat down on the settee beside the brazier and tugged Emily down beside him.

Other things were beginning to make sense now. The "nightmares" Emily had in the old part of the castle where the passageway was could have been real. Had Broderick actually entered her room with a knife and stood there watching her? Chills slithered down his spine.

The day Emily fell from the stairs... His uncle had been there talking with Everard from London. He would have had time to go back into the castle and loosen a board on the steps. It was Broderick who'd called Ian to the distillery because of a crack in a vat. Was that to make sure he wouldn't be present when the whisky had been put into Emily's tea to make her fall asleep when she needed to stay awake? The night that Emily had been poisoned, no one would have thought it suspicious to see their uncle with a glass of wine and marzipan, either. *Marzipan.* Ian felt a chill slide down his spine. Devon had just said that his uncle had brought marzipan to Isobel before she had been killed.

"I remember seeing Broderick in the hallway when I was going to the solar yesterday," Emily said.

"*What*?" Ian groaned. Yesterday, he'd announced he was going to Taynuilt. Broderick could have written the note and he would have had time to move the boards in the bog, since it was too wet to work very far. Emily would have trusted the ground was safe because the damn note had said it was.

"I did not think anything of it," she said. "There is a back door to the gardens so I assumed he'd come from there."

Fiona looked at her brothers. "What are we going to do?"

Ian looked grim. "We will set a trap."

Devon nodded. "Rory, Carr, and I will help."

"What kind of trap?" Fiona asked.

Ian shook his head. "I am nae sure yet. Let me think on it a wee bit."

"I have an idea," Emily said.

• • •

"*No*."

Emily sighed over the emphatic answer from Ian. She should have known that was coming. They were all still in Fiona's bedchamber, and his sister and Devon were both staring at her as well. If she was going to marry the man, he needed to know she didn't back down.

"It is the most practical—and easiest—solution."

Ian's jaw set. "I willna have ye using yourself as bait to lure Broderick into attempting to kill ye. Again."

"But you will be there to catch him," Emily replied. "It is not like you will really be called away from the castle."

"'Tis too much of a risk."

"It would be a calculated risk." Emily folded her arms across her chest. "At least we would know when to expect him to attack."

"She does have a point," Devon said.

Ian gave his brother a black look. "Did I ask for yer opinion?"

"He is right." Fiona scowled at Ian. "Better we ken when—and how—our uncle will attack than to have Emily caught by surprise." She pointed a finger at her brother. "At a time and place where ye may nae be able to come to her rescue."

Ian frowned. "I still doona like it."

Emily raised a brow. "If I am going to be a MacGregor, then I do my part."

Ian opened his mouth, snapped it shut, and then grinned. "Is that a *yes* then? Ye dinna actually say it earlier."

"It might be."

Devon looked at them both, then changed the subject. "We can ask Carr and Rory what they think of the plan."

Ian grimaced. "I suppose they will need to be told about Isobel, at any rate."

"And I think my sisters as well," Emily said. "I do not want them worrying or, God forbid, getting in the way."

He looked at each of them, his mouth a grim line. Finally he nodded. "Have everyone meet in the solar in ten minutes… and take care neither of our uncles are about."

"Thank you." Emily smiled at him. "For listening to me."

He grunted. "Something tells me this will nae be the only

time I do."

Her smile widened. "Of course not."

• • •

A quarter of an hour later they were all assembled in the solar. The bright sunshine streaming in the window did nothing to elevate Ian's mood. He still thought Emily's scheme was harebrained. And dangerous.

"Now let me make sure I understand." Carr had been pacing while Emily spoke, but now he stood still. "Ian is going to make known that ye are his leman—"

"I do not think you should cheapen yourself," Juliana interrupted.

"You will be ruined," Lorelei added.

"I didna think ye could *ruin* a widow," Rory said.

Juliana narrowed her eyes at him. "That is so typical of what a man would say."

Emily held up her hand. "Rory is correct, but this will be only temporary."

"Temporary?"

"Aye," Ian said. "Yer sister and I plan to marry once all this is over."

There was a moment of silence over that remark, then everyone started talking at once, only to be shushed by Emily. "Details later."

Lorelei looked puzzled. "Why not just announce your intention now?"

"Because we do not want to force Broderick's hand too soon," Emily answered. "If he thinks we are betrothed, he may try something immediately. If he thinks I am just a mistress, someone who can be discarded, he will feel he has time to plot something."

"Only *we* are going to plot that something for him,"

Fiona said.

"So..." Carr cleared his throat. "Ian and Emily are going to move back into the old chamber she occupied, claiming they want more privacy—"

"The one with the passageway?" Juliana asked.

Carr nodded. "Then Ian is going to receive a missive—that I will pen—asking him to settle a dispute between kin near Oban. That will take him away for the night, since 'tis nearly a day's journey either way."

"And we will have Hamish deliver the missive when Broderick is here so he will hear for himself that Ian must leave," Rory said.

"Only once Ian rides out, he will leave his horse with one of our crofters and double back on foot, using the postern gate to get in and taking the passageway to the chamber to lie in wait. Our uncle will most likely strike at night when all is quiet."

"But what if he does not wait?" Juliana asked. "Emily will be alone until Ian can get back."

Which was exactly what he was afraid of. "Aye. I think it too risky—"

"Doona fash," Fiona said. "I will make sure she is surrounded by people all day."

"And Devon and I will tell our uncles we want to discuss the distillery after supper," Carr said. "That will give Rory time to make sure Ian is already back and Emily safe."

"Broderick is not happy with me having a say regarding the distillery," Emily said, "so if Carr tells him it is a good idea that will goad him into acting as well."

Ian snorted his displeasure. "I doona think it wise to goad the man if he is already mad."

Emily gave him that look that he was already beginning to recognize. The one that said she knew what was best. He harrumphed. They were going to have words about that. A lot of words.

But first, they had a murderer to catch.

...

Several nights later, Emily lay fully clothed under the covers in her old bedchamber. What had sounded like a foolproof plan when they had all discussed it in the solar suddenly seemed not quite so brilliant.

Not that things hadn't gone according to plan, but a tiny bit of superstition—or maybe it was experience—hovered and niggled at her. Generally, whenever her life seemed to be moving along like it should, something invariably happened to make her plans run amok. So far today, nothing had. Hamish had delivered the message as they were breaking their fast, Ian had acted like it were a true emergency and left immediately. Carr had announced that he would be working on the accounting books much of the day, making it clear he would be around, while Rory had mentioned a few of the horses needed shoeing and he would be overseeing the farrier when he arrived. She and Fiona had spent the day with a half dozen maids going room-to-room to discuss what needed airing and cleaning.

And now, night had fallen. Carr and Devon had concluded their discussion with their uncles, and both Ian and Rory waited in the room with her. She couldn't see them, since the candle had been extinguished and the brazier coals banked, but she could hear steady breathing. Her own was shaky.

It seemed she lay there for hours—the bit of moonlight that had shone through the window had shifted position—when finally she heard a sound. It was hardly discernible...a soft *click*, but her ears were attuned to the silence like a fox awaiting a hare at a ground hole. Only she were the hare.

Although Ian and Rory were still quiet, she could sense

the tension in the air.

There was a slight creaking sound and slowly, the wardrobe door opened. Through her half-closed eyes, she could see a figure emerge. The moonlight glinted off the knife in his hand, and it was all Emily could do not to scream. Her nightmares had been real…

And then, all hell broke loose. Broderick was halfway to the bed when Ian tackled him. The man fell against the bedpost and managed to scramble out of his grasp and crawl onto the mattress. Rory grabbled for the knife as Emily scooted up against the headboard, wrapping her arms tightly around her knees as Broderick tried to slash her. The door to her bedchamber flew open and Carr and Devon burst in with their own weapons. There was a great deal of cursing from all of them as bodies thumped and collided, Ian practically lifting his uncle off the bed to throw him on the floor. There was a sickening crack and then silence, save for the heavy breathing. Then hands reached for her and Emily managed to stifle a scream when she realized they belonged to Ian.

"Hush." He smoothed her hair and pulled her close. "Hush. 'Tis all right now."

She clung to him as someone managed to light the oil lamp hanging by the door. "Is…is he dead?"

"Nae. Just knocked out," Rory said.

Broderick moaned and began to stir as Carr finished tying his hands with the rope he'd brought. "Let me go, ye fools!"

"Think again who the fool is," Devon growled at him as another figure appeared in the doorway.

"What is going on here?" Donovan asked, his eyes widening as he saw his brother on the floor and then his hands went up as Carr and Rory advanced on him. "Whatever Broderick was up to, I had nae part!"

"Our uncle just tried to murder Emily," Ian said.

"*What*?"

"And he murdered Isobel, too," Devon added.

Donovan looked at each of them and then down at his brother. "Is this true?"

"The whore cheated on me," Broderick spat out. "I loved the bitch and she cheated on me!"

An odd expression crossed Ian's face and then cleared. "So ye meant yerself when ye said Isobel cheated on the man who loved her." It was a rhetorical question and he got only a defiant look for an answer.

"But why try to murder Lady Woodhaven?" Carr asked.

"Because she is English." This time he did spit. "And she wanted the distillery. It was supposed to be mine. *Mine*. Donovan was going to sell me his portion when he retired. I had plans—"

"Nobody interrupted yer plans," Ian said. "Emily gave ye only an opportunity to make more profit."

"The damn English do nae keep their promises," he said defiantly. "Ye ken what the English have done to MacGregors for nigh two centuries! Ye are going to trust the damn bit—"

His words were cut off by Ian's fist. "One more word against Emily and there will be murder done here this night. *Yers*."

Broderick gave him a belligerent look but kept still. Donovan took a step closer to him. "Ye meant to kill Lady Woodhaven? I will hear it from ye."

Rory held up the knife. "He had this in his hand when he emerged from the passageway."

Donovan glanced at it, then back to his brother. "I will hear it from ye."

"Aye."

"Were ye also responsible for the whisky put in her tea and the hemlock in her wine?" Devon asked. When Broderick didn't answer, he crouched down and grabbed him. "I was blamed for both those things. My own brother doubted me. I will have the truth from ye as well."

"Aye," Broderick finally said. "I took the foreshots from the whisky so it wouldna smell."

"What are those?" Emily asked.

"They are part of the early distilling process," Ian answered. "Different boiling points are used to extract the alcohol and part of the first stage—the foreshot—is verra strong and has almost no odor." He turned back to Broderick. "And the hemlock?"

Again, he looked mulish and Devon's hand went to his neck. "Answer us while ye can still talk."

"I stole it from Old Gwendolyn's cottage," he choked out. "She never locks it."

Devon released his hold and stood up. "What are we going to do with him?"

"He should be turned over to the magistrate in the morning," Carr said.

"He will hang," Donovan said quietly.

"He should have thought of that before he tried to kill Emily," Ian said.

"But he did kill Isobel," Rory answered.

"Which I, for one, could overlook, considering her treacherous behavior and the fact that her father killed ours," Ian replied. "But I canna—and willna—allow Broderick to be a danger to Emily. Ye should also ken," he continued, "that we are going to marry."

"She is a Sassenach!" Broderick shouted.

Ian raised a fist, only Emily caught it. "Please. No more violence tonight."

He lowered it slowly. "What ye doona ken is that Emily offered—before my proposal—to return the deed to our lands if our name is cleared. All she asked was to stay in the castle and to share the profits." He looked at Donovan. "The land is going to be ours. *And hers*."

Donovan glanced down at his brother, then back at Ian. "If I give ye my oath—as a *MacGregor*—nae a Murray—that I will escort my brother to Glasgow and see that he is on the next ship that sails to the Colonies and…" He glanced down once more. "If Broderick swears he will nae return, would ye agree to banishing him?"

"I canna—"

"Yes, you can," Emily said. "I do not want to see a man hang, even if he hates me."

"Ye are more honorable than we are," Devon muttered.

"Not honorable especially," Emily answered. "I just do not want to start life as a *MacGregor*"—she turned to smile at Ian—"with MacGregor blood on my hands."

He studied her for a moment, then sighed and nodded to Donovan. "'Tis done then. Take him away."

As his uncle helped Broderick up and out the door, Ian looked at his brothers. "And I will have ye gone as well." He put his arm around Emily's shoulders and drew her close. "I would like to spend some time getting to better know my intended." He smiled at Emily. "Much better."

"We doona need to be told twice," Rory said and pushed his brothers out into the hall. "We'll send food up in a few days if we doona see ye."

Emily shook her head as she went to the door and bolted it after them, then turned to Ian.

"How much better do you intend to get to know me?"

He grinned and held out his arms. "Come here and I will show ye."

Epilogue

STRAE CASTLE, DECEMBER 1774

Emily looked around the Great Hall, glad to see so many of the neighboring clans had come to celebrate the reinstatement of Clan MacGregor—together with its name and tartan—by Parliament. Even the Duke of Argyll was present.

Of course, she had her *own* reason for celebrating. She was now officially a MacGregor as well. *Mrs. Ian MacGregor* as of four o'clock this afternoon when they'd gotten married.

"Happy, wife?" Ian asked, coming up beside her near the dais and handing her a glass of wine.

"Very much, husband." She looked over the packed hall once more. "It seems everyone is having a good time."

"They should be. We have our name back—and our lands, thanks to ye."

"I just wish Alasdair were here."

"Alasdair will be returning in the spring with some of our kin. And, if the Irish have rubbed off on them at all, they'll be wanting to celebrate our wedding again."

"It would be nice to have the neighboring clans gather again," Emily said. "The more friendships we establish, the better."

"I would agree with ye, although I am nae so sure yer sister does." He gestured with his glass. "Juliana seems to have an unwanted admirer."

Emily followed his direction. Neal Cameron was talking to her sister. Or attempting to. Fiona and Lorelei flanked her, the trio looking like determined warrior-queens. She shook her head. "I am surprised he evens remembers Juliana, as inebriated as he was at the Campbell ball."

"He's a stubborn arse."

"Well, Juliana can handle him." She spotted Rory standing not too far from the group. "I do wish she'd be kinder to your brother, though."

"Doona fash. Rory brings it on himself." Ian shrugged. "I think he enjoys roiling her temper."

"Perhaps something he should rethink then," Emily answered. "But I am glad Devon no longer *totally* hates the English."

"Aye. He is nae ready to forgive yer countrymen, but I think ye have made him see there is good on both sides."

"It really is too bad Broderick did not realize that as well."

"I think my uncle is a wee bit mad." Ian's mouth tightened. "He is lucky we did nae turn him over to the magistrate."

"At least he will not be returning, so let us put the past where it belongs." Emily smiled at him. "Tonight is cause for *our* celebration. And I think your clansmen agree." She gestured around the room. "Although that might be the result of kegs of ale and barrels of whisky."

Ian's expression relaxed as he looked over the crowd. "Aye, liquor does play a role, and in a few hours most of them willna be standing upright."

Emily gave him a sideways glance. "*We* will not be upright, either, I hope."

Ian grinned. "Did I ever tell ye I like the way yer mind works?"

She managed to put a mock frown on her face. "I think you have disagreed a time or two with my ideas."

"Och, well. I doona like when ye put yerself in danger." He leaned closer, although with all the noise in the hall no one would hear him. "But the only danger ye'll face tonight is to be a wee bit sore in the morning."

"You are expecting me to move about tomorrow morning?"

He grinned again. "Only in our bed."

She couldn't help but smile. Not a night had passed since he brought her back from the bog that she hadn't been sore the next morning. But it was a most pleasant soreness.

"Do you think we might get started on that soon, husband?"

His grin widened as he took her glass and set it down on the table with his. In one swift movement he bent and lifted her into his arms, causing her to give a startled squeak.

"I see nae reason to wait, wife."

And with those words, he strode out of the Great Hall and to their chamber, where the door would remain bolted well into the next morning.

About the Author

Cynthia Breeding is an award-winning author of twenty-one novels and twenty-eight novellas. She currently lives on the bay in Corpus Christi, Texas, with her absolutely-not-spoiled bichon frise, and enjoys sailing and horseback riding on the beach. She also loves traveling, with Scotland a favorite destination.

Also by Cynthia Breeding…

A Rake's Redemption

A Rake's Revenge

A Rake's Rebellion

Rogue of the Highlands

Rogue of the Isles

Rogue of the Borders

Sister of Rogues

Rogue of the High Seas

Rogue of the Moors

Discover more Amara titles...

Her Accidental Highlander Husband

a *Clan MacKinlay* novel by Allison B. Hanson

Marian, Duchess of Endsmere, is on the run from the English Crown after killing her abusive husband in self-defense. She has only one safe place to go—her sister's clan in Scotland. When one day a disheveled lass runs from the forest with an English bounty hunter right behind, War Chief Cameron MacKinlay feels compelled to protect her by claiming she is his wife. But he certainly didn't intend to marry her for real!

Highland Conquest

a *Sons of Sinclair* novel by Heather McCollum

To finally bring peace to his clan, Cain Sinclair will wed the young female chief of their greatest enemy. Only problem: Ella Sutherland may be clever, passionate, and shockingly beautiful, but what she isn't is willing. Every attempt Cain makes to woo her seems to backfire. The only time they ever see eye to eye is when they're heating up Cain's bed, and the only thing Ella truly wants is the one thing he cannot offer her: freedom. But when a secret she's been harboring could threaten both clans, Cain must decide between peace for the Sinclairs and the woman who's captured his heart.

The Viking's Captive

a novel by Ingrid Hahn

If Thorvald captures the princess and brings her back to his jarl, he gets his land back. Easy. Even if the beautiful spitfire makes him question everything. Alodie impersonates the princess in order to save her from the bloodthirsty Northmen. Easy. What is not easy is Alodie's pulse racing for the handsome captor she'd just as soon hate, especially when Thorvald finds out she is not who she said she was. That can lead to death for them both.

Highland Obligation

a *Highland Pride* novel by by Lori Ann Bailey

Due to a violent attack, Isobel MacLean will do anything to keep her family safe—except marry infuriating Grant MacDonald. She wants justice, not a damn husband. Unfortunately, we don't always get what we want… Grant MacDonald is determined to tame the hellion wife he was forced to wed. And he'll need to use every tool in his arsenal to distract his alluring wife from her quest for vengeance…before it's too late for them both.

Made in the USA
Monee, IL
03 November 2024